THE GRANDBURG SERIES
Edge of Memory

Books in
THE GRANDBURG SERIES

EDGE OF MEMORY

(future installments)
UNFINISHED BUSINESS
FULL CIRCLE
THE BREAKFAST

THE GRANDBURG SERIES

Edge of Memory

Book One

Janifer C. DeVos

BOOKLOGIX

Alpharetta, Georgia

ISBN: 978-1-6653-0747-5 - Paperback
eISBN: 978-1-6653-0748-2 - eBook

These ISBNs are the property of BookLogix for the express purpose of sales and distribution of this title. The content of this book is the property of the copyright holder only. BookLogix does not hold any ownership of the content of this book and is not liable in any way for the materials contained within. The views and opinions expressed in this book are the property of the Author/Copyright holder, and do not necessarily reflect those of BookLogix.

Library of Congress Control Number: 2023921511

⊚This paper meets the requirements of ANSI/NISO Z39.48-1992 (Permanence of Paper)

1 1 1 3 2 3

For Verna

*Who woke me up
to rock mysteries, bird song,
the magic of growing things,
the beauty of harvested peppers,
and to what might happen along the river
after dark.*

*You encouraged me every time you asked,
"How's the book?"
You affirmed my decisions every time you said,
"That sounds sensible."*

*You are such a blessing.
I thank the Lord often for putting us
next door to each other.*

Chapter One

The cold front blew out of the northwest and passed silently over the dark crosscurrents of the Grand River into the park. Cool air intermingled with warm. An energized breeze traveled along the river's eastern edge and nudged pine, oak, and maple limbs to bounce, needles and leaves to dance. And then, gradually, the front moved through the woodland acres of the park and into the sleeping town of Grandburg. Wind caught and carried fountain spray far beyond the edge of the Tilden College lagoon. Gusts crisscrossed the downtown streets, picked up bits of gutter refuse, tossed them up and cast them down again. A fresh surge parted and reparted the orange fur of a stray tabby hunting behind the Alley Cat Bar and Grill.

The wind gathered speed as it traveled up the steps of City Hall, slammed against the wood-faced entry doors, and hurled itself back down the steps again. It blew past the hospital, through the town's two parking garages, and startled the police officer stepping outside for a quick smoke. It pushed riderless swings back and forth in deserted school playgrounds. With each passing windy breath, flagpole chains clanked in irregular metallic beats. The wind swept on into sleeping neighborhoods.

A jagged fork of lightning flashed high above the tree line of the park. The sliver of new moon was swallowed by a sea of billowing clouds. Distant thunder cracked and rumbled. Rain came. Large drops smacked cement, windows, doors, lawns, and gardens. Steam rose from the streets as the drops came down smaller, harder, faster.

Solomon Rigby opened his eyes with a start when thunder rattled his bedroom window. Raindrops increased to earnest drumming overhead, and he sat up, swung his feet out from under the sheet and onto the floor. He gripped the mattress edge and closed his eyes again.

Why am I sitting on Sarah's side of the bed?

It took a few seconds for the fog to lift from his brain. Then he remembered. He'd been alone in this bed since January. January, February, March, April, May—the longest five months of his life. A wave of grief passed over him. The sound of increasing rainfall brought him back to the present moment.

"I wonder what time is it?" he said into the dark.

"Guess I better make sure the boys are okay and check the upstairs windows," he muttered to himself. He turned on the lamp.

Soft yellow light flooded Solomon's corner of the bedroom. His blurred reflection looked back at him from Sarah's vanity table mirror. He ran one hand through his thinning, sand-colored hair and reached for his glasses. Once he'd pushed them up on his nose, the father of two sons, college professor, and widower looked back. He studied his reflection in the mirror.

I wonder what Sarah would say about the beard and mustache? He smiled. He knew exactly what Sarah would say, because she'd said it, last December, when he'd broached the subject one morning over breakfast.

"It's certainly your right to do whatever you want with your face," she'd said matter-of-factly. "But let me be clear. I do not kiss men with facial hair." She'd taken a sip of coffee and looked pointedly over the rim of the coffee cup at him. Seven-year-old Sam had giggled. Older brother Jonathan had subverted his grin by taking a large bite out of his toast.

The December kitchen scene evaporated as Solomon looked hard at his reflection. He thought for the one thousandth time how he'd never imagined he'd be sitting here without his Sarah.

Another lightning flash reflected off the mirror. Its fleeting brightness sliced across his internal lament. He stuck his feet into his slippers, stood up, and shuffled over to the half-open window. Glad to find the sill dry, he closed the window and headed into the upstairs hallway. A nightlight at the far end of the hall gave just enough light for Solomon to see shapes and shadows. No light came from under either of his sons' bedroom doors.

Good, he thought. *Maybe they'll sleep right through.*

Solomon decided to check Sam's window first. He gently pushed open the bedroom door. Lightning lit up the room long enough for him to see Sam huddled in his bed, arms pulling his knees to his chest.

"Hey, buddy, you're awake." Solomon came around the foot of Sam's twin bed, where Snickers, the family cat, was tucked nose to tail in a snug ball. He bent down to turn on the small lamp on the bedside table, creating an oasis of light surrounding Sam and his pillows. Solomon could see the tension on his son's face. Lightning flashed again, and to his surprise Sam started counting.

"One alligator, two alligator, three alligator—" Thunder cracked. "Three miles away," Sam said softly and gripped his knees tighter.

Solomon sat down next to Sam on the bed. The window would have to wait. "Three miles away?"

"Ms. Ko taught us." Sam looked at his dad. "If you count between the lightning flash and the thunder, you can tell how many miles away a storm is."

"Well! Good to know."

Solomon reached out and pulled Sam close, unsettling Snickers. She uncurled herself, stretched, and jumped to the floor. Thunder crashed again, and she disappeared under the bed. Solomon could feel Sam shaking.

"Hey, Sam, it's okay. We're safe. This is just a plain old thunderstorm. No watches, no warnings.

This house has made it through over fifty years of storms."

"But Dad," Sam persisted, "sometimes they don't know what's coming."

Yes, thought Solomon, *yes, like in January. There was no warning that day.*

Solomon felt Sam's weight shift more firmly against him. Lightning flashed again.

"One alligator, two alligator—" they counted together. Thunder interrupted the count.

"It's getting closer," Sam said, brown eyes wide, looking up at his dad and then back down again.

"And how are we right now?" Solomon spoke calmly into his son's brown hair, hugging him even closer. "We are dry. We are safe. The electricity is on. Rain will make the grass grow. I predict you and your brother will have the pleasure of mowing that grass in the very near future."

Sam looked up into his dad's face, the corners of his mouth curving into a tiny smile.

"Hey, how come everybody's up?" a sleepy voice spoke from the doorway.

Solomon looked up and saw his older son standing there, green-striped pajamas hanging loosely on his tall, slender frame.

"Jon, go close your bedroom window, would you please? I'm sure it's raining in."

"Already done, Dad," he said. He yawned and ran his fingers through thick brown curls.

"Good. Close your brother's."

Jonathan crossed to the window and pulled it

shut. He came and stood at the foot of Sam's bed just as lightning triple-flashed.

"One alli—"

Thunder boomed overhead.

"I'd say the storm center is upon us," Solomon said to Sam.

"Dad, let's sing. Can we sing?" Sam asked urgently. "'Dona Nobis Pacem.' That's what Mom always sang with us."

"Okay, but I'm not sure how it goes." Solomon looked uncertainly from Sam to Jonathan.

Thunder reverberated overhead. Solomon felt Sam's body press even closer to his.

"Jon, start us off!"

Jonathan started singing, catching his little brother's eye, inviting him to join him.

"Do-na no-bis pa-cem pa-cem . . ."

Sam picked up the melody a few notes in and sang along confidently with his brother. Solomon managed to sing along, just a note or two behind, until they came to the third part of the round. When they launched into the last line, he wasn't prepared for the quick succession of notes. The resulting vocal train wreck made them all laugh.

"So much for peace!" Solomon said, grinning at his sons.

"It's not the same with all boys," Sam said to no one in particular.

Solomon looked expectantly at Jonathan. His older son was never without some clever quip or comeback. But Jonathan was silent.

Lightning brightened the room for a second or two.

"One alligator, two alligator, three alligator, four alli—" they counted together. A more distant rumble of thunder cut them off.

"It's getting farther away," Sam said, relieved.

Solomon checked the clock radio next to the lamp. "Four hours before it's time to get up, boys," he said. "Think you can fall back to sleep?" He looked at Sam.

"Yup," Sam said. He crawled back under his covers and flopped back into his pillows, took a deep breath, exhaled, and closed his eyes.

"What about you, college man?" Solomon looked up at Jonathan, marveling yet again at how he had seemingly grown overnight into the young man standing in front of him.

"If I can't fall asleep, I'll study for a while," Jonathan said.

Solomon leaned over and kissed Sam's forehead. "See you in four," he said. "How does a Rigby sleep?"

"Sound and deep," Sam answered.

He turned off Sam's lamp and followed Jonathan out into the shadowy hallway. Solomon watched Jonathan walk away from him and recognized his own longish legs in his son. He saw himself in Jonathan's broad shoulders and strong arms. But the curly head of brown hair was definitely from Sarah.

Jonathan walked into his room and closed his

bedroom door without looking back. Solomon stood alone in the hallway and considered the closed door. He shook his head and walked back to his own bedroom. He sat down on the bed and slid his feet out of his slippers. The wood floorboards were cool against the soles of his feet. The rain overhead was just a gentle patter now. He stretched out in the middle of the bed and stared at the ceiling. He loved his boys. He was proud of his boys. Solomon closed his eyes and thought about Jonathan. Something was bothering him. Was it the grief that wrapped itself around them all? What else could it be? Solomon knew he'd never get back to sleep if he allowed himself to dwell on this now. Sam's alligator counting came to mind and Solomon silently thanked Ms. Ko for Sam's good second-grade experience.

Second grade. I'll think about my second-grade year. Who was my second-grade teacher?

He drifted off to sleep as he revisited a classroom he'd not seen in almost forty years. It was raining there too.

Jacoba Dahm was wide awake when the storm rolled through her neighborhood. Earlier in the evening she'd fallen sound asleep on top of a stack of papers she'd been grading. She'd awakened a couple hours later with a miserable crick in her neck. But after she'd gotten into bed, head resting comfortably on her pillow, she couldn't fall asleep. Tuning in to the smooth jazz station didn't help. Listening to a contemplative outreach podcast didn't help. Counting her blessings alphabetically didn't help. She'd resisted getting back up until lightning flashed repeatedly outside her bedroom window and thunder crashed. That got her moving.

"Better unplug my laptop," she said to herself. "And the TV too." She was glad she'd closed the windows before going to bed even though her little house was stuffy now. She walked barefoot down the hallway to the bedroom she used as an office, where she disconnected her laptop before hurrying to the living room. A loud clap of thunder sounded right over her head. Once she'd unplugged the TV, she stood in the middle of the room, not sure what she wanted to do next. Rain pounded over her head.

I'm going to go sit on the porch. It'll be cooler out there, she thought. *I should be okay as long as rain doesn't blow in. I wonder if I could see the rain gauge with the flashlight?*

She crossed the short expanse of beige carpet to the tiny dining room, navigated the narrow space between the wall and the dining room chairs, and entered the kitchen. She was glad she always kept the stove nightlight on; she could see everything by its bright glow—the round oak pedestal table and matching chairs in the middle of the room, the maroon countertops and stainless-steel sink under the window, where she had an excellent view of her backyard. She opened the turquoise drapes covering the sliding-glass door to the screened-in porch and picked up the high-beam flashlight she kept by the door, flicking it on and off again out of habit.

Good! Still nice and bright.

The kitchen light's glow spilled ahead of her onto the porch. Jacoba reached down and took the long piece of wood out of the track of the door. Cheap but effective security. When she'd asked the local handyman to cut the piece of wood when she'd moved in a few years before, he'd laughed. "You don't need that," he'd said. "This is Grandburg!" But Jacoba had needed it. She needed to know the only people in her house were the ones she'd invited.

Jacoba flipped up the door's thumb lock, pushed the heavy glass panel to the left, and stepped down into the screened-in cement square. Falling rain thundered on the aluminum roofing.

Sure feels better out here!

She breathed in her backyard's rich, wet aroma. The outer edges of the room's periphery glistened when she turned on the flashlight and pointed the beam in front of her. Rain diamonds shimmered on the screens. A sudden gust of wind carried cold, rainy spray across her face. She stepped over to her lounge chair hoping she'd be out of range.

I wonder how much rain has already fallen?

She swung the flashlight beam in the direction

of the rain gauge located just beyond the screen, but she couldn't see it. She turned off the flashlight and stared out into the dark. No lights on at her backyard neighbor's house.

Hope Verna doesn't get water in her basement from this.

She sat down on the edge of the lounge chair, swung her feet up, shifted into the taut nylon seat, and leaned back until her head hit the top of the chair. The drumming rain started to slow down. Jacoba could hear the splash and gurgle of the gutter downspout at the corner of the house. She felt herself relax. She closed her eyes.

I wonder if I could sleep out here.

Lightning flashed beyond the porch. Thunder rumbled a few seconds later, the sound less immediate than before.

I wonder if it will be too wet for the kids to be out on the playground?

She shifted in the chair, stretched her legs all the way out and crossed them, left ankle over right.

May . . . already.

Drowsiness crept up on her.

This school year has gone by so fast.

She sighed and settled back into the lounge chair.

It's been good . . . a good year . . .

As she started to nod off, a little voice spoke one word:

Except . . .

Dr. Miller, the school principal, rose up in her

mind's eye, immaculately dressed as always: paisley silk tie, white button-down shirt, silver cuff links, gray suit coat and all. Miller was a short man, all business.

Dr. Robert Miller gets a C as an administrator, and he most certainly is not a friend. But it's been a good year, she insisted.

She stretched her arms out in front of her, her long fingers reaching out into the night. She yawned, crossed her arms, and settled lower in the chair.

Mrs. Pratt has been a great room mother. And this has been my best year ever for creative bulletin boards, thanks to Jeremy. I hope he'll help me tomorrow . . . oh, wait, it's tomorrow already. Hope he'll help me today after school.

Rainfall slowed and stopped. Jacoba felt herself slipping into that delicious zone on the edge of sleep.

"Good year," she said sleepily into the cool porch air.

Except . . . the little voice insisted again. *Except for the little incidents of mischief all year.*

Jacoba opened her eyes and shook her head. "Boys will be boys," she said into the dark. Mrs. Pratt had said that to her more than once. Every time she put an incident of "boys being boys" behind her, another little something would happen: playground fights among boys, unpleasant discoveries of pages torn out of boys' textbook, and one or two pencils snapped in half. And last week the twins' backpacks had disappeared and then re-appeared, looking a whole lot worse for wear. That was the first time a girl's possessions had been involved.

May, she thought suddenly. *It's May. In a few more weeks these children won't be mine anymore. It will all be over for another year.*

And with that sad but comforting thought, she nodded off.

The large glazed jelly donut in front of Simon Roe oozed cherry filling onto the plate. He reached out a finger to take a taste. As he leaned closer to the plate, he heard someone calling him. He kept his eyes on the sweet treat in front of him and continued to reach, but the voice was insistent.

"Sime, wake up! Sime!"

The combination of the urgent voice accompanied by a loud clap of thunder caused him to open his eyes, an action he immediately regretted. Instead of the jelly donut, he saw his own dark bedroom. His wife was leaning over him, speaking into his ear.

"Sime, wake up! I think I left the kitchen window open. It's pouring!"

Simon rolled over, let out an exasperated sigh, and pushed himself up on his elbows.

"Seriously, Dar, you left the kitchen window open? Your husband is a police detective, and you left the kitchen window open? Do you know how embarrassing it would be if someone climbed through that window and robbed us? I'd be the laughingstock of the force!" He flicked back the sheet and sat on the edge of the bed. Dar turned on the lamp on her side.

"No one has climbed through that window since the boys were young," she said calmly. "And just think, a trip downstairs and back will give you a head start on your step count for Thursday."

Simon shook his head and gave a tiny grunt of annoyance. A thunderclap directly overhead and the sound of pounding rain prompted him to grab his robe and head for the stairs at the end of the hall. He reached for the light switch at the top of the stairs as lightning illuminated the staircase and thunder crashed. He flipped the switch up and down, up and down again. No electricity.

Not again!

Simon put his left hand on the smooth wood banister and his right hand flat against the wallpapered stairwell wall. He'd lived in this house for over thirty years. He could manage these stairs in his sleep, and when the boys were babies, that's exactly what he'd done. He smiled at that memory.

So long ago, but it also seems like yesterday. Thirty years in Grandburg. Thirty years in this house. Thirty years on the police force. Thirty years.

He reached the bottom step and walked through the little hallway into the kitchen. The window over the sink was wide open. Rainy wind rippled the starched white café curtains. Simon leaned over the sink, closed the window, and touched the sill.

"Wet," he said. "Flashlight first, and then a towel." He felt his way along the counter edge until his hand bumped a drawer handle. Just as he opened the drawer and found the flashlight, the electricity came back on. The refrigerator started to purr. The nightlight in the far corner glowed. Simon turned on the kitchen overhead light. He opened another drawer and pulled out a red-and-white-striped dishtowel. It took only a moment to wipe up the rainwater on the windowsill. He draped the wet towel over the gooseneck faucet of the kitchen sink and looked longingly at the refrigerator door.

No snacks. You are doing so well. Don't blow it.

He looked at the flashing display on the microwave.

I wonder what time it is? When do I get to eat again? No snacking!

He grinned at himself. Those last words sounded more like Dar's than his. Just as he turned to head back to the stairs, the power went out again. Simon felt his way to the staircase and climbed carefully back upstairs.

I wish I had a dollar for every time the power's gone out since we moved here. I hope things are okay at the Village.

Brockway Retirement Village was just north of their neighborhood. He and Dar had a running joke about getting a condo there. They wouldn't even have to get a moving company. They'd just move all their belongings one carload at a time. The boys could move their furniture for them.

Retirement.

Simon pushed the thought away. He heard the refrigerator rumble back to life a second time just as he reached the top step.

"Okay, you are on, now stay on!" he spoke sternly into the air.

"Simon? Who are you talking to?" Dar's voice called from their bedroom.

"I'm talking to the electricity," he called back.

He rounded the corner to their bedroom and saw his wife sitting up in bed with her pillows behind her, a legal pad on her lap and several sheets of paper on the quilted bedspread. He sat down on his side of the bed, which was now partially covered by her paperwork. He looked at her, eyebrows raised in question.

"I'm showing a very special house in the morning."

"What house isn't very special to you, Dar? You'll be great. You're always great!"

"I want to sound confident and convincing." Dar sat up straighter and turned the papers in her hand toward him. "I'm reviewing some details."

He slid under the covers and rolled over on his left side, creating a tsunami effect with Dar's paperwork.

"Simon Roe! Really!"

"Come on, Dar, please. I don't have to be up until six thirty." Simon's eyes were already closing. "Let's go back to sleep." He snuggled into his pillow and pulled the bedclothes farther over his shoulder. Dar's papers fell into even more disarray.

Dar pulled the papers into a pile and set them on her bedside table. She looked at her quilt-covered mound of a husband.

"We're getting old, Sime. Old. Remember what we used to do when we both woke up at three a.m.?" She bent closer to his ear. "Sime?" she said playfully.

Simon didn't answer. He was sound asleep, the jelly donut of his dreams just out of his reach.

Chapter Two

Jeremy put down his pencil with a satisfied thump. Papers rustled all around him as his classmates worked on the afternoon writing assignment. He knew he was supposed to proofread his poem one more time, but he didn't do it. He was finished. He'd just written the most important poem of his life. This poem was his statement to his family and friends, to the world really, about how he, Jeremy Davis, planned to do things "from this time forward and forevermore." He looked at the last lines of his poem and quietly repeated the words.

"From this time forward and forevermore. No more fear, hurray!" He smiled. The power, the promise, the hope in those sentences filled him with confidence.

Jeremy slid his chair back, picked up his paper, and headed to the front of the room to turn it in. He walked a little faster as he passed Billy Barnes's desk. He was relieved to see Billy's head bent close to his paper, completely focused on what he was writing. When he came to Ms. Dahm's desk, he reverently placed his poem on top of several others in the assignment tray.

Jacoba Dahm looked up from her work and smiled at him. Jeremy noticed how her smile traveled up from her mouth to her eyes, always encouraging, always welcoming.

"Another Jeremy Davis classic?" she asked as she hastily clipped a stack of papers together.

"My best ever!"

Jeremy's grin parted the sea of freckles on his face. The thick brown hair he'd so carefully combed that morning had inched down his forehead and over his eyes. His white uniform shirt and khaki pants had looked better that morning too. Now his shirt advertised the chocolate fudgesicle he'd enjoyed at lunch, and his pants bragged about his glorious muddy slide into second base during recess.

"Well, Jeremy, you've written some really good poems already. What's the title?"

Jeremy retrieved his paper and held the poem up so Jacoba could see.

"'This time forward and forevermore,'" she read aloud. Her eyes darted from the words on the paper to Jeremy's face. "I look forward to reading it."

Jeremy grinned and replaced his poem on top of the pile.

"Say, Jeremy, I'm going to put up a new bulletin board after school today. Want to help me? You have the magic touch—my bulletin boards have never looked so good!"

"I can't, Ms. D, not today. Tomorrow?"

He suddenly wanted to tell her what he was planning to do after school, but he couldn't get the words from his brain to his tongue fast enough.

"Okay, Jeremy, tomorrow then. Having your help is worth a twenty-four-hour wait." Jacoba's gaze traveled past Jeremy to the clock on the back wall.

"Oh, my goodness! Look what time it is!" She pushed away from her desk and stood up to address the class.

"Friends, the dismissal bell will ring in about five minutes. Before you leave, your poems should be on my desk, and your homework assignments copied in your homework pads." Jacoba headed for the classroom door.

Jeremy started back to his desk only to come nose to nose with Billy Barnes. Jeremy and Billy were well matched physically, but Billy's quickness and mean spirit gave him an advantage. Before Jeremy could move out of his way, Billy shoved him hard against the sharp corner of the teacher's desk.

"Oh, so sorry, Jeremy." Billy looked Jeremy straight in the eye, his expression mocking.

Jeremy gritted his teeth, his hip smarting. Under his breath he whispered, "From this time forward and forevermore . . . from this time forward and forevermore." Billy had done this to him before—pushing, shoving, or tripping, leaving a bruise here, a cut there. Jeremy wasn't the only recipient of Billy's attention, but lately he'd been receiving a lion's share of it. And Jeremy was afraid to tell. He'd seen what had happened after Jake and Maddie's parents had talked to Billy's parents. Just a few days later, Jake and Maddie's backpacks had been mysteriously stomped and mutilated. No, he wasn't going to say a word.

As Jeremy walked back to his desk, his classmates gathered their belongings, pushed past each other to put their poems in the assignment tray, and either flipped open or slapped shut assignment pads. He slid into his chair and pulled his bike helmet out of his backpack. He double-checked his homework pad to be sure he'd copied tonight's assignment correctly, and then pushed the pad and his binder deep into his pack. Sixty seconds before the dismissal bell rang, the room was whisper quiet. Jake and Maddie caught his eye from three rows over and mouthed the words, "Bike rack." He nodded back and gave a thumbs-up. Afternoon freedom was almost within his grasp. And not just any afternoon, but the afternoon when he would launch "Operation From This Time Forward and Forevermore." His anticipation grew with every click of the classroom clock's second hand.

Yes, absolutely, positively I'm doing it this afternoon, and then everything will be better.

He pulled his backpack onto his desktop, zipped it shut, plunked his helmet on top, and wrapped his arms around it. When the bell rang, he and his classmates rose from their seats and formed an orderly exit line, a discipline that had taken Ms. Dahm several weeks to establish at the beginning of the school year. Jeremy liked all the ways Ms. D created and maintained order in their fourth-grade day. He passed by her, backpack and helmet in his arms, out the classroom door and into the crowded hallway.

"You're helping me tomorrow, don't forget!" she called after him.

"I won't!" Jeremy called back over his shoulder.

Tomorrow . . . I wonder if tomorrow is going to feel different? Tomorrow Operation From This Time Forward will be in full swing. This afternoon's mission will be history. Mission accomplished. Wow.

Energy surged through him. He tried to locate Maddie and Jake in the throng of students heading out into the May afternoon. Not spotting them, Jeremy continued down the hallway, turned the corner into the main corridor, scanned as always for Billy Barnes, passed the glass-windowed front office, and finally exited through the double doors of Grandburg Elementary School. He breathed in the warm May air, squinting his eyes in the bright afternoon sunlight. He impatiently raked his fingers through his hair to shove it off his forehead. Jake and Maddie waved to him from the bike rack as they unlocked their bikes.

He hurried to join them and dropped his backpack next to his bike. He swung his helmet up on his head and fiddled in frustration with the helmet's chin strap.

"Not again!"

"Here, let me try." Jake reached over and tugged on the strap. He stopped after a couple attempts.

"Jeremy, I'll break it if I pull it any tighter. It's all frayed."

"I'll tell my dad. He'll know what to do about it."

Once they'd hoisted their backpacks on their shoulders, the three friends walked their bikes past the crossing guards. Farther down the sidewalk they hopped on their bikes, feet to the pedals.

"Come on, guys!" Jeremy yelled. "Let's take the long way! Last one to Connor Avenue has to carry my backpack tomorrow!"

He pulled out ahead of the twins. Jake and Maddie were quick to catch up, though, and for the next few minutes they laughed their way toward home, weaving in and out of formation, speeding up, slowing down, and dismounting several times to roll their bikes across intersections. Connor Avenue finally came into view. All three heads bent down with chins tucked, bodies hunched over handlebars. Furious peddling propelled them forward. Jeremy was out in front again, his orange handlebar streamers flapping wildly with each downstroke of the pedals. Suddenly his helmet flew backward off his head, narrowly missing his friends. Jake and Maddie streaked past him and stopped triumphantly under the Connor Avenue street sign.

Jeremy brought his bike to a wobbly stop,

jumped off, and rolled his bike back a few yards to retrieve his helmet from the grass.

"Dumb strap! Guess I'll be carrying my own backpack tomorrow." Jeremy laughed. *And you won't believe the difference you'll see in me! From this time forward and forevermore!*

"See you!"

The twins headed south on Connor Avenue and Jeremy headed north, helmet back on with the broken chin strap dangling. He pedaled the short distance to his street. Aptly named, Ravine Circle backed up to the yawing ravine where the usually sedentary Winding Creek flowed. The creek created a natural dividing line between downtown Grandburg and the residential neighborhoods. Jeremy could see the ravine's upper lip from his kitchen window if he stood on tiptoes. He always stayed a respectable distance from the dizzying drop down into the creek bed when he played in the backyard.

Jeremy pedaled to the only single-story house on the circle. He rode up the little sidewalk, dismounted, and scooted the bike up the three cement porch steps. Once he'd leaned the bike against the porch rail and set his helmet down on the rattan seat of a weathered white rocking chair, he unzipped an inner compartment in his back-pack. After a little fishing, he pulled out his house key and unlocked the frosted glass–paned front door. Once inside, he was aware of the coolness, the quiet of the house. He put the house key in his pocket and looked at his watch. He only had a few minutes to spare before his daily check-in call to Grandmother Davis.

Jeremy hurried down the short hallway to his bedroom, threw his backpack on his bed, ran back to the kitchen, and turned on the TV in the corner. The game show host's baritone burst into the kitchen midsentence.

"—our last question before a brief break."

Good! Right channel and a couple minutes to go before the commercial. Enough time to get milk and a cookie.

Jeremy hit the mute button on the TV remote. His eyes darted from the kitchen counter to the TV screen and back again as he poured himself a glass of milk and popped open the dented cookie tin. He had just enough time to dunk a chocolate chip cookie twice and gobble it down before the game show went to commercial. As soon as the commercial began, he wiped his hands on his pants, reached for the phone, and hit speed dial #1. He listened as it rang on the other end. Once, twice . . . and . . .

"Hello?" Suspicion sparked out of the receiver into the kitchen.

Jeremy winced. "Hi, Grandmother Davis, it's me, Jeremy. I'm home now." He turned to look at the clock hanging above the sink. He knew he had sixty to ninety seconds before both the commercial break and the phone call would be over.

"You tell your father my lawn needs to be

mowed." The voice on the other end of the line was loud. "I can't do it myself anymore."

"Grandmother, maybe I could mow your lawn, but not today. Today, I'm—"

A derisive snort on the other end of the line interrupted him. "You, mow? I don't think so!"

Jeremy's shoulders sagged. His fingers gripped the phone receiver more tightly. He surprised himself when he said, "From this time forward and forevermore . . ."

"What? What in the world are you talking about, Jeremy?"

Jeremy felt his resolve welling up and pushing against his ever-present shyness. "Remember the movie we watched, Grandmother Davis? The hero said, 'From this time forward and forevermore.' Well, I've decided—"

Grandmother Davis cut him off. "The next round is starting!"

Click. She was gone.

Jeremy set the receiver back in its cradle. He aimed the remote at the television and turned off the set. After dunking two more cookies in a second glass of milk, he rinsed his glass and put it in the dishwasher. Then he took a deep breath and headed for the front door.

As he walked through the living room, he stopped in front of the framed family photo hanging above the fireplace. He looked up at his parents and studied their faces. He thought he looked more like his mom than his dad. He had his mom's freckles and brown hair. Their chins and eyes matched. Jeremy looked down at his hands. He did have his dad's long fingers. His mom called them piano fingers. There was no piano in their house, and now, at this moment, Jeremy wondered if his dad even played the piano.

Jeremy remembered when the picture had been taken: last summer in the park. Large oak trees and a picnic table were in the background. The three of them were smiling in the picture.

"Should I leave Mom and Dad a note telling them where I'm going?" he asked himself, still looking at the photo. "Nah, there's no need. I'll be back before they even get home."

Once he was out on the porch again, he plunked his helmet on his head, walked his bike back down the three porch steps, rolled it along the front walk, and mounted it. He pedaled his way back to Connor Avenue and headed north toward the park. He crossed Winding Creek Road, and was, as always, a little awed by St. Gregory's, the Catholic church on the corner. Jake and Maddie went to church there. They'd invited him more than once, but he hadn't gone.

Maybe after today I will. When I'm done today, things will be different. I will be different.

Jeremy veered off Connor Avenue after passing the church corner and took the bike trail through a weedy field to the pedestrian bridge over Cherry Street. He rolled across the boards of the bridge, and his bike picked up momentum as it bumped down the brick exit ramp. The pedestrian bridge ended within a few yards of the road that led to the rear entrance of the park. In another minute he was pedaling past the rusted double gate and the empty guard hut that stood sentinel at the park's entrance.

Jeremy stopped just beyond the gates to catch his breath. He could hear traffic sounds from Cherry Street but he was alone on the perimeter road—no other cars, bikers, or joggers. He looked all around, wanting to take in every detail of this place, this stretch of time, so he would always have a memory of what it had been like before his life changed.

"From this time forward and forevermore!" he shouted into the air. He pushed off and started pedaling again, steering the bike with one hand and making a fist with the other. Pumping the air, his clenched fist accenting each word, he chanted, "No more fear! No more fear! No more fear!"

He breezed along, the spicy scent of pine trees wafting past him. The perimeter road's incline was gradual but steady. Suddenly when he looked to his left, instead of pine trees and grassy slopes, he saw the river sparkling in the afternoon sun. The Grand River wasn't blue. It was more the color of his mother's morning coffee after she'd put cream in it. When he reached the first scenic overlook, he stopped a minute to rest his legs. He closed his eyes and faced into the late afternoon sun.

"From this time forward and forevermore!"

He started pedaling again. The road changed from a gradual incline to a gently rolling expanse. He pedaled up and coasted down, pedaled up and coasted down. The orange streamers on the bike handles fluttered and rested, fluttered and rested.

"No more fear! No more fear!" he chanted in time with his pedal strokes.

In another three minutes he topped another hill and spotted the Prayer Trail sign anchored in the gravel by the roadside. The sign's arrow pointed down the grassy embankment and into the woods. He pedaled past the sign, remembering the first time he'd been to the trail. He'd come with his boys' club. The boys, several dads, and Mr. Barfield, their leader, had walked from the rear entrance parking lot to get there. Mr. Barfield had gathered them together in front of the bronze memorial plaque in the clearing at the base of the trail. Several boys had reached out to touch the raised lettering on the plaque. Jeremy had seen "Native American" and "1800s" from where he had been standing.

"Native Americans considered this trail to be sacred. Who knows what 'sacred' means?" Mr. Barfield asked.

Jake Hirsch and his dad were standing next to Jeremy. Jake raised his hand. Mr. Barfield smiled and nodded at him, inviting an answer.

"Sacred means holy, set aside for God." Jake looked from Mr. Barfield's face to his father's.

"Thank you, Jake. Yes, sacred means holy, set

aside for God. Native Americans came to the prayer trail to talk to God. Their name for God was 'The Great Spirit.' Native Americans were still using this trail in the mid-1800s. They would stop and speak to God or listen to God, The Great Spirit, along the trail. We don't know exactly how they marked the sections of the prayer trail. They may have built small stone towers at each stopping place. When I was your age, someone gave the curves on the prayer trail names in English and put a post at each turn. We're going to walk the trail just the way the Native Americans did: reverently, slowly, quietly."

Then Mr. Barfield led the way. He stopped at the first post and waited for the rest of the group to get there. Jeremy walked with Jake and Jake's dad.

"We start with praise." Mr. Barfield lifted his hands and looked up into the sky. "God, you are great. You are mighty. You are holy." He lowered his hands and looked from face to face. "Do any of you have words of praise to say?" But no one else spoke. After a minute, they headed up the steep incline to the second post.

"Now we thank God for our blessings. You can say your words out loud or just in your mind." Mr. Barfield bowed his head. The others followed his example.

Jake's dad said something out loud, but his voice was so low Jeremy couldn't make out his words. Jeremy looked sideways at his friend.

Jake's lips were moving and his eyes were closed. Jeremy closed his eyes too.

Dear God, I'm thankful for this place, for this afternoon, for my mom and dad, for Jake and Maddie, for Mr. Barfield, for Ms. D . . .

After a couple minutes the group started moving again, curving up to the third post.

"Here we listen." Mr. Barfield looked encouragingly at each boy. "Maybe God will speak to you."

Jeremy closed his eyes and listened intently. *God? I'm listening. I'm here.*

He heard the park speaking all around him: pine branches rustling in the breeze, a blue jay's harsh call. He even heard the clock in downtown Grandburg chime the hour. He peeked in Jake's direction. His friend was smiling, eyes tight shut.

Jake knows God better than I do. I wonder what God is saying to him?

Very shortly Mr. Barfield moved them on to the fourth post, where they were to wait for a sign that their prayer time was over and they could start the journey back down to the bottom. Persistent low giggling caused Mr. Barfield to speak a sudden, profound, "Amen!"

"Amen!" Mr. Hirsch echoed.

"Amen!" came from another dad at the far side of the group.

Jeremy was sorry the experience was ending. He wasn't quite ready for it to be over.

Mr. Barfield led the group back down at a faster pace. A minute later a couple boys sprinted ahead with Billy Barnes in the lead, only to be reined in by Mr. Barfield.

When the group had reached the bottom, they were all a bit out of breath, their calf muscles stretched and aching. They'd continued on through a stand of pine trees to get back to the jogging trail that ran parallel to the park's perimeter road and retraced their steps to the parking lot. On the way home, Jeremy had asked Mr. Hirsch the question that had occurred to him during the walk back.

"Mr. Hirsch, what happened to the Native Americans? Are they still around? I've never seen any Native Americans in Grandburg."

Jake had chimed in, "Yeah, Dad, what happened?"

"That's a story for another day, boys," Mr. Hirsch had said, a serious expression on his face.

Jeremy continued to pedal along the perimeter road, the rear entrance far behind him now. Thursday-afternoon shadows lengthened across the blacktop. He had biked here with Jake and Maddie soon after the boys' club outing. The three of them had taken the perimeter road all the way to the second scenic outlook where the Prayer Trail sign pointed to the top. They'd turned off onto the little gravel path that took them to the top of the trail and stopped at the fourth post. They'd leaned over their handlebars to get a better look at the steep descent.

"You would have to be so brave to ride your bike down that trail," Jake had said with a mixture of awe and fear. "If you were brave enough to ride down that trail," he'd declared, looking wide-eyed from Jeremy to Maddie, "you'd be brave enough to do anything."

Jeremy had nodded in solemn agreement, the seed of an idea sinking deep into the fertile soil of his imagination.

"You would be stupid to ride down that trail," Maddie had said with firm superiority. "This trail is meant to be walked. It isn't meant for a bike." She had turned and looked pointedly at both boys. "Don't even think about it—either one of you!"

"Yes, Mother," Jake had mocked.

The boys had laughed. Maddie had continued to give them both stern looks. Eventually they'd turned their bikes around and gotten back onto the perimeter road. They had biked the rest of the way around the park and then home.

And the seed had taken root, sprouted, and grown.

Jeremy looked ahead and saw the parking lot for the second scenic overlook. When he reached the overlook, he turned off the perimeter road and onto the gravel path that led to the Prayer Trail. When he got close to the fourth post, he put his feet on the ground and balanced his bike. The Prayer Trail in front of him curved down, down, down into the pine forest. He thought about how old this place was. In his mind's eye he pictured Native Americans solemnly walking up the prayer trail to this top post, the Wait post.

> *From this time forward and forevermore.*
> *No more fear.*
> *If you were brave enough to ride down this trail, you'd be brave enough to do anything.*
> *Brave enough to stand up to Billy Barnes.*
> *Brave enough to stand on the edge of the Winding Creek ravine.*

He wished now he'd told Jake and Maddie what he was planning to do. He wished they were here with him. He wanted witnesses to what he was about to accomplish, but more than that, right this minute, he wanted encouragement. He could feel little fingers of fear tickling his brain as he eyed the steep slope.

"Should I wait? Should I go?" he spoke anxiously into the air, looking up into the bright blue sky. A red-tailed hawk glided overhead, carried by an upper-level current. Suddenly the hawk shifted from lazy glide to purposeful flight.

That's it! That's my sign! Time to go!

Jeremy pushed off and started pedaling. As he left the Wait post behind, he shouted, "From this time forward and forevermore!" He started to put his fist in the air, but the bike's speed increased with the steep slope of the trail, and he needed both hands to steer. Downward momentum pulled him quickly from Wait to Listen. Then the Prayer Trail veered to the right and descended more steeply toward the Thank post. Jeremy took his feet off the whirling pedals and let gravity carry him.

Grandmother Davis will like the new Jeremy.

"From this time forward!" he shouted. The words were dashed against his teeth with a force that also pushed his hair back from his face. His hands gripped the handlebars tighter, and he crouched low, his chin almost level with his knuckles. The orange streamers on the bike's handles flared out parallel to the pathway, jerking and bouncing with the bike. Jeremy held on for dear life as he and his bicycle streaked past the Thank post.

"No more fear . . . no more fear . . . no more fear . . ." He desperately mouthed the words.

He could see the beginning of the Prayer Trail now, the Praise post and the large bronze plaque just beyond it. He hurtled down and careened past the Praise post, moving faster than he ever had in his whole life.

He knew he was going too fast. He tried to straighten back up but couldn't.

In desperation he squeezed both hand brakes. The wheels locked. A mighty jerk jolted through his body. The bike pitched forward like a bucking bronco, sending him headfirst over the handlebars. As Jeremy catapulted through the air, he felt his helmet fly off.

Oh no. Oh no.

Chapter Three

Jonathan Rigby stepped into the upstairs hallway, tennis shoes in hand. He pulled his bedroom door almost but not quite closed behind him. He couldn't risk even the smallest click. Both Sam and his dad were light sleepers. The dim glow of the hallway nightlight allowed him to see the two other bedroom doors. Closed. Good.

At the top of the stairs, he shifted his shoes to his other hand so he could hold on to the rail. His shoulder brushed the wall as he made his way down and stepped off the stairs onto the slate floor of the entryway. The stone's coolness seeped through his socks. He cautiously sat down on the bottom step to put on his shoes. Once both laces were tied, he looked at the dark wall just ahead of him. He knew the front door was there. He stood up, took three steps forward, reached out with his right hand, and found the doorknob. It was cool and round under his fingers. He was going to turn that knob, open that door, and leave. He checked his phone. He needed to hurry. His dad would be getting up shortly.

"Okay, Jon," he said softly, "go. Go now. Do what you've got to do."

The knob didn't turn as he'd expected. He

tightened his grip as a wave of anxiety swept over him. He tried it again.

"Oh, for crying out loud, you idiot!" he whispered to himself in exasperation. "It's just locked."

He slowly flipped the deadbolt and unlocked the door, pulling it open just far enough for his thin frame to slip through before stepping out onto the shadowed front porch. He winced at the tiny click when he closed the door again. Then he turned to gaze into the predawn dark all around him. This place had been home for all nineteen of his growing-up years. And now he was leaving. He had to go. He didn't have any other choice. Not after what his dad had said.

Anger, hurt, disappointment, and disbelief took turns flooding his brain. It wasn't like Jonathan hadn't expected some heated opposition from his dad regarding his plans for the future. Months ago, he and his mom had considered the best way to bring his dad on board. But now there was no mom to help him. And last night Dad had come down with bone-crushing force on his dream.

Jonathan took the three porch steps in quick time. Mugginess seeped into his clothing. Sweat trickled down his backbone to the waistband of his blue jeans. He looked back at the closed front door and pivoted neatly around, his determination rising. He paced purposefully down the front sidewalk to the driveway that ran along the side of the house and took the car keys out of his jeans pocket.

He opened the door of his father's aging car and slid into the driver's seat. As he reached around the steering column to insert the key into the ignition, he realized he'd forgotten something.

"Oh no!" he exhaled the words. "I left my backpack on my bed!"

He rested his forehead on the steering wheel, not quite believing his own ineptness. He lifted his head and stared at the side of the house.

"This is it," he said, his words loud and decisive. "This is it! I'm going! I'm going now!"

"Going where, Jon?" a sleepy voice spoke from directly behind him. "Can I come too?"

Jonathan whirled around. He pushed against the passenger seat's headrest with his hand and stared into the dim recesses of the backseat. No, no! This couldn't be happening!

"Sam? Sam! What in the world are you doing out here?"

It was light enough now for Jonathan to make out his little brother hunkered down in the center of his blanket nest in the backseat.

"How did you get out here? The front door was locked!"

"I didn't come out the front door. I came out the back door. Who even uses the front door?" Sam stroked the cool, satiny surface of his green comforter. "I was hot upstairs, so I came out here."

"You were hot." Jonathan waited, letting the three words hang in the air, hoping heat was all that had brought his little brother to the backseat.

"Well, yes, I was hot, and the yelling . . . well, the yelling . . ."

"The yelling?" he repeated softly.

Sam's words came out in a rush. "The yelling woke me up, and I couldn't get back to sleep, and I was hot, and I decided to come sleep out here."

Jonathan turned back around. He gripped the steering wheel with both hands and pushed himself hard into the driver's seat. What a mess.

"So, where are you going, Jon? Can I go? Does Dad know you're taking the car? Why was he yelling at you?" Sam snuggled down, his head resting on his pillow.

Jonathan tilted the rearview mirror so he could see his little brother without getting a crick in his neck. With each of Sam's questions, Jonathan's burning exit energy shrank until it was just a smoldering ember in his chest. Dawn brightened the landscape, the outline of house and shrubbery no longer a dark, unified whole.

Sam broke the silence with another question. "What time is it, Jon? I'm hungry. Think Dad's started breakfast?"

Jonathan looked at his phone. "Six eighteen. Dad's definitely in the kitchen."

I should have left earlier. Why didn't I leave earlier? Another voice argued back. *Even if you'd left earlier, Sam still would have been in the car. What if you'd driven all the way to Byington with him asleep in the backseat? How mad would Dad have been then?*

Defeated, Jonathan pulled the key out of the

ignition and swung his legs out of the car. He stood up, finger looped through the key ring, closed his door, and opened the door to the backseat.

"Come on, squirt, let's go. I'll carry your bed."

Sam tumbled out, hugging his pillow. Jonathan pulled the comforter out of the back and slammed the car door. The boys walked up the driveway past a bank of hydrangea bushes and around the back of the house. Sam stopped on the bottom back porch step and turned to face his brother.

"If you give me your bacon, I promise not to tell Dad you were running away."

"Running away? I wasn't running away!" Jonathan made his voice as disdainful as possible, but he couldn't look his little brother in the eye.

"Bacon," Sam repeated, staring hard at his brother as they both moved toward the screen door. Sam got there first. He turned and looked up at his brother expectantly. Jonathan couldn't help but smile back.

"Okay," he said, "deal."

They stepped into the three-season porch. The screened-door spring twanged and snapped the door shut behind them. The earlier adrenaline rush that had carried Jonathan down the stairs and out the front door no longer propelled him. In its place he felt stinging disappointment creep behind his eyes and into his brain. He checked his phone.

6:30 a.m.

He should have been heading out of town toward Byington now, on his way to Uncle Mark and Aunt Marilyn's house. Well, that wasn't going to happen. And if that wasn't going to happen, then what was he going to do?

Light from the kitchen spilled onto the porch. Jonathan smelled coffee and toast. Sam walked ahead of him and opened the back door. Smooth jazz filled the bright yellow kitchen space. Snickers streaked past them, and the cat flap in the screen door snapped shut behind her. The boys stepped into the warm kitchen and dumped the comforter and pillow on a tall lattice-backed kitchen chair just as the weather forecast cut into the music.

"A beautiful spring Friday is on tap for Grandburg and the surrounding area today. High in the midseventies. There is an eighty percent chance of a brief afternoon shower. Keep that umbrella handy!" The music resumed.

The boys' father stood at the stove, black framed glasses perched on his nose, spatula in hand, his brown-striped bathrobe tied snugly around his waist. He turned toward the boys as they came into the kitchen, one salt-and-pepper eyebrow raised in surprise. He shoved his glasses closer to his face.

"What's this?"

"No big deal, Dad," Sam said quickly. "I slept in the car because I was hot, and Jonathan came out to get me."

Jonathan looked at his younger brother with a mixture of gratitude and amazement. Sam looked back with a knowing grin and mouthed the word, "Bacon."

Solomon harrumphed, shook his head, and turned back to the stove. He turned on the gas flame under the skillet.

"Eggs will be done shortly. Go wash up."

The rapid-fire pops of sizzling grease followed the boys out of the kitchen. They washed their hands in silence in the little bathroom just down the hall. Jonathan reached long arms around Sam to dry his hands on the towel.

They returned to the kitchen and sat down at the round table in their usual places: Jonathan near the back door, Sam to his left. Their father slid a fried egg each on two plates already laden with toast and grits. He set the plates down in front of the boys.

Sam bowed his head and launched into the breakfast blessing as he always did, his prayer rising above the bass guitar and saxophone coming from the radio.

"Thank you, God, for this food, for my dad who cooked it, and for my brother who—"

Jonathan gave Sam a swift warning kick under the table.

". . . who loves You. Amen."

Jonathan dug into his breakfast. When his father added three crunchy strips of bacon to his plate, he mumbled a thank-you but didn't look up. The three of them sat around the table, the only conversation the sound of silverware clinking against plates. When Solomon got up to put his plate and fork in the sink and pour himself more coffee, Jonathan picked up his bacon strips and put them on his brother's plate. Immediately Sam stuffed two strips into his mouth, chewed, and then washed it down with milk.

Solomon brought his coffee back to the table and sat across from the boys.

"You are listening to WTCG, broadcasting from the campus of Tilden College. Good morning, Grandburg. This is Adam Klein with this morning's news. Police are asking for your help in locating a missing ten-year-old boy, Jeremy Davis."

"Jeremy Davis!" Sam said. "He goes to my school!"

"Shhh! Sam!"

"Jeremy is about four and a half feet tall, brown hair, blue eyes. He was last seen on Thursday afternoon wearing khaki trousers and a white shirt, riding a blue bicycle in Grandburg's Winding Creek area. If you have any information as to his whereabouts, please contact the Grandburg Police Department."

Solomon got up and turned off the radio. He sat back down across from his sons. "His parents must be worried sick. I wonder what happened?" He looked from Sam to Jonathan.

Jonathan avoided his father's eyes. He scooped up and swallowed the last piece of fried egg.

"Homework all done?" Solomon asked Sam.

"Yes, sir."

"Lunches made?" His eyes went from one boy to the other.

"Yes, sir," Sam answered again. "I made mine last night."

Jonathan looked down at his empty plate. He'd not made his lunch because he hadn't thought he'd be in Grandburg for lunch today. He thought he'd be figuring out his next steps with his Uncle Mark.

"Jonathan? You have alternate lunch plans today?" His father looked inquisitively over the rim of his mug at Jonathan as he took another sip, right eyebrow raised again.

Does he know? Jonathan wondered, suddenly feeling sick to his stomach. *Does he know I was going to run away? If only Sam hadn't been in the car!*

Jonathan braced himself for more questions. But the questions didn't come. Solomon looked to the kitchen clock over the sink.

"Hey, boys! Time to move! Seven fifteen! The Rigby Express will be leaving in twenty-five minutes." He got up, set his mug in the sink, and hurried upstairs.

Jonathan stood up from the table and set his dish in the sink on top of his father's. He started to turn away, but then considered that the plates would still be there at the end of the day if he walked away now. He turned back to the sink and ran hot water over the dishes. After rinsing off the toast crumbs and specks of yolk and bacon grease, he put the dishes in the dishwasher. Then he started rummaging around the pantry shelves for lunch ideas. He caught his brother looking at him.

"Hey, Sam, you better get a move on. Last time

I checked, second graders weren't allowed to wear pajamas to school."

Sam got up, handed Jonathan his dirty plate and fork, and ran out of the room. Jonathan turned back to the sink when he was surprised by his brother's voice behind him.

"Jon . . ."

"Yes, Sam?"

Jonathan felt Sam grab and pull the belt loops of his blue jeans. He turned around, and Sam buried his face in his brother's shirt.

"Hey, hey, buddy! What's wrong?"

Sam looked up into his brother's face. His fingers moved from Jonathan's belt loops to his shirt, grabbing a fistful of material in each hand. Jonathan could feel his brother's knuckles pressing against his ribs.

"Don't leave, Jon," Sam whispered tearfully. "Please don't leave."

Jonathan knelt in front of Sam and looked him in the eye. For a split second he saw his mother looking back at him, but then Sam's tear-streaked face crowded out her image.

"Sam, I'm not going to leave."

"Promise?" Sam let go of Jonathan's shirt with one hand and wiped tears from his cheeks and chin.

"Yes, Sam." Jonathan took a deep breath. "I promise."

And he felt the promise anchor him to the spot. How could he leave Sam, his exasperating and dearly loved younger brother? He hadn't thought through the consequences of his leaving, but after last night's confrontation with his dad he knew exactly what staying meant. He suddenly felt like crying himself.

God! What now?

Jonathan stood back up, smoothed out his shirt, and tucked it back into his pants. "Go on, Sam. Get dressed. I have to put my lunch together."

Sam ran out of the kitchen and upstairs.

"Lunch, lunch, concentrate on that," Jonathan told himself.

When his father came back into the kitchen with his briefcase and umbrella, Jonathan had put an apple, a bag of chips, a peanut-butter sandwich, and three chocolate chip cookies into a bag. Lunch in hand, he turned to the place where he usually left his backpack only to remember it was still upstairs. He dashed past his father.

Solomon scanned the kitchen counter and yelled after his son, "Hey, Jon, I can't find my car keys. Have you seen them?"

Jonathan's brain slammed into overdrive. Car keys! Where had he put his dad's car keys? Were they in his pocket? Were they still in the car? He felt the blood rushing to his face.

Solomon walked over to Sam's comforter and pillow.

"These need to go back upstairs. Sam? Sam!"

When he picked up the bedding, the keys fell to the floor with a metallic clatter.

"Sam had my keys?" Solomon checked his watch. "Sam! Get down here! We're going to be late!"

Intense relief washed over Jonathan. Sam thundered past his brother. He grabbed his lunch off the kitchen counter, lifted his backpack off the hook by the door, slung it over one shoulder, and stepped out on the porch.

Jonathan bounded up the stairs two at a time. He grabbed his backpack, pulled clothing out and put schoolbooks in, and rushed back downstairs, snatching his lunch off the counter. He slid past his father on the porch. Snickers scooted back into the kitchen as Solomon turned to close and lock the back door. The three walked in single file to the car, the May morning bright all around them. With each step, Jonathan felt a quiet resolve growing within. No, he wasn't going to leave. But he wasn't going to let last night's argument stop him from pursuing his dream either.

"Dad?"

"Yes, Jonathan?"

"I'll drive."

He watched as his father started to say no, stopped walking, looked at his keys, and looked at Jonathan.

"Okay," he said and tossed the keys to him.

Jonathan smiled.

Score one.

Chapter Four

Solomon looked with approval at Tilden College's main entrance when Jonathan stopped for the red light on Remembrance Road. From the passenger seat, Solomon could see all the way to the lagoon with its three-tiered fountain center-piece. The empty sidewalks told all. First-hour classes had started already. When the traffic light changed to green, Jonathan turned onto the cam-pus main street and drove slowly past the coffee shop and bookstore on the way to Preston Hall. A few seconds later he pulled the car neatly into a staff parking space beside the white stucco three-story building.

Almost before Jonathan had taken the key out of the ignition, Solomon was out of the car and retrieving his briefcase and umbrella from the backseat. Jonathan put the keys down on the passenger seat and reached into the backseat. He wrestled a notebook out of his backpack and settled back down in the driver's seat. He balanced the notebook on the steering wheel and gave all his attention to the pages in front of him. Solomon pushed the rear door shut, leaned forward, and spoke into the open passenger-side window.

"I'll meet you back here at four, Jon. I have af-ternoon office hours today." His eyes fell on the keys in the passenger's seat. "Don't lose those. We only have the one set."

He didn't wait for a response, didn't see his son's slow shake of the head and downcast expression. Briefcase in one hand, umbrella in the other, Solomon turned and started the short walk from the parking lot to his office. He had only gone a few feet when two students rushed past him on the sidewalk, clutching coffee and backpacks.

"Morning, Dr. Rigby!" they yelled and raised their coffees in salute.

"Morning!" He raised his umbrella in a return greeting. "Shoot," he muttered to himself when he saw their coffees. "Forgot my travel mug."

As a matter of fact, he hadn't even thought about it this morning. Sarah never would have let him leave home without his coffee. Sarah wouldn't have let him leave home without attempting some sort of reconciliation with Jonathan after last night's argument either. Actually, Sarah never would have allowed the two of them to go to bed angry with each other in the first place. He pushed the thoughts away.

He followed the sidewalk to the broad cement steps of Preston Hall, quickly ascended them, and passed through the double doors into the cool, carpeted hallway. He stopped at the second door on the left, put down his belongings, took the office key out of his pocket, and unlocked the door. Morning sunlight poured in through the high old windows, casting rectangular grids of light onto the blue-green carpet. He surveyed the room's contents with satisfaction: teak desk positioned under one window, overfilled bookcases on three walls, and a conference area with three armchairs arranged around an oblong, glass-topped coffee table. The coffee table had been one of Sarah's garage sale finds. Sarah. There she was again. He could think of Sarah now without grief sweeping over him. He'd worried a little when he'd first noticed the pain had receded ever so slightly—did that mean he loved her less? Did it mean he missed her less? Did it mean he was starting to forget what the past had been like? No, he'd told himself. No. It just means you're traveling away from what was. And so is she.

"Dr. Rigby?" a young woman spoke tentatively behind him.

He recognized the voice of his research assistant and turned to face the tall, slender young woman who looked back at him through round-rimmed glasses. She cradled two large notebooks along with a thick textbook. Her dark-brown hair curled well beyond the shoulders of her Tilden College sweatshirt, and the straps of her capacious purse rested solidly on her shoulder.

"Ms. Pritchard! Good morning! I'm not forgetting an appointment, am I?"

"Oh, no, Dr. Rigby. I just want to ask you a couple procedural questions, if you have a minute."

"Sure. Come on in."

Solomon picked up his briefcase and umbrella and hurried over to his desk. He leaned his items against one end and motioned to the chairs around the coffee table. They sat down across from each other. Solomon folded his hands, silently lamenting the absence of coffee. Ms. Pritchard set down her purse at her feet and balanced her notebooks and text on her knees. She tucked her hair behind her ears, which caused her dangling silver spiral earrings to swing.

"Here's what I'm considering . . ." she said.

Her earnest expression and tone transported Solomon to last night's confrontation. In his mind's eye he could see Jonathan sitting next to him on the sofa. He could hear his gentle tenor voice hesitating, then becoming more and more strident as he tried to share his thoughts.

"So, Dr. Rigby, taking all that into consideration, what do you think?"

Solomon looked into the expectant face across from him. He hadn't heard a thing she'd said. He sat back in his chair. "Tell you what, why don't you take a little more time to think this through, and come back this afternoon."

The young woman looked back at him in surprise.

Solomon stood up, smiled brightly in her general direction without making any eye contact, and walked to his desk. "I'm sure by this afternoon you'll have it all figured out." He pulled out his desk chair and sat down. "But if you still need my input, I'll be here until four."

He popped opened his briefcase and lifted out his laptop. Next he extracted a stack of papers and set them down, never looking beyond the open lid. He could hear Ms. Pritchard gather her belongings and walk into the hallway. When the door clicked shut behind her, he raised his eyes and leaned back in his chair. Relief mixed with guilt engulfed him.

Solomon, Solomon! You cannot allow your work to be affected by what goes on at home.

Home. Last night's conversation with Jonathan rewound and began to play in his mind.

"This is what I want to do, Dad. Mom knew. Mom thought it was wonderful—that's what she said, 'Jonathan, what a wonderful thing to do with your life.'"

Solomon put his finger on his lips. Sarah had known. Sarah had approved. He shifted his weight and the chair rolled a little.

I never saw this coming. I knew something was on Jon's mind, but I never would have guessed it was this. Why didn't Sarah tell me? Maybe she did tell me, and I wasn't listening.

He willed himself back into the present to focus on the stack of papers in front of him. But last night wasn't done with him yet. He heard Jonathan's words again.

"This is what I want to do, Dad. I want to make God's work my work."

God's work! Shouldn't God's work have been to keep Sarah's car from going off the road? Shouldn't God's work have been to protect my family? Solomon could feel his grief and anger commingling. It was almost more than he could stand.

"This isn't helping," he said to the clock on his desk. And upon seeing what time it was, he hastily gathered his laptop and lecture notes and hurried out the door. American History wasn't going to teach itself.

Once Jonathan saw his father disappear into Preston Hall, he put his notebook back in his backpack and got out of the car. As he walked beyond Preston Hall he fingered the car keys in his jeans pocket. His father had let him drive that morning, had even left the precious single set of car keys with him. Those actions looked to Jonathan like concessions. But concessions weren't the same as approval. And Jonathan suddenly realized approval wasn't all he wanted. What Jonathan wanted most was his father's blessing. After last night, he was pretty sure he wasn't going to get either one.

Jonathan headed to the Fine Arts building. Once inside, he hurried to the lecture hall and slid into his usual spot on one of the upper-level rows. He nodded to fellow students as they sat around him and reached under their seats for the movable desk arm. He did the same and then pulled out his laptop, all set to take notes. Two lectures later, he was more than ready for a break.

Jonathan's classmates made a beeline for the student union building and the cafeteria. But Jonathan chose to follow a meandering path around one of the campus ponds. He hadn't gone far when he stopped at a shaded bench under some oak trees and sat down on the wide board seat. A light breeze ruffled the grass around his feet. He heard a shout followed by laughter coming from the other side of the pond. Then he heard a siren. He sat forward, listening intently. Funny how until his mother's death he'd never given sirens a second thought. It sounded to him like it was coming from the direction of downtown Grandburg. He wondered if the siren belonged to an ambulance, a police car, or a fire engine. Before he could decide, the siren faded out.

Jonathan looked out across the water. A lone duck quacked several times offshore. Jonathan leaned back and yawned. A deep-down tiredness crept into his mind and body. So did hunger. He reached into his knapsack for the chocolate chip cookies and was pulling them out when a voice spoke directly over his head.

"Hi! Mind if I join you?"

Jonathan looked up to see a young woman smiling hopefully at him.

"Hi!" He moved to make room for her to sit down next to him. Her dangling earrings bounced, and a sudden gust of wind blew their hair across both their faces.

"A little rain is on the way," the young woman said as she pushed her curly hair away from her face. "I checked the weather radar before I left the apartment." She offered Jonathan her hand. "I'm Mary, Mary Pritchard."

"Say, aren't you in my psychology class? You usually sit midway back, on the aisle."

"Yup, that's me!"

"I'm Jonathan. Jonathan Rigby." He held out the baggie of chocolate chip cookies. "Want one?"

"Yes, thank you." She bit into a cookie and let out a groan of satisfaction. "Oh, wow, this is wonderful." She took another bite, savoring the flavor. She looked at Jonathan with a critical eye, and then waved the half-eaten cookie in his direction. "Jonathan Rigby. You look just like your picture."

Jonathan stared at her in surprise. "What picture? Where have you seen my picture?"

"In your father's office on his bookshelf. I work for him."

Jonathan didn't know what to say. A rumble of thunder caused them both to look skyward. Storm clouds were gathering black and thick overhead.

"Time to head for cover, I think. It was nice meeting you, Jonathan. Thanks for the cookie." She popped the last bite in her mouth and stood up.

"See you in class, Mary."

A lightning flash sent them scurrying in opposite directions. As large raindrops fell faster and with more intensity, Jonathan spotted the prayer chapel ahead and sprinted toward the double doors. He pulled one door open and stepped into the dim worship space. The long, arch-topped windows on either side of the room let in sufficient light for him to make out the modest lectern, the kneeling cushions underneath the brass railing, and the roughhewn cross affixed to the stucco wall. He walked to the last semicircle of seats, sat in the third chair from the end, and let his backpack slide to the floor. The staccato over head was already lessening. He got back up and pushed open the small glass rectangles at the bottom of the windows to let in some fresh air. A breeze carried the sweet smell of rain mixed with wet, newly mown grass into the room. The rain slackened even more, quick to come and quick to go, so typical of Grandburg spring showers. Jonathan took his seat again and let the chapel's peace sink into his mind, his heart. His gaze came to rest on the cross and stayed there.

"Lord, I don't understand. Nothing is turning out the way I thought it would. I never imagined Mom wouldn't be here." Jonathan stretched both arms as far as he could reach on either side. "And Dad is angry. At me. At You. I don't know what to do."

His phone alarm broke into his thoughts. He had fifteen minutes before his last class of the day started. As he reached for his backpack, his eyes fell on an open Bible in the chair next to him.

"'I lift up my eyes to the hills—where does my help come from?'" He picked up the Bible and continued reading. "'My help comes from the Lord, the Maker of heaven and earth. He will not let your foot slip—he who watches over you will not slumber.'"

Jonathan closed the book and sat back in the chair. He looked over the empty rows of seats to the cross. "Lord, I know You aren't asleep, but I really do feel like I'm slipping."

His thoughts returned to the night before. He'd helped his father clean up supper. He'd been waiting for almost a month to show him the brochure from the diocese. When his father had come back downstairs after putting Sam to bed, Jonathan decided the time had come. He'd pulled the brochure out of his backpack and sat next to him on the living room sofa.

"Dad, I want to talk to you about something."

"Sure, son, what is it?" Solomon answered without lowering the newspaper he was reading.

"I'd like to go to this." Jonathan slid the multi-colored brochure into his father's view.

Solomon put the paper aside and took the brochure out of his son's hand. He pushed his glasses farther up on his nose and read aloud from the cover, "Discernment Summer." He frowned and then looked quizzically at Jonathan.

"Discernment Summer? What's this about, Jon? What's to discern? You've got three more years at Tilden and then graduate school."

Jonathan could feel his courage ebbing as his father flipped the brochure open, quickly scanned the inside and then the back.

"Jon!" Solomon started laughing. "This looks like a brochure for men considering the priesthood!"

Jonathan looked steadily at his father.

"You're kidding. You're thinking about becoming a priest?" His father stared back, all humor exiting his expression. His next words came out clipped and hard. "You have a good mind, Jonathan. I won't condone wasting it studying a bunch of nonsense." Solomon reached for his newspaper, located the article he'd been reading, and lifted the paper between them.

Jonathan felt his chest tighten. "Dad," he said into the newspaper wall in front of him, "it isn't nonsense! This *good mind* wants to work for God." He sat up straighter and launched into his prepared sentences. "Worship matters to me. Saying the words. Sharing the sacraments."

The newspaper didn't move.

"I want to pray for people, listen to them, encourage them, talk to them about spiritual things."

The newspaper remained firmly in place.

Jonathan leaned closer, voice raised in frustration. "I'm nineteen now. I don't need your permission."

The newspaper wall lowered abruptly. Jonathan's defiant eyes met his father's astonished expression.

"Well, no, you don't need my permission," Solomon said in a low, cold voice. "But nineteen is too young to even consider a decision like this. Once you've finished your undergraduate work at Tilden, we'll revisit this idea of yours. But until then, I don't want to talk about it. I don't even want to think about it." The words were couched in a decisive finality.

But Jonathan wasn't ready to give up. "Mom totally supported my becoming a priest. She said, 'Jonathan, what a wonderful thing to do with your life.'"

When Solomon didn't say anything, Jonathan started talking again, hoping his words were causing his father to reconsider. "Dad," he looked at his father with confident expectation, "I want to make God's work my work." There. He'd shared his heart. Surely that would be enough.

Solomon slapped the paper down between them on the couch. "After what happened to your mother, I'm not sure there is a God."

"Dad! You don't mean that!" What was happening?

"And another thing, you may be nineteen, but if you live in this house, you live by my rules. And I'm invoking a new rule right now: No more God talk from you."

Jonathan looked at his father in disbelief. "What do you mean?"

"Exactly what I said. I don't want to hear you mention God in this house. Am I clear?"

"Yes, sir." Jonathan could barely utter the words.

"It's late." His father's voice downshifted into finality. "Time we were both in bed."

Jonathan got up from the couch and walked swiftly into the hallway and up the stairs. He hurried past Sam's closed bedroom door and into his room. He laid down on his bed and rolled over to face the wall, his arms wrapped tightly around his pillow.

The five-minute warning beep on his phone pulled him back into the present.

"That's when I decided to run away," Jonathan said over the rows of chairs in front of him. "And as You know, that didn't work out, either."

He stood up, slung his backpack over his shoulder, and walked to the chapel door. He paused and then turned back toward the cross.

"I really need You to tell me what to do next."

Chapter Five

Simon looked down at his desk blotter with surprise and pleasure. He hadn't seen it in weeks. He leaned back in his chair and was congratulating himself when his associate/intern, Richard Barclay, hurried into the room. He started talking before he reached Simon's desk.

"Missing child, parents just called. Darrin and Beverly Davis. Over on Ravine Circle."

Simon stood up, and the two men moved quickly back out the office door and down the hallway. Simon caught sight of their reflections as they passed other glassed-in offices, Richard a step ahead of him. His dark, wavy head of hair and olive skin were quite the contrast to Richard's short salt-and-pepper hair, light skin, and freckles. Richard wore glasses. Simon did not, although he kept a pair of reading glasses handy. They were close to the same height, but Simon was visibly heavier. He shifted his gaze away from the glass. Well, he was working on the weight issue.

They took the two flights of stairs in quick time down to the parking garage. Richard pushed open the exit door, and the humid air hit them both. They could hear the late-afternoon traffic sounds beyond the confines of the garage. Simon checked his watch.

"The worst of the afternoon rush should be over by now. Shouldn't take us more than seven minutes to get to Ravine Circle."

In six minutes and fifty-eight seconds they pulled up in front of the house, and the door opened before they made it to the porch.

"I'm Darrin Davis." A linebacker of a man reached out to shake Simon's hand and then Richard's. He stepped back into the foyer and made room for them to enter. "This is my wife, Beverly."

"Thank you for coming so quickly," Beverly said. "We're so worried." She looked up at her husband.

"I'm Detective Roe, and this is my associate, Officer Barclay. Why don't we all sit down, and you can tell us what's going on."

Darrin and Beverly sat close together on the sofa. Simon and Richard settled into the recliners across from them.

"We got home before five." Darrin looked earnestly into the faces across from him as he started the narrative. "We both work at Grandburg Mutual, so we drive together. We expected to find Jeremy doing his homework at the kitchen table, as usual."

"He was here." Beverly picked up the conversation thread. "He checked in with my mother-in-law like he does every day. His backpack is on his bed. He had milk and cookies." She stopped. Tears trembled along the edges of her words.

Darrin continued. "We realized right away his bike was gone. We called his buddies, Jake and Maddie Hirsch, hoping maybe the kids had gone biking together after school." He shook his head, looking at his wife. "Even though Jeremy knows he's not supposed to do that. They said they'd parted ways at Connor Avenue right after school, all headed home." Darrin looked away. He struggled with his emotions, cleared his throat, and continued. "Then Beverly and I thought maybe he'd left something at school and had ridden back for it."

"He's so conscientious," Beverly said softly.

"I drove to the school and came back a couple different ways, thinking maybe he'd had a flat tire or crashed. No sign of him. That's when we called you. We also called the hospital right before you drove up. He's not there either."

"Mr. and Mrs. Davis, has Jeremy ever run away, or threatened to run away?"

Beverly and Darrin both registered visible surprise. "No, Jeremy has never run away from home. He's never talked about anything like that."

"How's his school year going?"

"He loves his teacher. And he seems happy most days." Beverly looked to Darrin, who nodded in agreement. She looked out the window. "It will be dark in a couple hours. He'll be out there, alone. Where could he be, Darrin? Where could he be?" Darrin reached out and took her hand. "Why didn't he leave us a note?"

"Mrs. Davis, if Jeremy had left you a note, where would he have put it?"

"On the kitchen table," she answered without hesitation.

"Officer Barclay and I would like to take a look around the house. Would that be all right?"

The Davises nodded.

Simon and Richard opened closet doors, looked under beds and behind furniture, checked the nooks and crannies of the basement, and spent extra time in Jeremy's room. Richard opened Jeremy's backpack.

"Looks like he had what he needed for his homework," he said after taking a quick inventory of its contents. "The assignments in the pad match the books in his backpack."

Simon was looking at the puzzles and books on a shelf at one end of the room. "Jeremy is one orderly kid! These puzzles are organized by number of pieces, and the books are arranged alphabetically."

Richard picked up a hairbrush on the dresser next to the bed. "DNA sample here. I'll get his toothbrush too."

"I wonder why he didn't leave a note? I'm going to look around in the kitchen again. Maybe it fell on the floor or is under something." Simon walked back down the short hallway past the living room and into the kitchen. He looked down and scanned the floor. Nothing there. He retrieved a yardstick he'd seen in the pantry and stooped by the refrigerator. He slid the yard stick under the fridge, hoping to discover a note from Jeremy, but all he got was an old shopping list, some pieces of uncooked elbow macaroni, and a penny. He slid the yardstick under the stove. Nothing.

As shadows lengthened, the officers moved their search outside. The men checked the garage and walked through the backyard to the edge of Winding Creek's deep ravine. They peered down but spotted neither bike nor boy at the bottom. When the men came back around to the front of the house, they saw an older couple dressed in matching sweatshirts on the front porch talking with Darrin and Beverly.

"Detective Roe, Officer Barclay, these are my next-door neighbors, Sue and Bob Murphy."

Simon stepped onto the porch and shook their hands. Richard came right behind him and did the same.

"I wish we had something useful to offer," Sue Murphy said, "but we were gone all afternoon. On Thursdays we babysit our grandkids."

"And the granddog," Bob Murphy added.

It was obvious to Simon the couple treasured the babysitting job. Bob Murphy nodded in the direction of Beverly and Darrin. "We've been neighbors for years. We've known Jeremy since he was a baby."

"Do you have any thoughts about where he might have gone?" the detective asked.

Mrs. Murphy shook her head. "No, no idea. He

is such a nice boy, shy, always so polite." She put her arm around Beverly. "You are doing such a good job with him."

"Say," Mr. Murphy said suddenly, looking hopefully at Darrin, "we weren't here to see anything, but I bet ole Mooney was on the lookout! He's probably watching us now!"

"Mr. Mooney is our street's one-man neighborhood watch," Darrin explained to Simon and Richard. "He sits and plays Solitaire right in front of the picture window for most of the day, and in between games uses his binoculars to spy on the rest of us."

Richard started to laugh but caught Simon's warning glare, and the laugh morphed into a sort of snorting cough.

"Officer Barclay, let's go introduce ourselves to Mr. Mooney."

Simon and Richard hadn't even made it halfway up Mr. Mooney's driveway when the garage door ascended. A short man hunched over a bright-red walker rolled out of the garage. The blue jeans and red flannel shirt he wore hung loosely from his fragile frame. He adjusted the baseball cap perched on his bald head while he looked eagerly from Simon to Richard and back to Simon.

"What's going on?"

Simon put out his hand. "I'm Detective Roe, and this is my associate, Officer Barclay. Did you happen to see Jeremy Davis come home from school this afternoon?"

"Why, yes, yes I did." Mr. Mooney's raspy voice carried well beyond them. He straightened to his full height, the red walker parked solidly in front of him. Even then Simon and Richard had to look down in order to meet his eyes. "He came home at the usual time, put his bike on the porch like he always does." Mr. Mooney stopped to take a breath. "I don't approve of that, putting the bike on the porch. That's not where bikes belong!"

"Did you happen to see Jeremy leave again?" Simon asked.

"I sure did, a little after three forty-five, maybe closer to four," Mr. Mooney said. "Today was unusual. Once he's home he never leaves again. He's a shy one, that Jeremy. But he's always respectful. Always calls me Mr. Mooney."

"Which way did he go?" Richard asked.

"He was heading toward the corner of Ravine Circle and Connor Avenue. I can't see beyond the place where our street curves."

Simon handed Mr. Mooney one of his cards. "Thank you, Mr. Mooney. Please give us a call if anything more comes to mind."

Simon and Richard recrossed the street and walked up the Davises' driveway.

"Mr. Mooney saw Jeremy come home and leave again," Simon said to the waiting group, "but he didn't see which way Jeremy went after he'd passed Mr. Mooney's house."

"Yeah, we could hear him from here," said Mr. Murphy, his sober expression matching his tone of voice. "Darrin, we're here for you. Anything you and Beverly need, just give us a call."

"You know we'll be praying," Mrs. Murphy added. She reluctantly stepped away from Beverly and the Murphys headed down the sidewalk.

"If Mr. Mooney saw Jeremy, I wonder if any other neighbors saw him." Simon looked questioningly at Beverly and Darrin.

"I think the neighbors beyond the Murphys and the Mooneys all work until five p.m. or later."

"Well, we'll check in with them, just in case they were home." Simon turned to Richard. "Why don't you walk down the street and see what you can find out."

Richard nodded and headed back to the street.

Simon followed the Davises back into their living room. Beverly sat on the edge of the sofa, head down, hands clasped in front of her. Darrin sat next to her. He threaded his arm through hers and pulled her close. Beverly managed a short laugh through tears. "When Jeremy gets home, he's going to be grounded for the rest of his life!"

Simon took out the little spiral pad he always used for notes and flipped it open. "What did Jeremy wear to school today?" he asked quietly.

"White shirt, khaki pants," Beverly answered. "That's the school uniform. He's a fourth grader at Grandburg Elementary."

"And the color of his bike?"

Both parents answered together, "Blue."

"Do you have a picture of Jeremy?"

"Yes, right here." Wiping her eyes, Beverly walked to an end table and picked up a framed photo. After unsteadily bending back the metal prongs that held the photo in place, she extracted Jeremy's school picture.

"This is my Jeremy," she murmured as she handed the picture to Detective Roe. Her eyes stayed on the photo as Simon took it from her.

"I'd like to talk to Jeremy's teacher."

"Jacoba Dahm is his teacher. I have her phone number and an email address right here on my cell phone." She handed Simon her phone, and he copied the information.

"Who else would have had contact with Jeremy this afternoon? You mentioned his grandmother?"

"Yes, my mother, Madge Davis. She lives a few blocks away," Darrin said. "On the corner of Erickson Way and Weekly Street."

Simon wrote down her address. "And the friends he rode bikes with?"

"The Hirsch twins, Jake and Maddie. They rode bikes to and from school together today. They ride together most days if the weather is nice." Beverly looked at Darrin. "They live right down the road on Connor Avenue. I've got their contact information on my phone too." Beverly found the information and handed the phone back to Simon.

Simon copied the information down and then handed Darrin one of his business cards. He leaned forward and spoke to both parents. "You can call me anytime. I may not be able to answer right away, but I will always get back to you."

Darrin and Beverly both nodded. Then Beverly started to cry.

"Oh, Darrin," she sobbed softly. "I'm so scared."

Simon stood up to leave. "Finding Jeremy is the most important job we have right now. I'm not going to promise you everything will be okay. But I can promise you that Officer Barclay and I will do everything we can to find Jeremy."

"Thank you, Detective Roe."

"No need to get up," he said matter-of-factly. He walked quickly out the front door and onto the little porch. The evening air was warm. He was glad it was May. If Jeremy was alive somewhere in or around Grandburg, he wouldn't be cold tonight.

Simon walked down the sidewalk to the driver side of the car and looked up the street. He could see Richard walking toward him.

"Anything?" he asked when he joined him by the car.

"No. One neighbor didn't even know the Davises had a son. The other neighbors all got home after five p.m., just like Mr. Davis said. Nobody on that end of the street has security cameras."

Simon checked his watch. "I want to talk to Jeremy's grandmother and his biking friends. The Hirsches live close by. Let's go there first and then swing over to Jeremy's grandmother's house. After that we'll talk to Jeremy's teacher, Ms. Dahm."

Simon drove slowly down Ravine Circle, traveling the same stretch of road where Mr. Mooney had seen Jeremy earlier.

"And here's where the mystery really begins," he said as he peered left, then right, then left again at the stop sign on the corner of Ravine Circle and Connor Avenue. "Which way did Jeremy go? Left, or right?" Seeing no oncoming traffic, Simon turned right onto Connor and headed for the Hirsch house. "Going this direction would take him to his friends' house, and a little farther down to the big truck stop."

"And if he went north, he'd bike past St. Gregory's and the high school parking lot and then come to the park."

"There used to be a bike path behind St. Gregory's. I wonder if it's still there?"

"Yes, it's still there. It leads right to the pedestrian bridge."

"The 'be-on-the-lookout' has probably already gone out, but why don't you call in and request extra eyes on the truck stop and around St. Gregory's."

Richard took out his cell phone. By the time he'd finished making the request, Simon had pulled into the driveway of the Hirsches' two-story red-brick house. The broad cement driveway was covered with multicolored chalk renderings. The men stepped around rainbows and winged creatures on their way to the front door.

Richard rang the doorbell. Thundering footsteps advanced on the other side of the door. Then the door opened wide, and a sock-footed boy stared at them through the screened door. Before anyone could say anything, a man wearing blue jeans and a long-sleeved shirt joined the youngster, one hand coming to rest on the boy's shoulder and the other on the door's edge.

"Good evening, gentlemen, may I help you?"

Simon held up his ID. "Mr. Hirsch? I'm Detective Roe, and this is Officer Barclay."

Neil Hirsch pushed open the screen door and offered his hand to the officers.

"This is my son, Jake." Jake solemnly shook hands with both men. "I'm guessing you're here about Jeremy. Darrin Davis called here earlier to ask if Jeremy was here. He hasn't come home?"

"No, he hasn't," Simon answered. "We'd like to talk to your children about Jeremy, if we could."

"Darrin and Beverly must be beside themselves. Please, come in." Neil held the door open for the men to enter. He turned to his son. "Jake, go get your sister and your mom."

In short order Neil introduced his wife, Naomi, and the family sat down on the pink, floral living room sofa. Jake and twin sister, Maddie, were sandwiched between their parents. Simon recognized Naomi's dark hair and dark eyes duplicated in the twins. He took a seat across from them in a comfortable wingback chair. Richard pulled out the long piano bench just to Simon's left and sat down.

Simon addressed the twins matter-of-factly. "You rode your bikes home with Jeremy after school today, right?"

Jake spoke up first. He sat up straighter next to his mother while she absentmindedly brushed his hair off his forehead. "Yes, we met at the bike rack and we rode home—"

"The long way," Maddie piped up as she snuggled closer to her father.

"Yes, the long way," Jake continued. "Jeremy's helmet flew off—"

"It almost smacked us!" Maddie interjected, her eyes wide. She looked up at her dad. "We were racing."

"And when we got to Connor Avenue," Jake continued, "Jeremy rode toward his street, and we rode home, here."

"Did Jeremy say anything to you about going somewhere else later this afternoon? Somewhere besides home?"

The children shook their heads and muttered a bewildered "no" almost in unison.

Simon turned to Richard. "Officer Barclay, do you have anything you'd like to ask Maddie or Jake?"

Richard put both hands on the edge of the piano bench and leaned toward the twins. "Was Jeremy in a good mood this afternoon? Or did he seem worried, like he had something on his mind?"

The twins looked at each other first, then at Richard. "He was happy. He even laughed about losing the race," Jake said.

"I'd say that was a good mood," Maddie added decisively.

"Can you think of where Jeremy might have gone after he went home? Because he did go out again on his bike. We know that for sure."

"Jeremy's not allowed to go anywhere after school. It's the biggest rule ever," Maddie said firmly.

"But he did go out again, he broke the rule." Richard's voice was quiet, his tone even, nonjudgmental. "Where do you think he went?"

"Jeremy doesn't go anywhere by himself," Jake said with conviction. "We ride bikes together, we go places together. He wouldn't go anywhere alone."

Richard looked at Simon. "And when you ride together, where do you go?"

"To school, from school," Jake said.

"The short way, the long way," Maddie added.

Jake looked up at his mother when he spoke next. "And sometimes we ride to the park, but only when we ask first."

"We rode to St. Gregory's once," Maddie said. "Oh, but Jeremy wasn't with us."

Nothing more was offered. Jake and Maddie looked at Simon and Richard and then at their parents, serious expressions on both their faces.

"Well, thank you for talking to us," Simon said.

As he handed his card to Neil and Naomi, he leaned toward the twins. "If you think of anything that might help us find Jeremy, tell your mom and dad. They'll call us."

"Your thoughts, Officer Barclay?" Simon addressed his colleague as he carefully backed out of the driveway.

"I'm thinking we should request a check of the video cameras for the high school parking lot and the two entrances to the park. I'm not sure if St. Gregory's has a camera in their parking lot, but if they do, it might show part of the bike path. That path runs along the back of their campus."

"Good idea."

"I'll call Elizabeth right now and get the ball rolling."

"Get her to put together a news release for TV and radio, too, while you have her on the phone. Thank you, Lord, for Elizabeth!" Both men laughed.

"I remember when there was no Elizabeth," Simon said in all seriousness when Richard ended the call. "An investigation did not move at lightning speed in those days, let me tell you."

"Was that before or after the invention of the printing press?" Richard teased.

"Very funny, Mr. Barclay, very funny." Simon turned onto Ridley Street and headed east. "I'll take Ridley to Erickson Way. We'll go right past the elementary school."

"Wish we'd spot that blue bike," Richard said

as he looked out the window. He sat back and wrapped one hand around his seatbelt. "I'm picking up on a repeating theme. Jeremy is not a risk-taker. He likes routine, order. No surprises. For him to leave home this afternoon makes me think he had a plan, a compelling reason to go wherever he's gone."

"I agree. And I wonder if his plan included someone else."

"Maybe someone who didn't have his best interest at heart," Richard added soberly.

Simon didn't answer. He slowed down when he saw the stop sign on the Ridley/Erickson Way corner. In another minute they were out of the car and on Grandmother Davis's porch steps. The green-painted screened door to the porch was locked. Both men heard a TV game show coming from inside the house.

"Do you see a doorbell?" Richard looked without success for something to push.

Simon rapped the screened door sharply with his knuckles. "Mrs. Davis? Police officers! Mrs. Davis!"

The TV sounds abruptly stopped.

"Mrs. Davis?" Simon repeated his knock. He and Richard heard the front door open.

"Mrs. Davis? Police officers. We're here to speak with you about your grandson, Jeremy."

A short, dark figure shuffled across the unlit porch to the screened door.

"Keep your voice down!" an angry woman

growled through the screen. "The whole neighborhood knows you're here!"

"Mrs. Davis?"

"Yes, I'm Mrs. Davis. Has Jeremy come home?"

"No, he hasn't. That's why we're here. We want to talk to you about your conversation with him earlier in the afternoon."

They could see her shape more clearly now as she peered through the screen at them. She didn't unlatch the door. "What do you want to know?"

"What time did Jeremy call you this afternoon?"

"Must have been at around three forty-five, during my game show's commercial. He always calls then."

"Did he say anything about leaving the house, about going back out on his bike?"

Simon and Richard heard a derisive snort on the other side of the door. "No. I find it hard to believe he's gone anywhere. He's such a scaredy-cat! Have you been to his house? Looked in the garage? The backyard?"

"Yes, Mrs. Davis, we've searched there, and we've talked to the neighbors. Jeremy was seen leaving the house again, presumably after he'd talked to you. We don't know where he went once he got to Connor Street."

"Well, quit wasting time talking to me! How hard can it be to find a ten-year-old boy in a little town like Grandburg?" Mrs. Davis stepped back from the screen and moved toward the front door.

Richard called after her, "Mrs. Davis, did

Jeremy say anything odd or unusual to you this afternoon?"

"Just about everything that boy says is odd or unusual! Especially since he's been in fourth grade!"

The front door slammed, and in less than ten seconds the TV set was blaring again. Simon and Richard looked at each other.

"Wow," Richard said. "Grandmothers have changed since I was a boy."

"I think Mrs. Davis is the exception, not the rule," Simon said wryly.

They walked back to the car. Evening was arriving in earnest now. The streetlights along Erickson Way came on in one simultaneous blink. The drive to Jacoba Dahm's house took less than five minutes.

"I don't see any lights on," Richard peered through the windshield. "Think she's home?"

"I hope so."

They walked up the short sidewalk to the turquoise front door. Richard rang the doorbell. They both stepped back, and after a brief wait a light went on in the living room. The porch light went on overhead.

"Who is it?" a muffled voice called out.

"Detective Roe, Ms. Dahm. We'd like to talk to you."

They heard the click of the deadbolt. The front door opened.

"Oh, my goodness! What a surprise! Please, come in."

"This is my associate, Officer Barclay."

"How are your boys? Oh, but they wouldn't be boys anymore. They probably have children of their own!" Jacoba Dahm ushered the men into the living room. As they sat down Simon studied the woman across from him. She had the same contagious enthusiasm she'd had when his sons were in her classroom over fifteen years ago.

"You're right, Ms. Dahm. The boys are men now, but I'm not a grandfather . . . not yet."

"What brings you to my door on a Thursday evening?"

"Jeremy Davis is in your class, isn't he?"

"Yes, he is. Has something happened?"

"Jeremy is missing," Richard said. "He left home on his bike after three forty-five. He's not come back."

"Oh, no! His parents must be beside themselves!" Jacoba looked at Richard, then Simon, then Richard again. "How can I help?"

"Could you walk us through Jeremy's day with you today?" Simon pulled out his notepad.

"Certainly." Jacoba folded her hands in her lap and closed her eyes. "Okay. Math and Reading in the morning with a short recess break. Lunch and then writing workshop. We're working on a poetry unit right now. Jeremy was very pleased with his poem. When he turned it in, he told me it was his best ever."

"I'd like a copy of that." Simon looked across at Jacoba.

"Yes, of course." She continued. "I'd wanted Jeremy's help putting up a new bulletin board. I'd not remembered to ask him until he walked past me at the end of the day. He told me he couldn't help me today, but he would help me tomorrow."

"How would you characterize his mood when you spoke with him?"

"He was happy," she answered without hesitation. "Happy," she repeated. "He was full of that energetic optimism fourth graders have."

A cell phone ring suddenly broke into the conversation. Richard looked at the screen.

"It's Elizabeth," he said to Simon. "Excuse me." He went back out the front door to take the call.

Simon didn't wait for Richard's return before asking the next question. "I'm assuming you've met Jeremy's parents?"

"Oh, yes, on several occasions."

"And how would you characterize their relationship with their son?"

"They love him. They are very supportive, very encouraging. And they are interested in how the classroom system works. I'm sure if they didn't both have day jobs, they'd be more involved in our classroom activities."

"So, no red flags about an unhappy home life?"

"No, none whatsoever."

Richard came back into the living room. "Elizabeth needs us."

Simon got up immediately and took his card out of his pocket. "Should anything else come to mind that might help us figure out where Jeremy has gone, please call."

Jacoba took the card in both hands. "I hope you find him safe and sound."

Simon and Richard walked quickly down the sidewalk and got back into the car.

"Elizabeth got access to the high school parking-lot security camera," Richard said as they put on their seatbelts. "A boy on a bike showed up in several frames. Time stamp is four fifty-eight p.m. He was on the bike trail headed north—"

"Toward the park," Simon finished.

"Yes, toward the park."

Simon started the car. "What about the park entrance security cameras and the guard huts at both entrances?"

"No cameras at the entrances. Guard huts, yes; guards in the huts, no."

"Okay, I say we take Cherry Street to Park Road. I'm guessing he used the back entrance to the park since he was on the bike trail by the high school."

Simon looked at the clock on the dashboard. Eight p.m. As he turned onto Cherry Street the orange and gold sky broadcast the news that Thursday was coming to a close. They passed under the pedestrian bridge and took the immediate right onto Park Road.

"No one's on the pedestrian bridge," Richard said, craning his neck to see.

"All right, Jeremy," Simon said under his breath, "you can show yourself at any time."

Simon stopped at the junction of Park Road and the park's perimeter road.

"And here we are, faced with the same problem we had on Connor Avenue: Which way did he go? Left, or right?" Richard looked at Simon and then back out the car window. "If he went left, he'd be traveling north along the river. That part of the road is hilly. A nice challenge for bikers. And the jogging trail runs parallel to the road. He could have decided to ride on that."

Simon took his foot off the brake, and the car rolled through the stop sign, past the empty guard hut. A streetlight winked on just behind them. The road ahead was unlit. Simon flipped on the high beams and opened all four car windows.

"Okay, I'll keep my eyes on the road, you look to the side. I'll drive as far as the third scenic outlook and turn around. You can scan the riverside when we come back."

"I can see all the way to the jogging trail," Richard said as he aimed the car's exterior flashlight out and down. "And listen to those frogs! Quite the chorus tonight."

They'd traveled almost all the way to the third scenic overlook when another car came over the hill from the opposite direction. Simon recognized the driver. The two vehicles slowed, then stopped, one pointing south, the other north.

"Mr. Barfield! What are you doing out here?"

"Same as you, I bet. Looking for Jeremy Davis. We got the heads-up he was missing a little bit after five p.m. He's one of my boys. I couldn't go home without looking. I've been all the way around the park twice. I've driven through all the parking areas, and I stopped by the cemetery, the chapel, and the campground. No sign of him. If he's in the park, he's gotta be deeper in the woods. And that would be so out of character. Jeremy's not one for solo adventures, unlike another young man I remember."

Simon laughed. "A story for another time," he said in Richard's direction. He looked back to Mr. Barfield. "This is my associate, Officer Barclay."

The men nodded to each other.

"Well, Mr. Barfield, if you've covered all that ground, I think we'll turn around and look along the riverside. If we don't find Jeremy, then it's time to call in Beau."

"Good idea. You can't go wrong with Beau," Mr. Barfield said.

"Beau?" Richard asked.

"Beau, the best tracking dog this side of the Grand River," Mr. Barfield said. "It's a shame we don't have rangers here anymore. A private security firm checks the perimeter twice a day, but that outfit isn't worth much." He closed his car window and drove away.

Simon chuckled. "Mr. Barfield runs the camping office for the park. Has for years. He was my son's boys' club leader. He does a great job mentoring kids." He steered into the third scenic overlook parking lot, slowly turned the car around, and started back south on the perimeter road. Richard directed the high beam down toward the river.

"The woods and undergrowth are so thick here," he said after the car had traveled a few hundred feet. "Wait! I saw a flash!"

Simon pulled onto the gravel shoulder. Richard aimed the high beam down the hill, pulled another flashlight out of the glove compartment, and opened the door. He was almost out of the car when Simon spoke up.

"Stomp your feet, Mr. Barclay," Simon directed. "Snakes feel the vibration and go in a different direction."

"Snakes?" Richard sat down and pulled his feet back into the car.

"Just stomp your feet. You'll be fine."

Richard hesitated, took a deep breath, and got out. He moved tentatively down the overgrown embankment, stomping all the way.

"It's just a hubcap," he yelled. He made his way with some difficulty back up the slope, hubcap in one hand, flashlight in the other. After he stowed it in the trunk, he rejoined Simon, and they continued their riverside search. Richard had stomped his way to retrieve three more hubcaps before they were within sight of the back entrance guard hut, but there had been no sign of Jeremy or his bike.

Simon drove under the streetlight and put the car in park. He pulled out his cell phone.

"Hey, Elizabeth, this is Detective Roe. Officer Barclay and I are in the park looking for Jeremy Davis. I'd like to get Beau over here. What's his status? Sure, I'll hold." Simon looked out his window. Beyond the streetlight's limited range, it was pitch black. Crickets chirped alongside the vociferous frog chorus. A branch snapped close by. When Elizabeth came back on the line and started talking, Simon frowned.

"Okay, thanks for checking for me." He looked at Richard. "Well, that's disappointing. Beau is working over in the next county. He won't be available until tomorrow, midmorning at the earliest."

"There's only one dog?"

"There used to be three, but . . ."

"Budget cuts," Richard finished the sentence for him. "So, now what?"

Simon tapped out a slow rhythm on the steering wheel. He stared through the windshield into the dark. "Let's walk along the jogging trail and listen. Maybe we'll hear Jeremy calling for help."

They parked in the back entrance parking lot, grabbed flashlights, and took the little path to the jogging trail.

"I've biked this several times," Richard said as they stepped onto the gravel surface. "It's well maintained, but the woods around it are dense in places. Going off trail in the dark would not be a good idea."

Forty-five minutes later they were back in the car.

Simon fastened his seatbelt. "I think our next step, since we can't get Beau, is to get the fire department out here to do a ground search early tomorrow morning." He pulled out of the empty parking lot and took Park Road back under the pedestrian bridge. Four minutes later they drove into the precinct parking garage. By midnight search plans for the morning were in place. Simon came and stood next to Richard's desk.

"Come on, Mr. Barclay, I'll give you a ride home and pick you up at around six thirty."

Right before one a.m. Simon slid into bed as gently as possible so as not to awaken Dar. He was exhausted, but the events of the last hours were loud and alive in his mind. The Davis situation could still have a happy ending, he reasoned. But his optimism was diminished. His gut told him Jeremy was in the park. But where?

Chapter Six

Simon was up, dressed, and talking to Dar when his cell phone rang. He put it right to his ear. He didn't need caller ID to tell him it was the precinct on the other end. No one else called him at 6:15 a.m.

"Roe," he said. He listened and shook his head. "I'll be right there. Thanks." He hung up and looked solemnly across the table.

"A child's body has been found in the park."

"Oh, Sime."

Within five minutes Simon pulled up to the entrance of the Park View. Richard climbed into the front seat with a mumbled hello. His sleepy demeanor changed when Simon told him about the child's body on the jogging trail.

"What? We walked a long way on that trail last night!"

"I know."

Simon drove onto park property, turned onto the perimeter road, and followed it past the gift shop, the chapel, and the cemetery. Just beyond the back entrance parking lot an officer stood next to the guard hut. Simon pulled alongside him and lowered his window.

"Good morning," he said.

"Good morning, Detective. You'll see our

people by the Prayer Trail sign just beyond the first scenic overlook."

"Thanks."

Simon headed north on the perimeter road. Tall pines dotted the shaggy grass slopes that dropped steeply away from the road. The grass was badly in need of mowing, another silent witness to budget cuts. Early morning sunlight flickered and flashed off the Grand River, visible through the trees on their left.

"Looks different in the morning light, doesn't it?" He scanned the tangle of undergrowth Richard had fought through the night before.

They passed the first scenic overlook parking lot and shortly after spotted the sign for the Prayer Trail with familiar vehicles parked under it. Simon pulled in behind the Grandburg EMTs. When he got out of the car, he felt the gravel press through the worn soles of his beloved brown shoes.

Simon and Richard walked past the paramedics sitting in their vehicle, completing paperwork on their laptops. They nodded to each other.

Richard pointed down the slope. "I see yellow tape."

"That's where we want to be," Simon answered.

They left the gravel shoulder and stepped into the knee-high grass.

"Time to do a little stomping again, Mr. Barclay," Simon said as they descended the slope. The tall grass and their stomping ended abruptly when they came to a stand of pine trees and the jogging trail. Simon suppressed a groan. His knees hurt—confirmation that he needed to lose weight, which he really wanted to ignore.

A police officer was completing the rectangular yellow-tape perimeter around the body. Tree trunks served as anchors for the tape. The yellow rectangle incorporated a portion of the jogging trail as well as several yards of grassy area on either side. Simon and Richard stepped to the chest-high tape's edge at the same time and saw the body of a child, arms carefully folded across his white-shirted chest, legs in khaki pants stretched out straight. A blue bike rested on the ground beside the body.

Simon looked sadly at Richard. "Guess we can call off the search."

"I don't get it! We walked at least this far last night!" Richard looked in the direction of the body, the bike, and turned back to Simon.

Another officer and a young man in jogging shorts stood just beyond the body outside the yellow rectangle. When they saw Simon and Richard, they walked toward them.

"Detective, this is Thomas Callen. Mr. Callen found the body."

"I'd hoped he'd just stopped to rest." The jogger turned to the body. "But then, when I got up close . . ." His voice trailed off.

"Thanks for calling us, Mr. Callen. Do you run in the park often?" Simon asked, his notebook out and open.

"I try to get here several times a week," Thomas Callen said. "I'm a student at Tilden. I usually run before my morning class." He looked at his watch. "Guess I'm going to be a little late today."

"What time did you start your run this morning?" Simon asked.

"Right before six. I overslept. I should be on the trail by five forty-five if I'm going to make it to the third scenic overlook and back before class."

"Have you seen anyone else around here this morning?" Richard asked.

"No. I'm usually the only runner going north on the trail this early, but I often meet folks coming north on my way back."

Movement by the body caught Simon's eye. He recognized Tamara Lyons, the investigator for the coroner's office, stooping over the body and then kneeling next to it. Simon had worked with Tamara Lyons for most of his time as a Grandburg detective. He was always glad when he had her concise observations to work from. He turned his attention back to Thomas Callen.

"Have you ever seen that boy before?"

"No."

"If we have any more questions, what's the best way to reach you?"

"My cell phone."

Simon wrote down the number, thanked him again, and turned back toward where the body lay. He reached out, lifted the yellow tape, and invited Richard to duck under it ahead of him. When they were close enough to see the body clearly, Simon recognized the face immediately.

"Jeremy Davis," he said sadly to Richard.

The investigator's assistant joined them and started taking pictures of both the body and the bike. Tamara Lyons stood up with graceful agility, rolled the rubber gloves off her hands, and stuck them in her blue jeans pocket.

"Ms. Lyons, have you met my associate, Officer Barclay? He's an intern from Tilden College."

"No, we haven't met." Tamara Lyons extended her hand to Richard.

Simon watched as they shook hands. The firmness of the Lyons handshake was known to everyone in the department. Richard didn't flinch under the pressure of those powerful fingers, but Simon did see his eyes widen. Greeting over, Ms. Lyons raked her fingers through the short curls of her gray hair. Simon looked at her expectantly. She looked back down at the body and started talking.

"Male, Caucasian, probably nine or ten years old. Broken neck. Marks under his chin, possibly from helmet straps, even though he's not wearing a helmet now. Skull is in good shape, at least from the exterior point of view. Moderate facial lacerations. Lots of grass, pine needles, and dirt on his clothes, especially on the backside of his pants. One of his shoes is missing. His clothing is dry, as is the ground underneath and all around the body. Also, the bloodstains on his face tell me the body's been facedown for a while."

"So, what are you thinking?"

Ms. Lyons looked down at the body, a thoughtful expression on her face. Then she looked at both men. "On the surface, it looks like a boy's biking adventure gone tragically wrong. Cause of death: broken neck. Manner of death: accident." She shook her head sadly. "But since when does a little boy fall off his bike and break his neck while riding on a well-maintained trail? And how does he land, oh so sweetly posed, by the side of the trail with the bike resting right beside him?" She looked from one man to the other. "Somebody put him here."

A light breeze flowed along the jogging trail, ruffling grass and pine branches. A red-tailed hawk cried out overhead, soaring left, then right, then left again.

"Well, until we know for sure this was an accident . . ." Simon started.

"We treat it like a murder," Richard finished.

Simon turned to Ms. Lyons. "Could I use one of your photos to get an ID from the parents?"

"Certainly." She called over her assistant. While they were viewing the photos, two attendants maneuvered a gurney down the hill to the trail and waited on the other side of the police tape.

"There, that one's good. It looks like he's sleeping."

"I'll email it to you as soon as I get back to my computer," the assistant said.

"Thanks."

"Those poor parents," Ms. Lyons said, looking down at the body again. "My heart goes out to them." She beckoned to the gurney attendants. They came under the tape, and body and gurney were back up the hill and in the van in a matter of minutes. In the meantime, Simon and Richard had gotten the bike back up the hill and put it in the trunk.

Richard turned to Simon. "What's next, Detective?"

"Let's take a walk and see what we can find." He retrieved the canvas bag he always kept in the trunk. It held a generous supply of evidence bags and markers.

As they made their way back through the high grass to the jogging trail, Richard said suddenly, "Say, this is one time the budget issues might work to our advantage! If someone dragged the body from one place to another, we should be able to see that trail in the grass."

They started a slow, deliberate search, their backs to the jogging trail where the body had rested. They traveled deeper into the pines, eyes on the pine-needle carpet that replaced the tall grass.

"Found something!" Richard called out. He turned back around and looked in the direction of the area they'd just come from. Simon took a few careful steps in his direction.

"I see two distinct scuff lines in the pine straw here," Richard said. "And I can see the lines continuing in both directions."

Simon came and stood next to him. "You're right."

They walked alongside the line of plowed pine straw. Richard suddenly reached down and eased an object free from between two close-growing pine seedlings.

"Shoe!" he said, holding it up triumphantly.

Simon held open an evidence bag, and Richard dropped it in. Simon handed Richard a numbered marker, and Richard set it beside the seedlings.

They followed the drag marks a few more feet and stepped out of the stand of pines into a clearing. Directly in front of them they saw the large, bronze plaque, and a few feet beyond it a signpost with the word "Praise" written on it.

Simon turned around and looked back toward the jogging trail. "There used to be a clearly marked path from the jogging trail to this area."

Richard took a few steps back toward the edge of the clearing. "I can see it," he said. "It's just not been mowed in a while." He looked down. "What's this?" He reached down and retrieved a long, shiny orange bicycle streamer. Simon pulled out another evidence bag and numbered marker for Richard.

Simon continued his slow walk, eyes down, scanning the pine straw. "The dirt's all scuffed up here, really shows through the pine straw." He took a few more steps. "I see his helmet!" He lifted it off the ground using a thick tree limb. Another numbered marker went down in its place.

Richard walked over to the Praise post and looked beyond it to the ascending trail. He turned to Simon. "You don't suppose he rode down the Prayer Trail?"

"I was just wondering that very thing," Simon answered.

"If Jeremy rode down all three legs of the Prayer Trail with no slowdowns or stops along the way, he'd have been flying by the time he got here. There's no stopping," Richard said almost to himself, shaking his head. "You have to ride it out and hope you don't crash."

"So, am I hearing the voice of experience? Have you ridden the trail nonstop from top to bottom?"

"Yes, when I was fourteen." Richard wasn't smiling at the memory. "I would have had four years of growth on Jeremy and a bigger bike."

"And why did you do it, Officer Barclay?"

A breeze caused whispering among the pines. The tall grass hissed and swayed. Richard looked sheepishly at Simon.

"Two reasons. I wanted to impress a particular girl in my class, and I also wanted to prove to my two older brothers that their little brother was as tough as they were."

"And did it work?"

"No, actually it backfired," Richard answered with a wry grin. "The girl told me I was an idiot for doing it and never spoke to me again. And when my parents found out, they punished all three of us boys: my brothers for not stopping me, and me for doing something so stupid and so dangerous."

Simon shook his head and chuckled. He shaded his eyes against the glare of the morning sun and looked up past the Praise post. "Let's walk to the top and see what we find. Maybe Jeremy didn't ride down by his own choice." He silently apologized to his knees.

Eyes on the ground, they slowly ascended the trail. They found fresh bike tracks at two of the turns. Once they'd reached the top they stood a few feet from each other, carefully searching for some evidence of struggle.

"I don't see anything. You?" Simon looked over at Richard.

"No. Nothing."

They descended again. Simon's aching knees and the thin soles of his shoes didn't make the trip back comfortable. He was glad when they reached the Praise post again. He turned to face in the direction of the jogging trail.

"Okay, we've found the shoe, the helmet, the spot where Jeremy tried to stop, and a drag trail. Let's assume the drag trail starts where Jeremy's body came to rest. Did the bike land next to him? On top of him?"

Both men, heads down, started a slow walk a few feet apart. Simon shook his head and frowned.

"I don't see anything," he said. "The pine straw is too thick. And it's dry here. No footprints."

"Got something!"

Simon handed Richard a latex glove. Richard slid it on, ran his finger along the ground, and straightened up.

"Grease—from the bicycle chain." He reached out to Simon.

"Well! Good eye, Officer Barclay! And if the bike happened to land on top of the body, there might be traces of grease on the clothing."

The bell from the City Hall clock tower started to toll.

"Eight a.m.," Simon said. "I'd like to get to the Davises by nine. I'm glad the body's found, and the agony of waiting will end when I tell them. But the body found means their boy isn't coming home."

Richard shook his head sadly.

When the men finished the field assessment, they headed back to the precinct. Once Simon was back at his desk, he opened his email, where the photo of Jeremy was already waiting. As soon as he had printed it, he and Richard headed back out the door.

Simon drove slowly up Main Street and turned right at the community garden. Two sisters from St. Gregory's Convent were weeding one corner of the garden. Several of the plots were already boasting leafy green growth. River Street took them past the convent, the school, and the church. When they got to the corner of Connor and River Street, Simon wished the street were longer so he'd have a little more time to prepare himself. In another two minutes they were parked in front of the Davis house. He undid his seatbelt, took a deep breath, and got out of the car. He and Richard started the short walk up the sidewalk to the porch.

"Do you suppose Mr. Mooney is watching?" Richard asked, deliberately not looking that way.

"Probably," Simon said as he reached out to ring the doorbell.

Darrin Davis answered the door. When he saw Simon standing there, hope flashed for an instant in his eyes. But when Simon's solemn expression registered, the hope vanished.

"Mr. Davis, I have news for you and Mrs. Davis." Simon's voice was gentle, sad.

Darrin nodded and opened the door wider to let the men in.

"Darrin? Who was at the door?" Beverly came out of the kitchen, a pink bathrobe wrapped around her. She stopped when she saw Simon and Richard. Then she took a step in Simon's direction and stared into his face.

"You've found him," she said softly. "Oh, Darrin. Oh, Darrin." She started to cry.

Darrin led her to the couch, tears coursing down his cheeks. Simon and Richard sat across from them in the same chairs they'd sat in the evening before. Simon waited a moment before he pulled the photo out of his jacket pocket.

"The body of a child was found this morning. Would you please look at this picture and tell me if you recognize him?" He held out the photo. Darrin took it. He positioned it so Beverly could see.

"Oh no, oh no, oh no." Beverly pulled the picture out of Darrin's hands, hugged it to her chest between crossed arms, and bowed her head to her knees.

"It's Jeremy," Darrin said, his voice breaking. "It's Jeremy."

"I'm so sorry," Simon said. "So sorry."

"Can we see him? I want to see him!" Beverly choked out.

"Yes, of course. As soon as the autopsy is completed, your son's body will be released to the funeral home. That could happen as early as tomorrow afternoon or Sunday morning."

Darrin looked at Simon. "Where was he? Was he hit by a car? Did he fall off his bike?"

"It looks like Jeremy rode his bike down the Prayer Trail and crashed at the bottom."

"The Prayer Trail? In the park?" Darrin was incredulous. "What in the world was he doing there?" He looked askance, first at Simon and then his wife.

"This whole thing is just crazy," Beverly said. She started to cry again.

The clock atop City Hall was chiming the ten o'clock hour when Simon and Richard returned to the precinct. Simon sat down at his desk, aware he'd carried some of the Davises' sadness back to the office with him. He suddenly wanted to call his sons. He wanted to hear their voices, to know they were safe. And he wanted to hear Dar's voice. He reached for his cell phone, then put it back down.

No need to make them anxious just because he was. The adrenaline surge that had carried him along for the past hours slowed and stopped. He yawned. His stomach growled. Breakfast—had he had breakfast, or just coffee? And he'd left home in too much of a hurry to grab the healthy snacks Dar had packed for him. He sat up in his chair. He knew what he wanted: a tuna-salad sandwich on whole-grain bread from the Alley Cat Bar and Grille. With a dill pickle wedge. And maybe an order of sweet potato fries. A small order. Yes.

"Okay," he said to himself, "I'll update the Davis news release, read through my email, call in my lunch order, and then walk over to pick it up." He looked around for Richard. "Mr. Barclay, I'm going to get something from the Alley Cat. Anything I can bring back for you?"

Chapter Seven

It was almost 11:30 before Simon hurried up High Market Street. Humidity heralding imminent rain seeped into his clothes. Thunder rumbled overhead as he reached for the Grille's polished brass handles and pulled open the door. The air-conditioned blast from inside made him shiver. He walked up the gradual incline of the paneled entryway slowly enough to scan the framed cat art featured on the walls. Nothing new caught his eye.

"Detective!" The tall young woman with dark hair, dark eyes, and skin the color of creamed coffee greeted him from the hostess podium. "Here to pick up your order?

"Hello, Shantal. Yes, mine and Mr. Barclay's." Sudden pounding overhead caused them both to look up. "But maybe my 'to-go' needs to stay."

Shantal laughed. "No problem." She checked the seating chart in front of her. "And good news, your favorite booth is available."

With Shantal leading the way, they stepped down into the Alley Cat dining room, heavy rain visible outside the large picture windows overlooking River Street. They walked down the wide aisle between several round tables and chairs. The bar counter and stools to their left were empty. Across from the bar, five booths jutted out from a stone wall. A different cat presided over each table, its large color portrait hung on the stone, and its name on a brass plaque at the bottom of the frame. Shantal stopped in front of the booth sporting the portrait of a seal-point Siamese named Mezzo. Simon slid happily into the familiar seat. Shantal was right; this was his favorite booth. From here he could see everyone who entered, and he could hear a lot of the conversations at the tables in the middle of the room. If he was really in the mood for a challenge, he practiced lip reading from the mirror reflections behind the bar.

"I'll get your order, Detective, and Mr. Barclay's too." As she turned, she almost collided with another woman coming up right behind her.

"Oh, Ms. McKay! Sorry!" Shantal scooted out of the way of a solidly built, steely-eyed woman wearing a black pantsuit with a bright-red blouse.

"An order is missing, again!" the woman said to Shantal, and then unceremoniously dumped a rock the size of a grapefruit on the edge of Simon's table. She waved a small cardboard rectangle in his face.

"Detective Roe! Look at this!" Her alto voice brimmed with indignation. "It was under that rock on the takeout table."

Simon quickly removed the booth's dessert menu from its clip. "Jackie, stick that in here."

"Oh, right! There might be fingerprints on it!" The longtime manager of the Alley Cat reverently stuck the cardboard into the clip and slid into the seat across from Simon.

Shantal looked at them both, raised one penciled black eyebrow, and turned toward the kitchen. Simon recognized her expression immediately. It was the same one Dar gave him when he asked questions with a little too much enthusiasm about one of the properties she was showing.

"'IOU for chicken fingers and honey barbecue sauce,'" Simon read aloud from the cardboard. He studied the loops and swirls of the cursive writing as he put the menu clip back on the table. "So, Jackie, what's going on?" He looked across at the manager.

"This is the third time this month an order of chicken fingers has disappeared," she said. "The other two times cash was left under this rock to pay for the order taken. But this time, no money, just the IOU." The manager pointed to the rock. "That rock is from our patio. I use it all the time to keep the screen door open when we're serving a large party out there. Can you get fingerprints off rocks? Oh, wait, my fingerprints are on there too!"

"Sometimes we can get prints off rocks," Simon answered. "Explain the takeout system to me."

"Orders come over the phone. Shantal usually takes the call, fills out an order form, and sends it to the kitchen. Filled orders are put on the table outside the kitchen."

Simon turned around to spot the table.

"You can't see the table from here," Jackie told

him. "It's behind the wall of the fifth booth. Folks pay when they pick up the order."

"And if Shantal is busy?"

"Then I handle the takeout traffic. During the lunch rush I work the cash register too."

Shantal came alongside their table and put down Simon's order along with Mr. Barclay's. Simon thanked her and pulled out his credit card.

"Shantal," he said as she took the card from his hand, "how many chicken finger takeout orders have you had so far today?"

She thought for a moment. "I'm not sure," she said. "I've taken a boatload of lunch orders since we opened at eleven."

"How does our bandit know which bag or box to take?" Simon asked them both.

"I write the name in all caps on the order form," Shantal said. "The kitchen crew staples the order to the bag or tapes it to the top of the box with the name showing." She pointed to Simon's boxed order. "See?"

Shantal left with Simon's credit card, and Simon looked across the table at the manager. "So, do you want to come to the station and file a police report?"

Jackie shook her head. "No, it's not worth it. All that time and paperwork for something that costs less than ten dollars? No. But if it happens again, I might reconsider. And, hey," she continued with her characteristic enthusiasm, "since an IOU was left at the scene of the crime, maybe someone's planning to come back and pay up!"

"Stranger things have happened!" They both laughed. Simon held up the IOU on the menu clip. "Is it okay with you if I hold on to this?"

Jackie nodded. "Sure."

Simon slid the cardboard between the folds of a napkin and put it into his jacket pocket. "I'll take the rock too. It can go in one of your plastic bags."

Shantal came down the aisle with a party of two. She pushed Simon's credit card and receipt across the table as she passed by. Simon signed the merchant receipt and pocketed his receipt along with his card. He looked toward the patio and saw it wasn't raining anymore.

"Guess I can walk back to the office," he said. "But I'd like to look around a bit on my way out, just for my own satisfaction, if you don't mind."

"I'd appreciate it, actually."

As the two stepped into the aisle, Jackie said, "I heard about the body in the park. I bet you are on that case." She looked respectfully at Simon. "You'll figure it out. You always do."

"Thank you for your confidence," he said, the Roe poker face firmly in place.

Conversations rose from the tables, the lunch rush in full swing. The manager got a plastic bag and neatly scooped up the rock without touching its surface. Simon slid out of the booth, and Jackie handed the rock to him by the bag's loops. He easily balanced lunches and stone. He paused for a quick look at the takeout table. Jackie pushed open the screen door for him, and he stepped past her onto the patio.

"Thanks again for your help," she said. "Enjoy your lunch!" The screen door snapped shut between them.

Simon walked past round tables, their striped umbrellas trimmed with water droplets. He inhaled the earthy after-rain aroma Grandburg always had as he made his way to the raised deck on the patio's far edge. He climbed the four wide wooden steps and was rewarded with a spectacular view of the Grand River. He followed the wide ribbon of river south all the way to the Highway 10 bridge, where he saw three cars crossing over to the next county. He turned and looked north to the public beach and boat ramp only a block away. Just beyond the beach a dense line of pine trees marked the edge of the park. Looking down through the cracks in the deck flooring, he could see the old train tracks that ran parallel to the river. He straightened and faced the umbrellas again.

"It would be so easy to stroll inside the Alley Cat from here and grab a takeout order," he mused aloud. "Especially when it's busy inside. If I were going to skip out on paying my tab, that's what I would do." He started back down the steps. "And if I parked in the back parking lot, I could make a quick getaway."

He shifted his gaze north to River Street. "If I were on foot and ran west along River Street for just a few yards, I could duck into the alley and take it north to the back of the antique mall. And from there I could cross the creek and go into the park. And what about the other exit, the south exit?" he asked himself, facing that direction. He only considered it for a moment. "If I were the thief, I wouldn't take it. Too many buildings and people in that direction. Something or someone might slow me down or stop me or even recognize me."

Simon heard the City Hall clock chime the three-quarter hour. Time to get back to the precinct. He left the patio, walked through the parking lot, and headed south on Highmarket. When he finally sat down at his desk he set the bag-wrapped rock next to his inbox. He took the napkin-wrapped IOU out of his jacket pocket, slid it into a clear plastic evidence bag, and propped it up next to the rock. He flipped the cardboard piece over, keeping the clear covering taut, and studied it as he took a couple bites of his sandwich. There was something familiar about that cardboard rectangle.

Suddenly it came to him. He was looking at an old bookmark from The Cat's Meow. Dar had over a dozen in her bedside table drawer. He could just make out the faded imprint of a Cheshire cat, the bookstore logo, on the side opposite the cursive IOU.

"Interesting!" Simon said into the empty office. "So, we have a person who writes in cursive, likes chicken fingers, has shopped at The Cat's Meow, and is currently experiencing a cashflow problem." He triumphantly bit into a sweet potato fry, which, even cold, tasted delicious.

I wonder if the chicken finger bandit will pay up, he thought as he chewed and swallowed.

Richard came around the corner, saw Simon eating, and immediately rolled his desk chair up to one side of Simon's desk. Simon pushed Richard's lunch toward him.

"Mr. Barclay," he said after he'd swallowed the fry he'd been munching, "why leave an IOU if you don't intend to pay?"

"My Uncle Gus has a saying," Richard said as he sat down and opened his order, "'I'd rather owe it to you than cheat you out of it.'" He unwrapped his smoked turkey sandwich. "What are we talking about?"

Simon grinned and brought him up to speed. "I think the bandit has a conscience," he concluded. "After all, the two other orders were paid for."

"That's assuming the orders were placed by the same person."

"Good point, Mr. Barclay!" Simon said as Richard stifled a yawn. He wondered if he looked as "together" as Richard did. That yawn was the only thing about Richard Barclay's appearance that hinted at how little sleep they'd had over the last twenty-four hours. He picked up the bookmark. "I'm going to send this down to the lab along with the rock and let the techs have a go at them." He put the bookmark back down again.

"So, Detective Roe," Richard leaned forward in his chair, his sandwich half consumed, "what's my assignment for the afternoon?"

"Well, Mr. Barclay, here's what I'm thinking. You do some reconnoitering in the park while I go over to Grandburg Elementary and talk to Ms. Dahm again."

"Sounds good," Richard said. "I can cover the perimeter road up past the second scenic overlook and the jogging trail on my bike." He reached out tentatively for a sweet potato fry. Simon pushed the takeout container in his direction.

"Help yourself," he said. "You'll be saving me from myself if you finish them."

Richard popped a fry into his mouth and continued. "Then I'll walk the area where we were this morning."

Talking stopped and they finished eating. A short time later they were back in the car on their way to the Park View so Richard could pick up his bike.

"Let's meet at the picnic tables at the back entrance at around five or so," Simon said as they pulled up under the Park View canopy. "We can exchange information then and decide if we're done for the day or need to go back to the office."

"Got it." Richard got out of the car and headed for the entrance.

Simon took Creston Avenue all the way to the school. He drove slowly to the far end of the parking lot and pulled into a parking space some distance from the school's front entrance. He needed extra steps to work off those sweet potato fries.

He walked past two rows of parked cars and stepped onto the sidewalk. The full bike rack brought Jeremy and the Hirsch twins immediately to mind. Simon looked at his watch. Yesterday at this time Jeremy had still been alive. He walked up the front steps and pushed the call button.

"Welcome to GES, how may I help you?"

Simon stepped closer to the call button, aware of the camera above it. He held up his ID.

"I'm Detective Roe. I'd like to speak with Ms. Dahm."

"Of course, Detective. Come on in."

Simon heard the click of the magnetic door release. He pulled the door open and entered a familiar wide hallway with lockers on each side and a highly polished floor. Nothing had changed since his boys had been here. Before he reached the front office's sliding glass window, the office door opened. A man a little shorter than Simon stepped into the hallway. His blue shirt and paisley tie harmonized with a light-brown suitcoat and pants. Simon admired his loafers.

"Detective Roe, I'm Dr. Miller, the principal." He extended his hand. "I'm assuming you're here about the Davis boy? So unfortunate. How can I help you?"

"I'd like to have a word with Ms. Dahm, if I could."

"Certainly. Right this way."

Their steps echoed in the empty hallway. Dr. Miller stooped to pick up a stray scrap of paper. His suit coat fell open and his tie slipped sideways. He carried the scrap to a large trash can in the hallway corner, threw in the paper, and with a slight frown squared his jacket shoulders and readjusted his tie.

"Ms. Dahm's classroom is just around this corner, first door on the left." Dr. Miller continued to lead the way. "So, the boy's body was found in the park?"

"Yes," Simon said.

"And it was an accident?"

"I'm sorry, sir, but I can't comment at this point. Ongoing investigation. You understand."

"Oh, yes, of course."

They stopped in front of a partially open classroom door. A large bulletin board covered with children's artwork hung next to it. A printed sign in the middle of the board read "We Remember Jeremy." Simon stepped closer to see the display. His eyes traveled from one drawing to the next. Several pictures were of a smiling boy, his bike and his friends close at hand. One showed him swinging a baseball bat, another sharing pizza with two other boys and a dog. Simon scanned the collection for a drawing of a biker on the Prayer Trail. He didn't see one.

Dr. Miller reached up to knock on the classroom

door frame just as Jacoba pulled the door all the way open. Dr. Miller stepped back.

"Ms. Dahm, Detective Roe is here to see you."

Jacoba looked sadly in Simon's direction.

"Ms. Dahm, I'm hoping you can help me with a couple details. It won't take long."

"Yes, of course." She turned around and led the way back into the empty classroom.

As Simon followed her retreating back, Dr. Miller brought up the rear. Simon turned back and addressed him.

"Thank you, Dr. Miller. I'll take it from here."

Dr. Miller stared at Simon, sniffed twice, and frowned in protest, but seeing dismissal plainly written on the detective's face, he turned and retreated into the hallway.

Jacoba took the chair from a nearby workstation and rolled it in front of her desk for Simon. "Here you go, Detective."

"Thank you." He pulled his spiral notebook out of his jacket pocket. "Ms. Dahm, I'm sure this has been a very hard day for you. I'm so sorry."

She nodded as she blinked back tears. "Very hard," she said, "for all of us." She looked sadly at Simon. "His parents. I can't even imagine." Tears trickled down her cheeks, and she reached for a tissue.

"Paint a picture of Jeremy for me. What kind of child was he?"

Jacoba sat back in her desk chair. Her answer came easily. "Jeremy Davis was a quiet, sweet boy.

Very creative. He enjoyed making up stories, telling jokes, writing poems." She stopped and reached for another tissue.

"Would he, maybe on a dare, do something like ride his bike down the Prayer Trail?"

"No," Jacoba said decisively, shaking her head. "Absolutely not. He isn't . . . wasn't the daredevil type, and neither are any of his buddies." She looked at Simon, her expression troubled. "Do you think he rode his bike down the Prayer Trail?"

"We're looking into all kinds of possible scenarios," he said. "Ms. Dahm, last night you mentioned a poem he'd written yesterday. I'd like to see it, if I could."

"Certainly. It's right here." But when she reached toward her inbox, her eyes fell on empty space where children's work should have been. "Oh, no." She looked back at Simon. "My para pro must have taken the writing assignment along with the math she's going to check for me. She's part time. I won't see her again until Tuesday." Jacoba pulled open the middle desk drawer and started fishing out scraps of paper and putting them on the desk blotter. "I have her phone number here somewhere."

"There's no urgency," Simon reassured. "When you get the poem back, give me a call. You have my number. I'll come by and get a copy." He looked out over the rows of empty desk chairs. "How many children are in your class?"

"Nine girls and eight . . . seven boys now, so sixteen," she said sadly.

"Do they get along with each other?"

"Yes, they do. But," she looked down at the desk blotter, "I've certainly repeated the phrase 'boys will be boys' often this year." She looked at Simon, her eyes wide. "Do you think another child may have been involved in Jeremy's death?"

"There's no indication of that, Ms. Dahm. As I said, we're looking into a variety of possibilities."

Suddenly fourth-grade chatter accompanied by fourth-grade students spilled into the room. Simon put his notebook back in his pocket and stood up. He smiled at Jacoba and squeezed past curious eyes as he exited the classroom. He lingered a moment or two in front of the bulletin board before he turned the corner to the main hallway. He waved goodbye to the secretary behind the glass window and walked out of the building.

The bright May afternoon called for sunglasses. He squinted and shielded his eyes as he walked back across the parking lot to his car. He wondered if Richard was finding anything of interest. As he sat down in the driver's seat, he thought about Ms. Dahm's "boys will be boys." He knew from experience with his own boys that a situation could get out of hand in a heartbeat. Is that what had happened with Jeremy?

He pulled out slowly from the parking lot and headed back to the station. There was just enough time to get some paperwork done before reconnecting with Richard. And then, two glorious days off. He hoped Dar didn't have great expectations. He needed some serious downtime.

Richard pedaled along the perimeter road past the unmanned guard hut and let gravity pull the bike toward the curve north. He easily negotiated the gentle inclines, and it wasn't long before he'd reached the first scenic overlook. He rode one lap around the edge of the parking lot and stopped at the picnic tables. He leaned his bike up against one of them and walked to the overlook edge.

The air was tinged with the smell of the river. The bright afternoon sunlight glinted off the water below, and he could hear the hushed murmur of moving water. He looked up and saw a red-tailed hawk leisurely riding the thermals high over his head.

"The heavens declare the glory of God," the words came unbidden to his mind. "Huh," Richard said to himself. "Now where did that come from?" He said the words out loud. "The heavens declare the glory of God." And he remembered: Eighth grade. St. Gregory's. His eyes followed the hawk's glides and swoops. He'd thought he'd left behind all his religious education when he left. Well. Maybe not.

Reluctantly he turned and started back toward

his bike. He'd almost reached it when he heard more than his own footsteps. He stopped. Someone was whistling. He could just make out the tune, "Camptown Races." He turned partway around, scanning the edges of the parking lot.

"Hello? Is someone there?"

The whistling stopped. Richard shrugged, mounted his bike, and pushed off. He skirted the parking lot once and started north again on the perimeter road. It wasn't long before he passed the sign for the bottom of the Prayer Trail and the spot where he and Detective Roe had parked that morning. He could barely make out the jogging trail through the trees down below. As he continued to ride north toward the second outlook, the incline increased. A car came up behind him and then passed him. He got a good look at the license plate. California. He wondered if any out-of-staters had seen Jeremy yesterday. The river disappeared and reappeared on his left, obscured by one pine stand after another.

When Richard got to the second overlook, he took the short gravel path that led to the top of the Prayer Trail. He thought about his fourteen-year-old self who had been in this exact spot what seemed a lifetime ago. Even though the incidents were years apart, he and Jeremy both had been here, astride their bikes, both deciding to ride down. He looked up and saw a hawk, maybe the same one he'd seen earlier, gliding in long, lazy spirals overhead. He heard another car pass by on the perimeter road. He dismounted and walked his bike to the Wait post. The Prayer Trail's descent started immediately beyond.

"Why did you do it, Jeremy?" he asked softly, looking down the steep slope. He remembered how grateful he'd been when he'd made it to the bottom in one piece. And now, at this moment, he was filled with gratitude all over again.

Richard turned his bike around and pedaled back to the perimeter road. When he came to where he and the detective had parked earlier in the day, he turned off the pavement and bumped down the grassy hill to the jogging trail. He spotted the place where the body had been discovered and was surprised to see a small tower of smooth, flat stones stacked at the edge of the path. He stopped beside it and noticed a bird's feather at the top of the tower, held in place by a larger, rounder stone.

"Huh," he said. "I wonder what this is about?" Just as he bent over to further examine the tower, he heard the angry chattering of a squirrel coming from the woods. He straightened up as a gray squirrel shot past him with a medium-sized curly-coated brown dog in hot pursuit.

"Hey!" Richard yelled. "Where's your owner?" He watched the squirrel and the dog race back toward the perimeter road. He looked around, expecting someone to come rushing after the dog. He laid his bike on the side of the jogging trail and ran back up the slope to the perimeter road.

"Hello? Hello?" Richard yelled.

A sharp whistle pierced the air. He heard the dog bark, and the whistle sounded again.

"Hello? Police officer! I'd like to speak to you!" he yelled back down the slope. He waited. All he heard now was the sound of wind in the trees and birds calling to one another.

Richard walked back to the jogging trail, pulled out his cell phone, and took a picture of the rock tower. He picked up his bike and rolled it to the clearing at the base of the Prayer Trail. He passed the spot where he'd found Jeremy's shoe. He saw the hollow in the grass where Detective Roe had found the helmet. When he got to the scuff marks in the pine straw, he turned and looked back toward the jogging trail. If Jeremy's bike and body had come to rest here, the tall grass between the clearing and the jogging trail would have completely obscured them from view. So, maybe somebody moved the body and the bike so they would be seen. But why not just call and report it, like Thomas Callen had done that morning?

When Richard biked back into the parking lot, Simon was waiting for him at one of the picnic tables. Richard launched into what he'd seen and heard during his park reconnaissance.

"Wish I'd seen someone when I heard the whistling. If the whistler was in the park yesterday, he or she might have seen Jeremy."

The City Hall clock chimed the half hour.

"Oh, and . . ." Richard pulled out his phone. "When I went back to the spot where the body was found, someone had built a sort of stone tower there, and put a feather on top. Here, I took a picture." He handed his cell phone across the table to Simon.

"Interesting!" Simon studied the photo. "A cairn. I wonder who did this?"

"A what?"

"Cairn. A Gaelic word. Means pile of stones. A cairn can mark a trail, or be a memorial." Simon handed the phone back to Richard. "Email the photo to me, and I'll put it in the case file."

"Done," Richard said after a few keystrokes. "What's next, Detective Roe? Shall I cruise the park until after dark?"

Simon laughed. "No, Mr. Barclay. I think it's time for both of us to go home. Want me to drive you and your bike back to the Park View?"

"Thank you, but no. I'll ride the bike home. Maybe I'll spot that dog."

"You coming in on Monday?" Simon asked.

"Final exam Monday morning. I'll come in after that."

"Well then, I can guess what you'll be doing all weekend!"

Simon watched Richard pedal out of the parking lot and turn up the perimeter road in the direction of his apartment. He was going to miss him when his internship was over at the end of the summer. Richard Barclay was going to make an excellent detective. Simon got back into his car and checked the time.

I'll be home by six. Dar will be pleased.

Jonathan was already in the car when Solomon walked out of Preston Hall. When he saw his father, he started the engine. Solomon barely had time to close the passenger door before Jonathan started backing out of the parking place.

"Which way, Dad?" Jonathan asked as he stopped for the light at the main entrance. "Remembrance or Creston?"

"Remembrance," Solomon answered. "Less traffic this time of day."

When the light turned green Jonathan took an immediate left. He was surprised by his father's choice. Remembrance would take them right past the cemetery.

As if his father were reading his mind he said, "I want to see the new condos at Gryzen's Greens."

Jonathan drove past the cemetery and turned right onto Ridley. The condos were set back from the street with a semicircular access drive of their own.

"Want me to turn in?"

"No, stay on Ridley. Let's not keep Sam waiting."

When they got to Grandburg Elementary, Solomon went in to get Sam, and Jonathan stayed in the car. He turned on the radio and local news blared out into the car's interior.

"The child's body found in the park earlier today has been identified as ten-year-old Jeremy Davis. The boy's body and bicycle were discovered by a jogger. Police are not commenting on whether this was an accident or—"

Jonathan hit the tuning button and smooth jazz came through the speakers. He invited the contrapuntal rhythms to take his thoughts to a different place: away from death, away from mysterious circumstances, away from disappointments. He looked toward the school's front entrance.

The double doors burst open and Sam came running out of the building. He rushed down the front steps, pulled open the back door on the driver's side, and threw in his backpack.

"Hi, Jon," he said. Let's go home! I'm starving!"

"Okay, Sam, I'm with you. But we can't leave without Dad. Where is he?" Jonathan looked into the rearview mirror at his little brother.

Sam leaned back and tried to touch the car's ceiling with his fingers. "Dad's coming."

"Don't forget your seatbelt," Jonathan said automatically. "Did you have Art today?"

"Yup. Dad's got my picture."

When Solomon came out of the building, manila art paper in hand, Jonathan started the car. He turned the radio off. Solomon slid into the front seat and wordlessly handed Jonathan Sam's picture. Jonathan stared at the sketch.

"Well, Sam. What made you draw him today?"

"I was wondering if he stayed with Jeremy Davis in the park. I hope so."

Jonathan swallowed hard and didn't look at his father.

"I feel sad even though I didn't know Jeremy very well," Sam continued. "The whole school is sad."

Jonathan reached over the seat and gave Sam the drawing. "Sam, I don't think you've ever mentioned this guy's name."

"He didn't tell me his name. He just said, 'Don't be afraid.' And he stayed with me until somebody came and got me out." Sam looked at the drawing. "I can't believe you didn't see him, Jon. Are you sure you didn't see him?"

"Sorry, buddy. No," Jonathan said for what felt like the one thousandth time, "I didn't see him."

Jonathan put the car in drive and pulled away from the curb. He didn't want to think about the January snow, the slippery road, the car crashing down an embankment, his mother dying. But the whole incident replayed in his mind.

"I wonder if angels get cold," Sam said. "It was cold that day in the car."

Jonathan turned the radio back on. The sounds of smooth jazz filled the car again. He turned up the volume. For once his dad didn't turn it back down.

Chapter Eight

Simon looked beyond the office partition to the rain-spattered windowpane and then back to his computer screen. He was tired, Friday-after-a-long-week tired. He checked the time: 5:30. He needed to leave now if he was going to stop at the Davis visitation on his way home. He'd promised Dar an evening out and had made dinner reservations at Radcliffe's. He'd have preferred Marcellino's. The chef at Marcellino's knew what to do with garlic, and Simon loved garlic. But Dar's not-so-subtle hints for an evening of elegance had led him to make a different choice. A loud sneeze from the other side of the partition interrupted his musings.

"Bless you!" he said into the air.

"Thank you, sir."

"I'm surprised you're still here, Mr. Barclay. I thought you'd be off somewhere studying."

"This corner of the office is a good place to study. Too many distractions at my apartment, and the campus library is packed."

"How many exams do you have left?"

"One more on Monday and a paper due Tuesday. I thought I'd stay here until the rain stopped or hunger motivated me to bike home, whichever came first."

"Well, I'm heading out now. Would you like a ride? I'm going to stop in at the Davis visitation. I could drop you and your bike off after that."

"That would be great! I'd forgotten the visitation was today."

Simon logged off his computer and put the file he'd been working on in the locked cabinet next to his desk. He headed for the door with Richard right behind him.

"It's days like today I'm glad we have a parking garage," Simon remarked as they made their way down the deserted corridor to the stairwell. "I wasn't too keen on the idea when they decided to build it, but I have appreciated it since, when the weather's been bad."

The humidity increased with each step down the metal staircase. By the time they'd clicked seatbelts and Simon had backed out of his designated parking space, mugginess hugged them both like an extra layer of clothing. Rain thundered on the windshield when the car pulled out from under the cover of the garage. Simon flipped the windshield wipers on high.

"Good thing you're not on your bike now, Mr. Barclay," Simon said as he turned left onto Center Street.

"No kidding. I'll be so glad when I have a car again. Grandburg is a great place for biking, though," Richard continued. "It's the weather that complicates things."

Simon turned on his blinker just before Port

Street. "We really need a public transit system here," he said. "City Council has talked about it, but the idea doesn't ever seem to get any traction." The blinker's musical two-note solo sounded again as he turned left onto Main Street.

"You'd think the need would be obvious with all the development in Brockway Heights and the growth at the college."

They waited at the stop light on the corner of Main and River. Simon's eyes left the traffic light long enough for a quick scan of the community garden plots. No weeders in sight. The rainfall slowed as they turned onto River Street. They passed St. Gregory's Elementary School and rectory on his side and the convent on Richard's side of the car.

The blinker sounded again as Simon pulled into the north parking lot of Billingsley Funeral Home. He cruised down the first row of cars looking for a place to park. A car backed out midway down the second row, and he steered around to pull into the space. He undid his seatbelt and surveyed the parking lot.

"Good. The rain's stopped."

They walked up the row, their shoes splashing through numerous shallow puddles. They climbed the four steps to the funeral home's wraparound porch. The house was one of five historic homes built along Winding Creek Road and had been a funeral home as long as Simon could remember. Dale Billingsley had been the owner for the last fifteen years. Simon approved of the subtle restoration work Dale was doing on the place. He'd been on this porch enough times to recognize the improvements.

Simon and Richard took their places at the end of the receiving line that snaked out onto the porch. The people standing just ahead of them turned, nodded, and then turned back to continue their wait. An occasional raindrop fell from the porch overhang onto the railing. Simon looked beyond the white porch railing with its ornate spindles to the sprawling St. Gregory campus across the street.

"Have you been inside the worship space?" he asked Richard, nodding in that direction.

"Been in there many times," Richard replied. "I went to St. Gregory's from kindergarten through eighth grade. Probably sat in every pew in the course of my time there."

In another minute or so they'd made it around the corner to the front doors. Footsteps behind them caused them both to turn around. Jacoba Dahm was coming toward them, her purse swinging in time with her stride. She was carrying a large book encased in plastic.

Before they could exchange greetings, the line moved again, and they stepped inside the funeral home. Simon looked into the crowded great room, his view limited by the meandering visitation line as well as other people standing at various places around the room. Then the crowd parted, and he caught sight of Darrin and Beverly Davis and the casket at the far end of the room.

He turned his attention back to Jacoba. She was carefully removing the plastic from around the book. Once it was free, she held it up for them both to see. "We Remember Jeremy" was hand-lettered in white paint across the turquoise posterboard cover.

"Are these the drawings you had up on the bulletin board outside your classroom?" Simon asked.

"Those are here, but so are others the children drew."

"May I?"

Jacoba handed Simon the book. "Oh, Detective Roe, Jeremy's poem hasn't turned up. As a matter of fact, I can't find any of the poems the children wrote last Thursday. I'm sure they'll turn up eventually. When I find them, do you still want a copy of Jeremy's?"

"Yes." Simon smiled at her. "I think I'm more curious now just because we don't have it in hand."

Jacoba smiled back.

Simon turned his attention to the book. He gave each picture a thoughtful viewing. Richard looked on with mild interest until Simon got to the fifth picture.

"There's the dog!" Richard exclaimed.

"The dog?" Simon looked at Richard and back to the drawing.

"The dog! The dog I saw in the park last Friday! Brown and blond, short, curly fur. That's the dog!"

Simon stared at the picture of three children on bikes with a small, curly-coated dog following them. He turned the page to check for the artist's name. "Well! Isn't that interesting?" He held the book so Richard could see. The name *Jake Hirsch* was scrawled across the back in blue crayon.

"I wonder if the Hirsches are here?" Simon scanned the room. "There's Dale. He'll know." He turned to Jacoba. "Ms. Dahm, may I take the book for a few minutes?"

"Certainly," Jacoba said.

"Thank you. Be right back."

Simon and Richard headed to the center of the room where a man of medium height with dark hair and a modest mustache was keeping a watchful eye on all the activity around him.

"Detective Roe!" Dale Billingsley greeted Simon. "I haven't seen you here in a while. And I'm thinking given your line of work, that's probably a good thing."

"You're right about that! I don't think you've met my associate, Richard Barclay." The men shook hands. "Dale, are the Hirsches here?"

"I saw them speaking with Mr. and Mrs. Davis a few minutes ago." The funeral director scanned the room with sharp, quick eyes. "There they are. They're standing near the exit sign."

Simon and Richard caught up with the Hirsches just as the family reached the door.

"Mr. and Mrs. Hirsch?"

"Yes?" Neil Hirsch turned to face Simon.

"Detective Roe, hello!" Naomi Hirsch rested her hands on the shoulders of Jake and Maddie.

"This probably isn't the best time, but I'd like to ask Jake a question, if I could?"

Neil and Naomi exchanged glances, and Naomi looked down at her son. She shook her head, a small smile played across her lips. "Well, Jake, maybe now we'll find out about those cookies that mysteriously disappeared earlier this afternoon."

"Mom!" Jake looked up at his mother in annoyance. Maddie giggled.

"Ms. Dahm was just showing us the pictures everyone drew about their favorite times with Jeremy." Simon flipped the book open to Jake's picture and tilted the book toward him. "Is this your picture?"

Jake left his mother's side to get a better look. He took hold of the bottom edge of the book with both hands. Maddie edged closer to her brother to peer over his shoulder.

"Yes, this is mine." Jake looked up at Simon. "Ms. Dahm said to draw our happiest times with Jeremy. My best times with Jeremy were the times we rode our bikes."

"And the dog?" Richard interjected. "Is that your dog?"

"Oh, no, we can't have a dog. Dad's allergic to dogs."

"And cats," Maddie chimed in regretfully.

"But there's a dog in your picture . . ." Richard said as he looked back and forth at both children.

Simon waited, aware of the need to get the book back in Jacoba Dahm's hands before much longer.

"Oh, that's Max. He's very friendly."

"Does Max live in your neighborhood?" Richard asked.

"No," Maddie said firmly.

"No," Jake said, "not exactly."

"Where are you riding in this picture?" Simon tried to sound as nonchalant as possible. "Are you riding in a particular place?"

Jake and Maddie looked wide-eyed at each other.

"Can we go home now?" Jake asked in a small voice. Maddie stepped back to her mother and reached for her hand. Jake was quick to grab the other one.

Mrs. Hirsch sent a quizzical look over the twins' heads to her husband, Simon, and Richard as she shepherded the children out the door. Mr. Hirsch waited until his family was out of earshot and then said to Simon, "Leave it to me, Detective. I'll find out the location and more about the dog. I've got your card. I'll call you."

"Thank you, Mr. Hirsch."

Simon and Richard kept their voices low as they took their place back in line.

"Max. Yes, that dog definitely looks like a Max," Richard said. "But what made them stop talking?"

Simon handed Jacoba the book of drawings. "Thank you, Ms. Dahm." He congratulated himself on excellent timing. The Davises and the casket were just a few feet in front of them now. Simon assumed the elderly woman sitting alone on a loveseat quite close to where they stood was Grandmother Davis.

The couple ahead of Jacoba stepped away from Beverly and Darrin and moved slowly toward the casket. Simon watched Jacoba step up to speak to the parents and hand them the book of drawings. He could see by their faces that they were touched by the book. Darrin took the book over to his mother and motioned for Jacoba to join him. Simon and Richard had a ringside seat for what happened next.

"Ms. Dahm, this is my mother, Jeremy's grandmother, Margaret Davis." He looked down at Mrs. Davis. "Mother, look at this wonderful gift from Jeremy's friends." He handed the book to her and turned to introduce Jacoba. "This is Ms. Dahm, Jeremy's teacher."

Jacoba took a step closer and offered her hand to the seated woman. "Mrs. Davis, I'm so sorry for your loss."

Margaret Davis stared first at Jacoba's hand and then up into Jacoba's face. Hard eyes met Jacoba's gentle ones. When Mrs. Davis didn't take Jacoba's hand, Jacoba let hers fall back to her side.

"So, you're Jeremy's teacher. Jeremy talked a lot about you." Mrs. Davis's words were cold, accusing, condemning. She opened the book to the first drawing, pursed her lips in disapproval, and snapped the book shut again. She thrust the book back into her son's hands. "Here, Darrin. I don't want to see this." Her voice was louder now. "I don't go for all this creative crap in the classroom!"

"Mother, really, this isn't the time or place—"

Margaret Davis launched her attack the instant he stopped to take a breath.

"All those stories you read the children, all the imagining you invite them to do—it just encourages irresponsible thinking. And irresponsible thinking leads to irresponsible behavior." Margaret Davis stood up as straight and tall as her aging frame would allow. She pointed an arthritic finger at Jacoba. "Jeremy was never a risk-taker. But nine months in your classroom changed him."

"Mother, please, your voice is carrying." Darrin was pleading now. Conversation in the rest of the room stopped.

"I don't care, Darrin! People need to know what this woman did. My grandson died because of what she teaches!"

The accusation hung in the air. Jacoba was too stunned to move. Dale Billingsley materialized next to Simon.

"Mrs. Davis, I've brought you some water." Dale walked briskly to the loveseat, and stepped between the others and Grandmother Davis. He caught Simon's eye as he handed the bottle to the elder Davis.

Simon leaned over and whispered in Richard's ear. "I'll get Ms. Dahm out of here. You stay and give Mr. and Mrs. Davis our condolences."

Simon walked up to Jacoba, took her elbow, and led her away from the loveseat and Margaret Davis. He led her out the front door to a bench on the edge of the porch. Jacoba sat down and dug a tissue out of her purse. Simon sat down next to her and gave her a moment to compose herself. Early evening settled all around them, humid and warm. A short distance away, the park's tree frogs were warming up for their evening concert. The City Hall clock chimed seven times. An older couple passed them and sent sympathetic looks in Jacoba's direction. A minute or two later, Richard came around the corner and stood close by, leaning on the porch post.

"Could she be right?" Jacoba turned to Simon, her face etched with shock and disbelief. "Could my encouraging creativity be the reason Jeremy is dead?"

Simon looked her squarely in the eye. "Ms. Dahm, Jeremy Davis is dead because he rode down the Prayer Trail. We'll probably never know why he decided to do what he did." He paused and then asked, "Did you ever suggest to him that he ride down that trail?"

"No! Never!" She shook her head, tears rolling down her cheeks. "I would never suggest a child do something like that!"

Simon nodded, keeping his eyes in line with hers. "Jeremy's choice led to his death. Tragic? Yes. Your fault? No." He let the words sink in. "A tragic death brings out the best and the worst in people.

The need to place blame can be very strong. I'm sorry you were on the receiving end of such unkindness."

Jacoba took some deep breaths and wiped her eyes. "Thank you, Detective," she said softly.

"Officer Barclay and I would be happy to take you home if you'd rather not drive."

"No, no, I'm fine, really. Thank you, though. I don't have far to go. I live just a few streets from here." She pulled her car keys out of her purse.

Richard followed behind them as they walked down the porch steps and took the short sidewalk to the parking lot. Simon saw tears rolling down her cheeks as she turned and walked away from them.

"She's really hurting," Richard said as they watched Jacoba get into her car.

"I hope Ms. Dahm has a good support system. She needs it now."

Five minutes later Simon pulled under the green-canopied entrance of the Park View. The four-story building's exterior gleamed as the setting sun's rays reflected off the damp red bricks. Once Richard had retrieved his bike, Simon waved goodbye and turned back onto Creston Avenue. The clock on the dashboard read 7:25. He'd make it home with just enough time to take a very fast shower, change, and whisk Dar out the door to Radcliffe's. He was looking forward to uninterrupted time across the table from his wife.

The sun was low in the western sky when

Simon and Dar pulled into Radcliffe's parking lot. He walked around the front of the car and opened the passenger-side door. Dar got out and smiled fondly at him.

"You are such a gentleman, Simon Roe."

He grinned. They strolled up the sidewalk to the restaurant's stone entrance arm in arm. Simon pulled open the heavy door and inhaled her perfume when she walked past him. They walked together down the short hallway, nodded to the lady at the door of the coat-check room, and rounded the corner on the dining area. The large windows along the entire west wall were aglow with sunset colors. Round tables, covered with white linen tablecloths and flanked by round-backed upholstered chairs, were spaced discretely on the two-level floor. A tuxedoed pianist was playing a Broadway showtune on the grand piano. The music mingled nicely with the low murmur of conversations. Just ahead of them a small antique table with a tall brass floor lamp next to it served as the hostess station.

"Detective Roe, Mrs. Roe! Good evening!"

"Shantal!" Simon said in surprise. "You work here too?"

"I'm subbing for my cousin, just for tonight." She checked the tablet she held. "Right this way."

Shantal led them across the carpeted main floor and up the two steps to the second level. She took them to a corner table with a view back into the room as well as out the windows to the golf course.

Simon pulled out the chair for Dar and sat across from her. Shantal lit the votive candle in the crystal globe in the center of the table.

"Here are your menus. Raul will be your waiter this evening."

"Shantal, I'm curious. Did the chicken finger bandit ever pay up?"

"Nope, he or she did not," Shantal laughed. "Raul will be here shortly. Enjoy your dinner."

Simon wondered how she was able to say "Enjoy your dinner" in such a warm, personal way when he knew she said those three words ad infinitum. He looked at Dar across the table. She met his eyes with a mixture of curiosity and expectation. He kept no secrets from her, nor she from him. That she didn't know about the chicken finger bandit revealed how little they'd been together during the last week. In between bites of yeast rolls and Caprese salad, Simon told Dar everything that had happened, from the chicken finger bandit to the Davis visitation at Billingsley's.

As Dar finished her crab cakes topped with mustard cream sauce, Simon sipped his minted iced tea and looked out over the dinner guests. Most of the tables on the first level were occupied. Dar picked up her goblet of tea and turned toward the piano as the pianist began to play a new selection.

"Oh, nice! Something by Peter White, I think." She didn't turn back around right away. When she did, her eyes were wide. "Sime," she said softly, "do you see the couple sitting just to the left of the piano? Tall, heavyset man; woman wearing a red dress, blond hair piled on top of her head."

Simon glanced over and then looked back at her. "Who are they?"

"William and Ursula Barnes. He owns the company that built the condos on the greens. Big success. All the units were sold before they'd dug half the foundations. Rumor has it Mr. Barnes wants to build more condos, and you'll never guess where!" She looked across the table at him, both eyebrows raised expectantly.

He looked back at her. "Out toward Stifler Farm?"

"Nope. You're cold."

"North of Grandburg, on the way to Byington?"

"Nope. You're still cold, very cold."

"North of Tilden College?"

"Nope, but you are getting warmer."

"Is he planning to renovate some of the old downtown warehouses?"

"Nope, but you are definitely getting warmer, almost hot."

"How about south of Highway 10, by the retreat center?"

"Nope. You're cold again." Dar sat back and smiled her best all-knowing smile.

"Well, Dar, the only other open-land area I can think of is the park, and I . . ." He looked across the table in astonishment. She was nodding.

He leaned forward. "You're kidding! He wants to build condos in the park?"

Simon looked across the tables to the Barneses and discovered they were leaving. Ursula walked out ahead of William. Simon watched as William pulled out his wallet, tossed several bills on the table, and hurried after his wife. The waiter arrived at their empty table right after they'd left, the black folder containing the unpaid check in his hand. When he spotted the money on the table he shrugged, picked it up, counted it, and stuck it in the folder. Simon turned back to Dar, who was following the little drama right along with him.

"They didn't stay for dessert," he said to her. "Who comes to Radcliffe's and doesn't have dessert?" He looked back to the Barneses' vacated table. The busboy had just started clearing their dinner away. "Mrs. Barnes hardly touched her food," he said. "I wonder what that's about?"

"Simon Roe! Really!" Dar said in mock dismay. "I can't take you anywhere."

"So, Dar," Simon dutifully brought his attention back to his own table, "where in the park does Mr. Barnes want to build his condos?"

"At the second scenic overlook, near the top of the Prayer Trail."

"What? There's so much wrong with that idea I don't even know where to start!"

The arrival of the dessert tray interrupted their conversation. They decided to share a piece of the house cheesecake. After they had consumed the last decadent forkful, Simon picked up where he'd left off.

"Condos in the park? No way. Well, it is a rumor, after all. Might not even be true."

"Sadly, I'm afraid it is true. And after seeing William Barnes in action when he proposed the condos on the greens, I've no doubt he'll get his way."

Chapter Nine

Jacoba opened her eyes and lifted her head off her pillow just enough to see what time it was. 5:30. Early even for her. She rolled over so she couldn't see the red glow of the clock's numbers, determined to fall back to sleep. But after twenty minutes or so of restless tossing and turning, she gave up. She swept back the covers, perched on the edge of her bed, and reached for the lamp switch. Once she'd slid her feet into her slippers she shuffled down the hallway, all the while anticipating that blessed first cup of coffee.

She stepped into the dark, stuffy kitchen and turned on the overhead light, glad she'd set up the coffee maker the night before. Power button pushed, the machine beeped, and seconds later coffee started dripping into the carafe. As soon as the carafe was full enough, Jacoba poured some of the fragrant dark brew into her mug, added a splash of soy milk and a little sugar, stirred it, and took the mug out the sliding glass door onto her screened porch. Cooler air greeted her. She sat down on the lounger, set the mug on the little table next to her, and made herself comfortable. She wondered if yesterday afternoon's rain would repeat itself. Grandburg's May weather could be so unpredictable. She wanted, *needed* bright sunshine today. She picked up the mug, held it in both hands, and took the first sip.

"Ah, the elixir of life!" Jacoba spoke the words aloud and smiled. Her friend, Marty, always said that when they had coffee together. She sat back and looked out into her yard. Several raised flowerbeds were visible in the dawn light. According to Verna, her backyard neighbor, previous owners of her house had always had a nice green lawn, but none of them had ever planted anything. Verna had been delighted when Jacoba had put in a couple rose bushes, several rows of daylilies, and three different kinds of mint. The burning bush she had planted last year was still little more than a twig, but the new butterfly bush hadn't disappointed. Verna had given Jacoba several treasures from her own yard: ferns, daisies, and daffodils that now grew along the edge of Jacoba's porch.

"Maybe I'll try growing some vegetables this year," she said to herself and sipped more coffee. Looking to the east, she could see the glow on the tree-lined horizon where the sun would make its appearance at any moment.

How were the Davises doing this morning, she wondered. Were Darrin and Beverly awake? Had they even been able to sleep? And Grandmother Davis? Her anxiety spiked.

"Think of something positive, something good," she said out loud, willing herself to close her mind's eye on the accusing vision of Grandmother Davis.

"Detective Roe didn't think Jeremy's death was my fault. But ... but ... did something I said or did contribute to Jeremy's decision?" Tears welled in her eyes. "Creativity ... imagination ... dangerous?" She looked unseeing at the porch screen. "Did I miss something? What if I could have stopped this from happening?" Tears overflowed onto her cheeks, and she pushed them aside with the back of her hand.

"Stop it! Just stop it!" she admonished herself.

Time for more coffee, breakfast, and a shower. The sun broke over the horizon and flooded the porch with eye-piercing brightness. Jacoba picked up her mug and went back inside.

She ate cereal she didn't really want and lingered longer than usual under the hot shower spray. Eventually she finished getting dressed and took an appraising look in the full-length mirror on the back of the bathroom door. A medium-height, slender woman in her forties looked back, no smile, brown eyes wide. Her gray-streaked brown hair flipped under, bangs cut just above her eyebrows. Silver loops swung from her ears, and red-framed glasses perched on her nose. She tucked her short-sleeved maroon blouse into her black slacks. Her fourth graders referred to this outfit as her "heads-up clothes." It seemed to them she only wore the maroon-and-black combo if something unexpected or important was going to happen. And when she wore her black jacket with the outfit, they were sure something extra special was in the works. Jacoba had perpetuated the notion. She frowned at her full-length reflection.

Is this an example of what Grandmother Davis would call "creative crap"? She winced. The words stung even when she thought them.

Jacoba turned off the bathroom light and went down the hall to the living room. She sat in her recliner, put up her feet, and reached for a typed page on the cherry end table next to her. She pushed her glasses farther up on her nose, angled the page out a little, and spoke into the room.

"Psalm 23. The Lord is my shepherd. I shall not be in want. He makes me lie down in green pastures, he leads me beside quiet waters, he restores my soul."

Jacoba stopped, lowered the page to her lap, and closed her eyes. She'd been surprised when Mrs. Davis had called her earlier in the week.

"Ms. Dahm, Darrin and I want you to read Psalm 23 in the service on Saturday," Beverly Davis had said. "Please. Jeremy loved your after-lunch storytime. It would mean so much to have you read aloud at his funeral."

Jacoba hoped Darrin and Beverly and even Grandmother Davis would find comfort in the psalm. She wanted comfort for everyone at the service, but especially for the Davises. She opened her eyes again and read the rest of the passage. After speaking the last line, she let the paper fall into her lap. She settled back into her chair, her arms folded, suddenly feeling very relaxed.

"I'll take a ten-minute power nap," she told her-self. She looked at her watch. "I don't have to leave here until ten thirty or so. I have plenty of time. Ten minutes, that's all I need." She closed her eyes and fell sound asleep.

When she awoke, she felt better, refreshed. She checked the time and gasped. It was 10:45. She jumped out of the chair, ran to the bathroom mir-ror for a quick look at her hair and makeup. She rushed through the house, grabbed her purse and keys, and headed for the back door. Midway across the kitchen she looked down and realized she was still wearing her slippers and didn't have her jacket. She raced back down the hall to her closet, got shoes on her feet, and pulled her jacket off its hanger. She darted into the living room to grab her reading. With purse, keys, reading, and jacket in hand, she got in the car and roared out into the street. She glanced down at the car clock: 10:50. She was sure she could get to Creekside Community Church in ten minutes or less.

At 10:58 car time, she pulled into the church's large parking lot, found a parking place mercifully close to the building, and put on her jacket as she hurried to the entrance. Fortunately, she'd been inside Creekside Community Church enough times to know where to go. As she crossed the large open foyer toward the sanctuary's double doors, she passed three easels holding photo col-lages. She would have liked to stop to look at the pictures but knew there was no time. She reached the sanctuary door just as Dale Billingsley came through from the other side. The funeral director held the door open for her and an instrumental version of "It Is Well with My Soul" spilled into the foyer.

Jacoba thanked him as she stepped past him into the back of the sanctuary. Floor-to-ceiling windows on three walls opened out onto the dense woods along Winding Creek. Row upon row of mourners sat surrounded by trees. She was glad to see such a strong show of support for Jeremy's family. Jacoba's gaze traveled up the center aisle to the casket in front of a modest oak podium.

So small, Jacoba thought sadly. *Fourth-grade-boy size.*

An usher handed her a bulletin with Jeremy's picture on the cover. She smiled back at the familiar face. She walked along the back row and headed down the side aisle, hoping to find an empty seat on the end of a row so she could get out easily when it was her turn to read. She came to an empty seat five rows from the front. She bent down to ask the person sitting next to the empty chair if the seat was taken and was pleasantly surprised when Naomi Hirsch turned to face her.

"Mrs. Hirsch! May I sit here?" Jacoba asked softly.

"Yes, of course."

"Thank you."

Jacoba sat down. Relief washed over her. She

opened her bulletin and looked for her reading. There it was, Psalm 23, fairly early in the service.

"Ms. Dahm, Ms. Dahm," someone whispered close by.

Jacoba looked up. The whisper came again and waving hands caught her eye. She saw Jake and Maddie leaning out on the other side of their mother in order to catch her attention. She gave a small bow from her chair. The children bowed back. She suddenly realized Mr. Hirsch wasn't sitting with the family. She leaned over and whispered in Naomi's ear, "Won't your husband need this seat?"

"No, he's one of the pallbearers. The guys are all sitting together."

Jacoba turned her attention back to the bulletin. She found the list of pallbearers right away: Neil Hirsch, Alan Barfield, and Bob Murphy. She wondered who would be giving the eulogy. Before she could read any further the music stopped, and she looked up to see Dale Billingsley next to the podium. He motioned for the congregation to rise. Everyone stood and turned to face the back of the sanctuary. Two black-robed pastors led the procession, a diminutive red-haired woman on the arm of a taller woman with short white hair. Jeremy's family came slowly down the center aisle behind them. Darrin and Beverly Davis were first. They held hands and looked through the windows into the woods. Grandmother Davis, a grim expression on her face, followed a few steps behind them.

Several young couples walked behind Grand-mother Davis. Two of the couples had elementary-age children in tow.

Are they Jeremy's cousins? Jacoba wondered. *Isn't there a Grandfather Davis? And where are Beverly's parents?*

As the family members filled the first row and part of the second, Jacoba looked toward the podium. The pastors stood behind it, whispering in each other's ears. Then, after handing the more diminutive woman a set of headphones, the taller woman took a seat on the front row. The pastor at the podium turned to face the congregation, put the headphones on her short red curls, and opened the laptop in front of her.

"Good morning, friends," she said. "You may be seated."

It sounded to Jacoba as though the room was sighing as the crowd sat down.

"We are gathered here today to celebrate the life of Jeremy Davis. The Davises have asked me to thank you for walking alongside them at this very difficult time." The pastor's confident, clear alto voice warmed her words, her sentences. "For those of you who are visitors to Winding Creek Community Church, my name is Denise Thompson. I'm one of the pastors here. These headphones and the laptop are my eyes. The good news is should you fall asleep during the service, I'll never know." A modest wave of chuckles rippled across the rows. Pastor Thompson waited until the congregation was silent again. Then her words rang out in the space. "Our help is in the name of the Lord, who made heaven and earth." The funeral had begun.

When Jacoba stepped in front of the podium to read Psalm 23, her hands trembled as she placed her script on top of the pastor's closed laptop. She tried to envision herself in her classroom after lunch, the book of the week in her hands, her students in front of her. She took a deep breath, looked right at Beverly and Darrin, and started to read, her voice quiet, calm, steady.

"The Lord . . . is my shepherd."

Part of her mind focused on the reading while another part of her mind noticed many of her fourth graders and their parents scattered throughout the room. She saw Dr. Miller sitting on the back row next to Billy Barnes and his parents. She kept her eyes moving when Grandmother Davis came into her line of sight.

"Surely goodness and love shall follow me all the days of my life, and I shall dwell in the house of the Lord forever." Her eyes rested on Darrin and Beverly again, and tears filled her eyes. "No tears, no tears," she said sternly to herself as she walked back to her seat. "Not until after lunch. After the luncheon you can go home and cry all you want."

She sat back down and Mrs. Hirsch reached over to pat her arm. "You read so beautifully," she whispered.

When it came time for the eulogy, an elderly

gentleman came down the center aisle and stepped up to the podium. His tanned, deep-lined face gave testimony to years of outdoor activity. He gripped the podium with large, gnarled hands, looked out over the congregation, and began to speak. His voice matched his face: weathered, rich, old.

"I'm Alan Barfield. I was Jeremy's Scoutmaster." He shifted his gaze and looked directly at Darrin, Beverly, and Grandmother Davis. "The Davis family and I go way back. Twenty years ago, I was Darrin's Scoutmaster. And further back than I care to admit, Jeremy's Grandfather Davis and I shared a desk in first grade. That's one of the fine things about living in Grandburg. Family roots and friendships can run deep. We enjoy each other's company in the good times, and we hold each other up when times are hard."

Mr. Barfield paused and looked out beyond the Davises. A smile started to redistribute the lines on his face. "This may come as a surprise to some of you, but the Davis family is not known for its love of the outdoors." Jacoba heard laughter come from the front row. "As a youngster, Darrin Davis always came on our overnight campouts with two large sheets of plastic: one to put under his sleeping bag and one to put over it. On one particularly memorable camping trip, Darrin brought along bear repellent. Unfortunately, the repellent had the opposite effect: a large brown bear came into our camp and made off with most of our food." Jacoba chuckled. Laughter rose and fell all around her.

"Jeremy was an unusual Davis. Jeremy enjoyed being outdoors. He would have loved this view of the woods." Mr. Barfield turned toward the windows and the woods beyond, and then back to the people in front of him. "Jeremy loved sleeping under the stars, but he always put plastic over and under his sleeping bag. We all know who taught him to do that." Laughter broke out again. Mr. Barfield took a breath and then continued.

"Jeremy was an unusual Davis in another way. If you ask a Davis a question, you'll get an answer, but it will be short and sweet. Most men in the Davis family hold firmly to 'let your yes be yes, and your no be no.' But not Jeremy. Jeremy was a poet."

Startled, Jacoba leaned forward.

"Jeremy loved to wrap words around his experiences, and he often did it by writing poems. I'd like to close with a poem he gave me a few months ago. He wrote it for a birthday I'd just as soon have let pass by unnoticed. But Jeremy found words to honor it. Here's what he wrote:

> *It's your day, Mr. Barfield.*
> *A day you should cheer.*
> *You've done so much living*
> *To get all the way here.*
>
> *If you count all the campouts,*
> *The hiking and such,*
> *You deserve a big trophy,*
> *Thank you very much.*

I like sevens and zeroes.
They are useful numbers.
Seventy candles on your cake
Will be a super wonder!

Thank you, Mr. Barfield,
For being you.
My life is better because you
Let your goodness shine through.

Mr. Barfield looked out over the congregation. "I plan to honor Jeremy's memory by letting my goodness shine through in as many ways as I can. I invite you to do the same."

Jacoba fought back tears as Mr. Barfield walked up the aisle back to his seat. She looked down at her bulletin. The service would be over soon. *One hurdle down, two more to go,* she thought.

After the commendation and blessing, the pallbearers carried the casket out ahead of the Davis family. When the last family member exited through the sanctuary doors, Mrs. Hirsch turned to Jacoba.

"Ms. Dahm, would you like to ride to the cemetery with us? Jake and Maddie want to go. My husband will be riding with the other pallbearers, so there's plenty of room in our car."

"Thank you, yes."

Jacoba let Mrs. Hirsch and the twins take the

lead. Ten minutes later they had piled into the Hirsches' car, twins in the backseat, adults in the front. Once seatbelts were fastened, Mrs. Hirsch pulled out of the parking lot and joined the line of cars following the hearse to the cemetery. The funeral procession snaked along Erickson Way's irregular curves to Remembrance Road.

"Here, Ms. Dahm," Maddie spoke from the backseat, "would you like one?"

Jacoba turned and came face to face with Maddie's outstretched hand. Resting on her palm was a small, oblong stone.

"After the casket goes into the ground, you throw it in," Maddie explained.

Jacoba took the stone from Maddie's hand. *R.I.P.* was painted on its smooth surface.

"Dad took us to the park last Sunday so we could get some stones," Jake said. "He helped us think of words that reminded us of Jeremy, and Mom helped us paint the words on them."

"Short words," Maddie added, "so they would fit. Mine says *park.*" She held out her own stone for Jacoba to see. "I'm going to miss our park adventures."

"And mine says *best.* Jeremy was my best friend," Jake said. "And Dad's got one in his pocket that says *scout,* well, because, you know why."

"And I've got one in my purse that says *bike,*" Mrs. Hirsch said. "When I picture Jeremy in my mind, I always see him on his bike."

"My stone has *R.I.P.* on it," Jacoba said, and before she could say more, Maddie spoke up.

"R.I.P., rest in peace. Dad knows how to say 'rest in peace' in another language."

"Latin," Mrs. Hirsch said.

"Latin," Maddie echoed. "But we don't know those words."

Jacoba turned back around and slid the stone into the outside pocket of her purse. When she looked up again, the high-arched entrance of the Grandburg Cemetery was just ahead. She watched as car after car passed under the arch and entered the cemetery grounds. No one spoke as their car idled in line and then began inching forward. The procession wound slowly around rows of gravestones, an occasional monument, and several low-fenced family plots. It finally came to a stop at the northeast corner of the cemetery. Through the trees Jacoba could see the newly plowed fields of Stifler Farm. As soon as Mrs. Hirsch parked, the twins were on the move. When Jacoba got out of the car Maddie was waiting for her. Jacoba offered Maddie her hand.

"Ready, Maddie?"

"Ready," Maddie answered quietly.

They walked around the car to join Jake and Mrs. Hirsch. Jake stood next to his mother, close but not holding her hand. Together they led the way, following other mourners up the grassy incline. When they reached the top of the hill, Jacoba could see a large canopy just ahead with several rows of chairs arranged underneath. Pastor Thompson and her associate stood next to a small podium. The pallbearers had already placed the casket on the mechanical device that would lower it into the ground. Mr. Hirsch joined them, and they walked to the chairs. Jake sat down on the edge of his folding chair and absentmindedly tossed his stone from one hand to the other. Maddie sat next to her brother and the two of them started a whispered conversation.

Jacoba sat next to Maddie and looked beyond them to see who else was there. She spotted Dr. Miller again and several families from school. Jeremy's family filed into the first row.

Once they were all seated, Pastor Thompson spoke into the microphone, the words echoing in the open air.

"Neither death, nor life, nor angels, nor principalities, nor things present, nor things to come, nor powers, nor height, nor depth, or anything else in all creation, will be able to separate us from the love of God in Christ Jesus our Lord."

She stopped for a moment and then continued. "Scripture says, 'We know that if the earthly tent we live in is destroyed, we have a building from God, a house not made with hands, eternal in the heavens.' Jesus said, 'Do not be afraid, I am the first and the last, and the living one. I was dead, and behold, I am alive forever and ever. Because I live, you also will live.'"

And then the casket was lowered into the grave. Everyone stood up. The funeral director led members of the Davis family to the grave's edge first. They threw long-stemmed red roses into the open grave. Jacoba felt Maddie's hand slip into hers. When it was their turn they walked the short distance to the grave, the rest of the Hirsch family right behind them. Jacoba tossed her stone into the hole as Maddie tossed hers. They heard two sharp cracks when the stones hit the casket.

"Goodbye, Jeremy," Jake said solemnly as he threw in his stone.

"Goodbye, *Jeremy's body*," Maddie corrected her brother in a whisper. "Dad said Jeremy isn't here anymore. Jeremy is with God now."

Mr. and Mrs. Hirsch tossed their stones into the hole.

Pastor Thompson's voice sounded over the gathering. "We commend to Almighty God our brother, Jeremy, and we commit his body to the ground; earth to earth, ashes to ashes, dust to dust. Blessed are the dead who die in the Lord, says the Spirit. They will rest from their labor, for their deeds will follow them." Jacoba lingered a moment and watched as flowers, rose petals, and more stones were thrown on the casket below. Some people tossed in clumps of dirt they'd picked up from the grave's edge. Maddie tugged at Jacoba's hand, and she turned away from the grave. They all walked back to their seats.

Pastor Thompson moved forward to the next part of the service. "Let us pray together: Our Father . . ."

Jacoba joined the low, rumbling blend of inter-generational voices speaking in unison. When the prayer ended Pastor Thompson waited for a moment and then offered another prayer.

She lifted her hand to give the blessing.

"The Lord bless you and keep you. The Lord make his face to shine upon you and be gracious to you, the Lord turn his face toward you and give you peace."

The mourners headed back down the grassy slope to their cars.

"Why don't you ladies take the front seats," Mr. Hirsch offered as they walked. "I'll sit with the twins."

They got into the car, and Mrs. Hirsch slowly maneuvered their vehicle back toward Remembrance Road. *Two hurdles down, one to go,* Jacoba thought as she looked out the window.

"Next stop, lunch!" Jake announced.

"I hope we don't have to stand in line for too long," Maddie said. "I'm hungry!"

"I hope they have mac and cheese. I love mac and cheese." Jake leaned forward as far as his seatbelt would allow and spoke to Jacoba. "Mom doesn't make it because Dad's allergic." He rolled his eyes and leaned toward his dad. "Dad's got a lot of allergies."

Mr. Hirsch narrowed his eyes and scrunched his eyebrows in mock sternness. "You should be grateful, young man, that I am not allergic to YOU!" Jake shrieked with laughter as his father tickled him.

Saturday traffic on Remembrance Road made leaving the cemetery more difficult than entering it. The line of departing mourners' cars moved ahead at a snail's pace. Just when their car's turn came to turn onto Remembrance, another funeral procession turned in front of them.

"Okay, kids," Mrs. Hirsch said, looking at them in the rearview mirror. "Let's name some positives. What's good about this moment?"

"Well, this is taking so long that we probably won't have to wait in line when we get back to church," said Maddie.

"I hope they don't run out of food," Jake lamented.

"That's NOT a positive," his mother reminded him.

"I know, I know."

They finally made it back to church, entered the sunlit foyer, and walked down the wide corridor to the large room that functioned as a fellowship hall and a gym. Today the basketball hoops were secured high overhead, and three rows of long tables were set up on the polished gym floor, folding chairs placed on either side. Four long tables in front of the kitchen held the food. Jake and Maddie charged forward in the direction of the food tables, but Mr. Hirsch called them back.

"Ladies first, friends," he said to the twins. "That means your mom and your teacher go ahead of you."

The twins groaned but stepped aside as Mrs. Hirsch and Jacoba picked up plates and started down the row of lunch meats, bread, salads, and casseroles. Following close behind, Jake zeroed in on the mac and cheese. He put two heaping mounds on his plate.

"Put a vegetable and a piece of fruit on that plate and you are good to go," Mrs. Hirsch said over her shoulder. "Maddie, same goes for you. A vegetable, a piece of fruit, and anything else you'd like."

Jacoba put several pieces of deli-sliced turkey on her plate, forked two fresh tomato slices, added a scoop of red-skin potato salad, and let her hand hover over a fragrant dinner roll. She decided to indulge in the roll but forgo the butter. Before leaving the food tables she took one long look at the dessert choices. She was definitely coming back for a piece of cherry pie. She followed Mrs. Hirsch down the row of tables closest to the food spread. The twins came right behind her with Mr. Hirsch holding a brimming plate high over their heads. Mrs. Hirsch put down her plate and directed Jake and Maddie to sit next to her. Jacoba and Mr. Hirsch took their plates around to the other side of the table and sat down across from Mrs. Hirsch.

"Napkins on your laps and thank God for your

food before you eat it," Mrs. Hirsch directed the twins. Jacoba watched as napkins went in laps, hands were folded, and eyes were closed for only a matter of seconds. Jake opened his eyes and dove into his mac and cheese with gusto. Maddie picked up a carrot stick and enthusiastically snapped off the end with her teeth. It wasn't long before Jake finished the last bite of mac and cheese.

"Dad, I'm done." He stood up and pushed in his chair. "Can I go to the playground?"

Mr. Hirsch looked at his son's plate. "Did you eat a vegetable and a piece of fruit, like your mother told you to?"

"Yes, I had a carrot stick and some apple slices."

"No dessert, Jake?" Mrs. Hirsch asked.

"No room. I'm filled to the brim with mac and cheese. Playground? Please?"

"Okay, but only for a few minutes. We'll be leaving shortly." Mr. Hirsch looked meaningfully at his son. "Yardwork awaits."

Jake shot from the table. Maddie stuffed carrot sticks in her mouth and chewed madly. She jumped out of her chair, mouth still full, and pointed after Jake. Her mother nodded and Maddie followed her brother out of the fellowship hall.

Mrs. Hirsch turned to Jacoba to explain. "Maddie and Jake went to preschool here. The playground was their absolute favorite thing about the whole experience. Someone put a lot of thought into creating that space."

"I've always heard good things about Creekside Preschool," Jacoba said. She looked down at her empty plate. "I really shouldn't, but the cherry pie on the dessert table is calling my name."

Mrs. Hirsch laughed. "I know. I'm hearing the siren call of the peach cobbler. I don't think I can hold out much longer!"

Jacoba got up and started walking toward the desserts when she saw Darrin and Beverly Davis get up from the table where they had been eating. Grandmother Davis remained seated with her back to Jacoba. She was jabbing the air with her fork, punctuating her sentences as she talked to the woman sitting next to her. Jacoba walked up behind Darrin and Beverly and put her hands on their shoulders.

"I just want to say again how sorry I am for your loss," she said when they turned to face her. "I will never forget Jeremy. He brought so much delight to my classroom." Jacoba surprised herself. She'd managed to say the words without crying.

"He loved fourth grade," Beverly said. "His year with you was one of his best school years ever. Thank you for that."

There, you see, Jacoba told herself, *they aren't blaming you for anything.*

Darrin motioned them to move farther away from the tables and then continued the conversation. "Ms. Dahm, I'm sorry for my mother's outburst at the visitation. She can be difficult."

Another family came up to speak to Darrin and

Beverly, so Jacoba stepped away and headed to the dessert table. Good! Three pieces of cherry pie were in the glass pie dish. Jacoba slid the smallest piece onto a plate. When she took her place at the table again, Mr. Hirsch had a half-eaten cookie in his hand and Mrs. Hirsch was savoring a small bowl of peach cobbler. Jacoba's enjoyment of her dessert was cut short when a sticky red glob of cherry filling slid off her fork and landed on her slacks.

"Oh, no," Jacoba groaned.

"If you dab that with cold water right now, you'll be fine," Mrs. Hirsch assured her. "The ladies room is just down the hallway."

Jacoba had just reached the ladies room door when she recognized Maddie's voice coming from around the corner at the end of the corridor.

"I won't say it, Billy! Leave me alone! You're mean!"

Alarmed, Jacoba hurried toward the voice. When she came to the corner she saw Maddie by the exit to the playground, her back against the wall. Billy Barnes towered over her, his back to Jacoba.

"Oh, you'll say it, Maddie Hirsch, or your brother gets a matching bruise to go with the one he already has."

Maddie saw Jacoba and called out, "Ms. Dahm!"

"I'm not falling for that!" Billy sneered as he moved even closer to Maddie.

"Billy! Stop!" Jacoba ordered, her voice stern and indignant.

Billy turned around in wide-eyed surprise.

Suddenly a man's voice roared from behind Jacoba at the other end of the corridor. "Billy! Car! Now!"

Billy sprinted past Jacoba. She watched as he raced to catch up with the retreating figure of his father.

At that moment Jake came into the hallway from the playground. "Come on, Maddie!" he said impatiently. "What's taking you so long? We don't have much time!" Then he saw the look on his sister's face. "What's wrong?"

"Nothing," Maddie said. "Nothing. Come on, Jake, let's go swing."

"Maddie, wait. What just happened?" Jacoba came and stood next to her. "Was Billy threatening you?"

"Maddie!" Jake looked at his sister in alarm. "Billy was here?"

Jacoba looked from one child to the other. "Something is obviously going on, and I want to know what it is."

"Maddie, Jake, time to go!" Mr. Hirsch called from down the hall. The children scooted past Jacoba. She followed right behind them, her mind in overdrive.

"Did the cold water work?" Mrs. Hirsch asked when Jacoba caught up with them.

"I never had a chance to try it," Jacoba said. "On

my way to the ladies room, I overheard Billy Barnes threatening Maddie."

"Not again," Mrs. Hirsch said, looking at her husband. "I was hoping we were done with this."

Jacoba stared at both parents. "What do you mean 'not again'? Done with what?"

"Billy, bullying the twins . . . but you know all about this, right?" said Mr. Hirsch.

"No, I don't know anything about this." Jacoba looked from one parent to the other, mystified.

"Dr. Miller hasn't talked to you about Billy?" Mrs. Hirsch looked almost as mystified as Jacoba did.

"No, he hasn't said a word to me about Billy Barnes. What's going on?"

Mrs. Hirsch's eyes narrowed. She looked down at the children and then at her husband, her lips set in a tight line.

Mr. Hirsch turned to Jacoba. "Ms. Dahm, we live right up the street. Let's continue this conversation there."

Hours later Jacoba sat on her back porch pondering what she'd heard in the Hirsches' living room. Billy Barnes had been bullying Jake and Maddie since last November. In mid-December, Naomi and Neil had spoken to Billy's parents. The Barneses had downplayed the situation. They had even implied that the twins were the bullies, not Billy.

The bullying had stopped after the December conversation but started again toward the end of

January. The Hirsches had gone to Dr. Miller in early February. He'd assured them he'd look into the matter and would make Jacoba aware of the situation.

Only Dr. Miller hadn't made Jacoba aware of the situation. She looked out beyond the porch screen. The Hirsches had gone to Dr. Miller in February. It was May now.

Why didn't Dr. Miller tell me? How did I miss bullying going on right under my nose? She felt sick to her stomach. *Who else has Billy been tormenting? Was Jeremy one of his targets?*

A warm breeze came through the screen. Shadows lengthened on the porch as daylight diminished around her. She thought about going inside, but her heavy heart kept her in her chair. *Good thing tomorrow's Sunday. I'm not ready to face Jeremy's empty desk, or Dr. Miller.* She looked across the backyard to Verna's. The kitchen light was on.

Jeremy's empty desk . . . Bullying in my classroom.

Grandmother Davis's accusation roared in her memory: "People need to know what this woman did. My grandson died because of what she teaches in her classroom."

Was Jeremy's death my fault?

Overwhelmed by it all, she started to cry.

Chapter Ten

Richard Barclay opened his eyes into the dark space under his pillow. Had he dreamt it or had he heard a baby crying during the night? And Ethel. What a pillow hog. He pulled his hand out from under the covers and checked the area over his head. No cat. Good! He came up for air and rolled over to admire the glow-in-the-dark stars and planets on the ceiling, leftovers from previous residents. When he heard the hiss and gurgle of the coffee maker he decided to get up. He stuck his arms through the sleeves of his bathrobe and walked out into the apartment's combination living, cooking, and eating space.

"Hello, cat," he said to the gray-striped furball in his chair. He went to the bank of switches by the front door and flipped the second one from the end. The kitchenette's tube lighting blinked a couple times and started to hum. In another minute he'd pulled a mug out of a cabinet, set it down on the slick surface of the breakfast bar, and filled it with fragrant black coffee.

"Paper," he said to himself after he'd taken a sip.

He walked to the front door and pushed back the deadbolt with his thumb. Ever vigilant should Ethel attempt escape, he opened the door just far enough to grab the triple-folded *Times* and shut it again. He sat down on the barstool and unfolded the paper. Ethel appeared at his feet and wound herself between the barstool legs.

"Well, Ethel. How was your night?"

The cat squinted her emerald eyes at him, sat down on the blue fleur-de-lis linoleum, and began the vigorous washing of her tail. Ten licks into the bath she stopped, strolled over to her food dish, and started enthusiastic crunching.

Richard decided he was hungry too. He poured bran flakes into a bowl and added milk after he'd given the carton's contents the sniff test for freshness. He looked wistfully at the empty banana hook on the counter, pulled a spoon from the utensil drawer, and sat back down at the bar. He dipped into his bran flakes and looked forlornly in Ethel's direction.

"How can I still have fifty pages of criminal law to read and notes from four lectures to review? I studied all day yesterday." He put another spoonful of flakes into his mouth. He chewed and struck a bargain with himself. *I'll finish this, have a little more coffee, read the rest of the paper, and then I'll study!*

When he finished his cereal, he offered Ethel the milk left in the bottom of the bowl. She conducted her own sniff test and walked away. Richard refilled his coffee mug and decided he'd be much more comfortable in the living room. He gathered the newspaper and coffee and switched off the kitchenette lights, glad to silence the annoying hum. He settled into his chair and reopened his paper, his coffee on the wooden TV tray next to him.

"It's too dark in here," he muttered to himself.

He turned on the brass floor lamp next to his chair. Nope. Still too dark. He crossed the carpet to the shade-shrouded picture window and tugged on the metal chain. Light spilled into the room as the shade inched up. Richard squinted against the glare as he took in his bird's-eye view of the park. From his third-floor vantage point he could see the shingled roof of the gift shop at the park's main entrance. No cars traveled the perimeter road at the moment. The glare off the clapboard chapel's metal roof caused him to squint even more. He could just make out the cemetery's uniform lines of white grave markers. But beyond that, an ocean of green completely hid the jogging trail and the park's back entrance from view. He marveled at what a difference the seasons made. Last December he'd been able to see all the way to the guard hut at the back entrance.

He sat back down for a little more time with his coffee and paper. He finished both much too quickly. He slumped in his chair and looked dejectedly into the room. He really didn't want to study any more. But he had to. He had to.

"Come on, Barclay," he said with forced enthusiasm. "You're in the home stretch. Read fifty pages, review those lecture notes, and you'll be done! You can do it!"

He reached down for the textbook he'd left on the floor the night before. As he straightened back up, Ethel leaped into his lap.

"Whoa! Ethel!"

Richard shifted in the chair to accommodate both book and cat. He pulled Ethel closer so he could open the book. He found the place where he'd stopped reading and picked up where he'd left off. He was finishing the third paragraph when a baby's angry wail filled the room.

"Oh, no." Richard looked at Ethel. She looked back at him and jumped to the floor. Richard got up and walked over to the picture window. The park beckoned. The wail grew louder.

"That's it. I'm going for a bike ride."

In a matter of minutes Richard was dressed and out the door. The baby's cries were even louder in the hallway.

Decision confirmed.

He quickly took the two flights of stairs to the first floor. He silently thanked James Brown, the Park View's manager, for letting him stash his bike and helmet in the custodial closet at the base of the stairs. He unhooked his bike from the wall where it hung, put the helmet on his head, and rolled the bike through the deserted lobby to the outdoors. It wasn't until he came to the other side of the Park View's green-striped canopy that he realized he'd forgotten something.

Shoot. My sunglasses! Oh, well.

He pushed the bike across Creston Avenue,

mounted it, and bumped along the well-worn shortcut into the park. The footpath ended just past the main guard hut at the perimeter road. Richard headed south, glad for the road's solid surface under his tires. He cruised past the chapel. And then his head started to ache.

Got to get out of this light. Ah! I know what I'll do.

At the cemetery's last row of grave markers, he left the road and pedaled the short distance through the grass to the shaded jogging trail. Peace settled over him as the bike carried him along. His headache receded.

May in Grandburg. Nothing like it.

He passed the back entrance and navigated the jogging trail's sharp turn to the north. A flash to his left grabbed his attention.

The river. Can't ride in the park without seeing the river.

He dismounted, walked the bike up the grassy embankment to the perimeter road. He remounted and pedaled to the first scenic overlook. He pumped past two parked cars with out-of-state license plates at one end of the overlook's small parking area.

After riding a few more yards he dismounted and leaned the bike against the same picnic table he'd used when he'd had his bike in the park for work. He took the short walk to the overlook's waist-high guard rail. Abundant spring rains had caused the river to breach its eastern banks and sprawl below him into the low-lying woodlands.

Near the center of the river where a narrow sand-bar was usually visible, Richard could only see rippling whitecaps. He shielded his eyes with his hands and looked all the way across the water to the other side of the river. Dense pine forest stretched in a jagged but unbroken line on the river's west bank. As he looked out over the mocha-colored expanse with its forested edges, a sense of awe washed over him.

God's grandeur, an interior voice whispered. He grinned to himself. Would the years at St. Gregory's ever let him go?

So big, so old, he thought. *The river, the forest, the rocks—here long before I was born, and long after I am gone.*

His head started to ache again. Time to get back into the shade. He got on his bike and pedaled back to the jogging trail. He biked past a jogger pushing a stroller and then a trio of walkers. He slowed down when he came to the spot where Jeremy Davis's body and bike had rested. The stone tower was still there, but no dog, no squirrel. He'd traveled well beyond the second scenic outlook when he noticed an abrupt decrease in daylight. He looked up.

Uh-oh. Rain's coming.

Twenty minutes later when he got back to the park's main entrance, he could smell rain. The storm clouds overhead guaranteed it. He looked across the green space to the Park View, grateful to be almost home. As he biked along the footpath to

Creston Avenue, he looked up at the row of third-floor windows. There was Ethel, perched in the second window from the end. Richard dismounted, crossed the street, came under the Park View canopy, and entered the still-deserted lobby. He rolled his bike into the custodian's closet and hung it up on its hook. He left his helmet gently swinging from the seat.

"Did I check my mail yesterday?" he asked himself. "Hmm, I don't think so. Might as well check as long as I'm down here."

He came back out into the lobby. The quiet was odd. On weekday mornings when he left for school or the precinct, the lobby bustled with adults going to work, children going to school, dogs on leashes, youngsters in strollers. The building manager's office door was always open. In the mornings Mr. James Brown was a one-man greeting committee with a good word for everyone. Richard could hear the man's rich baritone voice in his head. "Morning, Mr. Barclay. Ethel behaving?"

Richard walked over to the four-tiered bank of mailboxes on the north wall. He stepped up to his box in the third row and carefully turned the dial. Left. Right. Left. Door open. Box empty. A little disappointed, he closed the door again and spun the dial. His gaze shifted up to the fourth line of mailboxes. Only one of the doors had a combination dial.

"Huh. How did I not notice that before? Is there only one apartment on the fourth floor? Oh, maybe there's a penthouse up there!" He'd have to ask James Brown the next time he saw him.

Richard took the stairs back up to his apartment. When he came to the third-floor landing, he stopped to listen. He smiled. No crying. Just as he closed his apartment door behind him lightning lit up the room, followed by a rumble of thunder. Richard sat down in his chair. Ethel came by his feet as raindrops hit the picture window in vicious bursts. Lightning flashed and thunder crashed loud and close. He hoped they didn't lose power, not with the studying he still had to do. Hours of studying. He groaned. He suddenly wished the power *would* go out so he'd have an excuse not to study any more.

"Okay, forget about the book. Just review the lecture notes. After that, you can stop." He pulled his lecture notes into his lap. Lightning flashed, thunder cracked directly overhead, and the lamp winked. Richard got up to look out the window. The rain was coming down so hard he couldn't see much of the park at all. Crying came through the wall once more. Hiccupping sobs progressed rapidly to earnest wailing.

"Well, Ethel, there's no escaping. I guess it's time to break out the cotton balls. Tomorrow I'll pick up some earplugs." The cries grew louder. A new thought came to Richard.

"Ethel, I don't think earplugs will do the job. We just might have to move."

Jacoba got up with every intention of doing what she usually did on Sunday morning: attend worship at Emmanuel, maybe enjoy lunch out with friends, and later indulge in an afternoon nap. But a pervasive weariness slowed her movements and muddled her thinking. When it was time to get dressed for church, she had trouble deciding what to wear. The outfit she eventually chose rested heavy in her hands after she'd pulled it off the hanger. She sat back down on her bed for the third time and looked down at her bare feet. Her shoes were in her closet. They might as well have been in South America.

"I can't do this," she said to herself. "I don't have the energy for church—people, talking, singing. I can't. It's all too much." She'd thought her tears of the evening before had been the end of her crying, but more threatened to spill over.

"I'm staying home," she said to the turquoise curtains on her bedroom windows.

Jacoba put on her favorite blue jeans and pulled a short-sleeved pink T-shirt over her head. She walked to her living room and opened the front door, where warm, humid air surrounded her as she bent down and reached for the *Grandburg Times*. She took the paper to the kitchen and started a new pot of coffee. While it was brewing, she unfolded the newspaper and half-heartedly scanned the headlines. When the coffee was ready she poured some into a mug, tucked the paper under her arm, and went out onto the screened porch. She sat down on her lounger, put the paper down next to her, and took a couple sips of coffee. She looked at her watch. Linnea would be delivering her sermon right about now.

You have no real excuse for staying home, an accusing voice whispered. *You're not sick. Why are you sitting here instead of in church?*

"Oh, leave me alone!" Jacoba said defiantly into the air and paged through the *Times* until she found the comics. She sat back and started a leisurely read of her favorite section of the paper. When she'd finished, she folded the paper into some semblance of its former self and reached for her coffee. It was cold. She put the mug down and closed her eyes. Closed eyes took her right to her classroom.

Tomorrow would be the second Monday without Jeremy. All last week her students had placed flowers, action figures, toy cars, and even a teddy bear on Jeremy's desk. She wasn't going to touch those things. She couldn't imagine taking his name off the class duty roster or the milk carton mailboxes either. His name needed to stay in place, his memory honored. She would wait until the school year was over, the children gone, to change anything.

Her thoughts circled back to yesterday's conversation with the Hirsches. She admired Mr. and Mrs. Hirsch for going to talk to Billy's parents. The Barneses must have taken something they'd said to heart because the bullying had stopped for a little while.

Or did Billy just take a break from the twins and start picking on someone else?

She remembered Billy's reaction yesterday when he realized she'd been standing right behind him.

I wonder what Billy will do when he's face to face with me tomorrow?

She looked out into her backyard. She couldn't believe Dr. Miller hadn't talked to her about Billy. *I'll set up an appointment to see him first thing. You've got some explaining to do, Dr. Miller.*

The combination of a car door slamming shut and thunder rumbling startled Jacoba back into the present.

"Jacoba? You home?" a familiar voice called from her back gate. Lightning flashed and thunder cracked overhead. Large raindrops landed on the sidewalk.

"Marty!"

Jacoba jumped up to unlatch the porch's screen door. She held it open for the short, gray-haired woman in black slacks and a black-and-white long-sleeved shirt who hurried up the steps.

"You brought coffee!"

"Yup, the elixir of life." Marty held up the cardboard carrier holding two coffees.

Both women laughed. Rain pounded overhead, and the fine wet spray came through the screen into the porch.

"Come on, Marty, we'd better go inside."

Marty's eyes fell on Jacoba's coffee mug as she passed the lounge chair.

"Uh-oh, maybe I should have brought fruit juice instead of coffee."

"Are you kidding? There is no such thing as too much coffee!"

Jacoba led the way to the living room and sat in her recliner, while Marty stepped between coffee table and couch to plunk into her usual spot. She set the coffees in front of her, offered one to Jacoba, and took the other for herself. They raised their beverages to each other in salute and took appraising sips.

Marty drank a little more of her coffee before resting it on her knee. "So, are you okay, Jacoba? You've been on my mind all week."

Jacoba looked into the face of this friend. She knew Marty would listen and speak truth to her. She needed both those things.

"Marty, I've always thought I understood my students, at least most of them. I've always thought I knew what was going on in my classroom."

"And something has happened to change that?"

Jacoba nodded. "Yes. I found out yesterday that a little boy in my class has been bullying other students right under my nose. I can't believe I didn't see it." She paused for a moment. "And Jeremy . . . the boy who died . . . Riding his bike down that steep trail in the park was completely out of character." She lifted a stricken face to her friend. "Marty, what if I'm responsible for what he decided to do?"

"What? Jacoba! Where is this coming from?"

"Jeremy's grandmother. She said Jeremy died because of what I teach in my classroom." As soon as those words were out of her mouth, a giant glacier of emotion began to melt inside her. "All I've ever wanted to do was to get children excited about learning—to make learning fun, interesting." Tears fell faster than her fingers could wipe them away.

Marty hurried to grab a box of tissues off the kitchen counter and brought it back into the living room. Jacoba pulled out several at once, used them, and reached for more. She took a deep breath, then another.

"Jacoba, listen to me. You've been teaching how long?"

"Almost twenty years," Jacoba said softly.

"And in almost twenty years, has anything like this ever happened?"

Jacoba looked at her friend in surprise. "No."

"If being a creative, enthusiastic, dedicated teacher caused students to die, don't you think that would have happened in your classroom before now?"

"Wow, I hadn't thought of that." Jacoba sat up a little straighter, pondering Marty's words. "Thanks, Marty. Thanks."

The sound of chirping crickets erupted out of Marty's purse. "Oh, my goodness! So sorry. That's Bob." She pulled her phone out of her purse and checked the screen. "He's wondering where I am."

She quickly texted back and dropped the phone back into her purse.

"You and Bob still planning to leave me in charge next month?" Jacoba smiled a little and reached for her coffee.

"Absolutely! We couldn't go anywhere if you didn't step in to run the antique mall for June and July. I never worry when you're there."

"It's my summer dream job," Jacoba said with conviction. "No papers to grade! No lessons to plan. *Behind the Times* doesn't open until ten a.m., so I get to enjoy a more leisurely start to my day. And I'm forever amazed at what people buy! Cracks me up sometimes. It's really true that what's trash to one person is treasure to another." She put her coffee down. "I'm looking forward to working in the antique mall this summer more than I ever have."

Marty gave Jacoba a sympathetic nod. "I can believe that. A summer at the mall is just what you need." The chirping cricket sounded again from her purse. "Oh, Bob," she said in mild exasperation. "Guess I'd better get going, Jacoba. Feeling better?"

"Yes," Jacoba said. "Thanks for coming, Marty, and for listening. And for the coffee too."

"You're welcome. That's what friends are for!"

Marty left through the front door and ran through light drizzle to her car. Jacoba went back to the porch and her chair. She stared through the screen into the backyard and considered what

Marty had said. Her friend was right. She'd been a teacher for almost twenty years, and her creativity had never killed a student. It made solid, reassuring sense. But then she thought about what the Hirsches had told her yesterday afternoon. Self-recrimination came surging back. Doubt, guilt, regret swirled in her mind.

Stop this! No more crying! Jacoba told herself sternly. *No more crying!* But tears came anyway.

Neil Hirsch sank down into his favorite chair. Traces of charcoal smoke wafted up to his nose from his clothes. *The price one pays for grilling hamburgers,* he thought. *A peaceful end to a pleasant Sunday.* He shifted his weight left, then right. Something was wrong. The seat cushion underneath him was much more solid than usual. *Who has been sitting in my chair?* He laughed.

"This is what your life has become, Hirsch," he said to himself. "Lines from fairy tales are now a mainstay of your mental processes!" He shifted in the chair again, stood up, and pulled up the seat cushion. Aha! Jake's missing library book!

"Jake!" Neil called out. "Come see what I found!"

Jake thundered down the stairs and into the living room. Neil held up the library book. A large grin spread across the boy's face. "You found it! Thanks, Dad! Where was it?"

"In my chair, under the cushion."

Neil handed the book to his son and repositioned the cushion after administering a couple plumping punches. He sat back down and bounced a bit. "Much better!" He looked at Jake. "Do you and Maddie want to ride bikes to school tomorrow, or do you want to ride with me?"

Jake's answer was quick and quiet. "Ride with you. No bikes."

Neil nodded. "Okay, sure, buddy. Too soon for biking to school?"

Jake nodded back. "Too soon." He stood still, book in hand, eyes on his dad.

"Something on your mind, son?"

Jake looked down at his book.

Neil wasn't patient by nature, but he'd learned the benefits of patience where his children were concerned. He reached down to tug at his shoelaces and pull up his socks, buying them both some time. Jake moved to the couch and sat on the corner closest to his dad. Neil sat back in the chair and rested his elbows on the chair arms, the fingers of both hands resting against each other. He looked inquiringly at his son.

Jake looked back at his father, his expression serious. "Dad, I've been thinking about Jeremy."

"Mmhmm." Neil nodded his encouragement.

"Is it Sunday night in heaven? I hope there are bikes there. I'm really going to miss riding bikes with Jeremy," Jake said sadly.

Ahhhhh, Neil thought. *Finally! I've been waiting for an opening all weekend.*

"I know you will, Jake." He tried to sound as nonchalant as possible. "That was a great picture you drew of you, Jeremy, and Maddie riding your bikes. And the dog—what was his name?"

"Max," Jake said.

"Right, Max. Detective Roe and Officer Barclay sure were interested in Max."

Neil looked at Jake. Jake looked back, eyes wide, and then he looked down at the book in his hands. He started turning the book over and over. Neil envisioned the wheels turning in his son's head. He waited. The book finally stopped turning, and Jake spoke.

"Dad, we promised to keep Max and Miss Sally a secret. I wasn't thinking about the promise when I drew the picture."

"Miss Sally? Who is Miss Sally, Jake?"

"I can't say any more. Answering you would be breaking the promise." Jake pulled the library book to his chest and held it there with crossed arms.

"I'm proud of you for being a man of your word, Jake. But your mother and I want to know all the people in your life. We want to keep you and your sister safe, to protect you from danger."

Jake sat up in surprise. "Dad! Max and Miss Sally aren't dangerous. Miss Sally says she just needs her privacy to do her work in the park."

"Okay," Neil said, fighting to keep his concerns

under control. He looked at his son with a mixture of love and exasperation. "I think it would be a good idea for your mother and me to meet Miss Sally." He had a flash of inspiration. "What if you invited Miss Sally to come for supper one night?"

Jake started twirling his book again.

"Okay, Jake. No more questions from me. Time to get ready for bed."

Neil stood up as Jake pushed off the couch. When Jake brushed past his father, Neil reached out and gripped him in a bear hug, book and all.

"Love you, son."

"Love you, Dad."

Neil released his son and watched him round the corner to the stairs. Naomi wouldn't be happy when she heard about the twins' mysterious park friend. He'd tell her about it after the kids were in bed. And he was sure she'd want to be part of the conversation when he called Detective Roe tomorrow. He took some comfort in the thought that neither Jake nor Maddie had any reason to be in the park again anytime soon.

Solomon climbed the stairs to the second-floor hallway and turned in the direction of the shrieking and yelling. The commotion was coming from Jonathan's bedroom. When Solomon got to the doorway, he saw Jonathan leaning over his bed, his pillow in one hand and the edge of his bedspread in the other. He was pulling the bedspread, but a large lump under the covers was pulling back.

"Come on, Sam! Enough!" Jonathan yelled. "I have to finish my paper!"

A muffled but defiant voice came from under the bedspread. "And I have to finish my job here!"

"Job? What job?" Jonathan asked.

"I'm contaminating your bed with my brother cooties!"

Sam shrieked again and rolled around under the covers as Jonathan renewed his pulling.

"Boys! Boys!" Solomon intervened from the door. "Sam, time to get ready for bed. Weekend's over. Back to school tomorrow."

Sam popped out from under a tangle of covers, made one more exaggerated motion of touching as much of the surface of Jonathan's bed as he could, and then triumphantly walked over to his dad.

"Pj's on, teeth brushed. I'll be there in a few minutes," Solomon said.

Jonathan shook out the bedspread and let it fall back on the bed. He pulled his desk chair out and sat back down in front of his open laptop, his back to his father. Solomon came over to the desk and looked over his son's shoulder at the paragraphs he'd typed so far.

"So, how's the paper coming?"

Jonathan kept his eyes on the screen. "My summary is good. But my defending argument stinks. Dr. Summit is going to find a lot to laugh about in here."

Solomon felt a twinge of guilt. How many times had he and Dr. Summit made disparaging remarks about students' writing abilities? This time his own son's work would be on the receiving end. It wasn't a pleasant thought.

Jonathan resumed his typing, and Solomon went next door. Sam had crawled between his baseball-print sheets and was leaning back into his mountain of pillows. His feet didn't quite reach the snoozing Snickers curled up on the comforter at the foot of the bed. Solomon walked past the autographed poster of Sam's favorite baseball team and sat on the edge of the bed. Sam grinned at him, a thin line of toothpaste at the corner of his mouth. He moved over to make more room for his dad, and they began their evening ritual.

"So, Sam, what was the best part of your day?"

Sam pulled his knees to his chest and hugged them. "Best part was dessert tonight: chocolate ice cream with chocolate sauce."

Solomon nodded in agreement. "I'd have to say that was a high point in my day too. Okay, what was the worst part of the day?"

Sam stretched his legs back out and curled his hands around the sheet. "The worst part is happening right now. I'm too wide awake to go to sleep. Can't I please stay up a little longer?" And then he yawned in spite of himself.

"I saw that!" Solomon laughed. "Last question: How's your heart?"

"It's okay, Dad. But I miss Mom. I still expect to

see her in the kitchen or to have her here, tucking me in."

"I know," Solomon said. "I know. I still expect to see her too." He willed his brain to stay right where it was, not to go beyond this edge of memory. "Okay, Samster, sleep like a Rigby!"

"Sleep like a Rigby, sound and deep!" Sam chanted back as he snuggled down into his pillows.

Solomon got up and turned off Sam's bedside lamp. A baseball-shaped nightlight glowed in the corner.

"Do you want your door open, closed, or cracked?"

"Cracked, please," Sam answered. "Snickers might want to go sleep with Jon later."

Solomon pulled the door until only a cat-sized crack remained. He crossed the hall and walked into the dark master bedroom.

He turned on the lamp and Sarah-touches materialized: the peach-colored comforter, the light-colored draperies, the low chest at the end of the bed that held decorative pillows he didn't take out anymore. He looked beyond the bed to the chest of drawers between the window and the walk-in closet. He remembered Sarah's delight when she'd found it at the local antique mall the summer they'd moved here.

An artificial rubber tree filled another corner. If they wanted indoor vegetation, artificial was the only way to go thanks to Snickers's appetite for green, growing things. Solomon hadn't wanted a cat; he was a dog person. But when Snickers had appeared at their door, Sarah had promptly fallen in love with him. And Solomon hadn't put up much of a fight.

Solomon walked over to the window and shoved it open as high as it would go. The blinds rattled as a soft breeze wafted into the room. He looked out over his neighborhood. He could hear the hum of an eighteen-wheeler travelling down Remembrance Road on its way to US 10.

He thought about Sam missing his mom. Sunday evening was one of the times Solomon felt Sarah's absence most. Last fall Sarah had started bringing the kitchen calendar upstairs on Sunday nights. With the calendar between them on the bed, they'd talked, laughed, and tossed scheduling possibilities back and forth. Somehow, they'd always come up with a weekly plan that worked.

Now that was all up to him. Right after Sarah's death there had been disastrous weeks littered with forgotten appointments and tardy arrivals. He had started carrying the kitchen calendar in his briefcase. Slowly but surely the Rigby weekly schedule was getting back on track.

After he'd gotten ready for bed, he poked his head out of his bedroom door just in time to see Snickers slip out of Sam's room and trot down to Jonathan's. A narrow beam of light shot out into the hallway as the cat pushed open the door and disappeared into the room.

Solomon went to Jonathan's door and rapped his knuckles softly on the door frame.

"I'm going to bed, Jonathan. You want Snickers in here or shall I put him downstairs?"

Jonathan didn't turn away from the laptop to answer his father. "He can stay, Dad."

"Night, then."

"Night."

Guilt tapped Solomon on the shoulder for the second time that evening. He knew exactly where it was coming from.

If Sarah were here . . .

He cringed at the thought of what she would have said to him about how he had dismissed Jonathan's desire to seek the priesthood and his invoking of a new house rule. And she never would have stood for the resulting icy civility that existed between father and son now.

Light in the stairwell reminded Solomon he still needed to check the back door. He went downstairs, clicked off the floor lamp by his chair in the living room, and walked to the kitchen. Once satisfied all was as it should be, he went back upstairs to bed. He repeated the family's vesper mantra as he closed his eyes.

"Sleep like a Rigby, sound and deep."

Chapter Eleven

Jacoba stepped out into the hallway and pulled the music room door closed. She'd complained all year about having music first thing Monday mornings, but it served her well today. She walked the brightly lit hallway to the front office and entered. She expected to see Barb Globe, Dr. Miller's administrative assistant, on the other side of the high counter, but instead she came face to face with Dr. Miller himself.

"Oh, good morning, Dr. Miller. I was just coming to set up an appointment with you." Jacoba tried to keep her voice steady and calm. She attempted a smile, but her lips weren't cooperating. How different this moment would have been if Cassie Elliot were still principal. Cassie had been both boss and friend to her staff. Dr. Miller was the boss now, but he most certainly was not a friend.

"Ms. Dahm. I was on my way to talk to you. Your class is in music now, correct?"

"Yes, for half an hour."

Has something happened? Why does he want to talk to me? Her heart started beating faster. *Don't assume what's coming is bad. Don't assume. Step away from the bridge!*

Jacoba walked past him into his office and took the chair in front of his desk. She heard him close the glass-windowed door with a firm hand, not quite a slam but close. He walked past her, sat in his desk chair, and looked down his nose at her. A decidedly unprofessional thought popped into her head. *He looks like Mr. Spock on Star Trek. An older Mr. Spock.* The mental comic relief of that picture was short-lived. Dr. Miller's next sentences set her heart racing again.

"Since we only have a short time for conversation, I'll get right to the point. I've had a phone call already this morning from William Barnes. He called to complain about your treatment of his son on Saturday."

"What?" Jacoba stared at him.

"Billy told his father you allowed the Hirsch twins to make fun of him." Dr. Miller's tone left no question as to his presumption of her guilt. Jacoba's look of astonishment didn't seem to register with him.

"Dr. Miller, that's not what happened. Billy threatened Maddie Hirsch. As I was stepping in to intervene, Billy's father called him, and Billy took off."

Dr. Miller's icy regard didn't waver. Jacoba plowed ahead. "Dr. Miller, on Saturday afternoon Mr. and Mrs. Hirsch told me Billy Barnes is a bully, that this had been a problem all year and you knew about it. And they thought I knew about it. They thought you had told me months ago."

He looked back at her with a defiant expression,

his lips set in a tight, thin line. The resemblance to Mr. Spock really was uncanny.

"Dr. Miller, we've never had a conversation about Billy Barnes."

There it was. Truth on the table. No answer came from the other side of the desk. Why didn't he say something?

It was a full minute before Dr. Miller spoke. "When I became principal two years ago, GES was sadly lacking in a number of areas. Thanks to the generosity of William Barnes, several classrooms, including yours, now have computer labs. Internet access is available throughout the building. A new multifunction copier arrived in February, of benefit to teachers and support staff. Mr. Barnes and I are currently in conversation about adding a new wing of classrooms to the north side of the building." Dr. Miller looked pointedly at her. "I intend to do whatever it takes to ensure the Barnes generosity continues. Having William Barnes's financial backing means I don't have to wait for a community vote. I can get what I want now."

Jacoba couldn't believe what she was hearing. Dr. Miller checked his watch, looked past her, and stood up.

"I think I've made myself clear. I expect your full cooperation in this matter. Now if you will excuse me, I see my next appointment is here." Dr. Miller strode past her, opened the door, and disappeared into the outer office.

Jacoba got up and followed him out. She didn't

even look to see if Barb Globe was behind the counter as she left the office.

She headed back to the music room as questions swirled wildly in her brain. *Cooperate? How can I cooperate? Doesn't Dr. Miller realize he's enabling Billy? I know about Billy and the Hirsch twins, but are there others? Could Billy have had anything to do with Jeremy Davis's death?*

Jacoba stood outside the music room door and belatedly realized she'd completely misread Billy's demeanor when he had entered the classroom that morning. He'd assiduously avoided her. She'd assumed he was operating under a guilty conscience. Wrong. *One more time you didn't know what was really going on.*

Mrs. Warren, the music teacher, opened the door to reveal a line of eager faces. Christopher, today's line leader, looked expectantly at Jacoba.

"All right, friends," Jacoba said with as much enthusiasm as she could muster. "Brief time on the playground and then back to work!"

She walked alongside the line as it progressed toward the exit door at the end of the hall. She counted heads in front of her and then behind. Sixteen children in her class now, nine girls and seven boys. Billy Barnes was third in line with Lillian Pratt right behind him. Jacoba felt an overwhelming urge to snatch him out of the line and stick him in a corner for the longest timeout of his life. How could she protect the rest of the children from him? And how could she help him if she was supposed to ignore what he was doing?

I miss Cassie Elliot, she thought. Cassie Elliot's moral compass spun on the same axis as Jacoba's. *I wonder what she would say about all this?*

Joyful shrieks, bright sunlight, and laughter jumbled together as Jacoba stepped out onto the sidewalk. Hand over her eyes, she walked closer to the swings. She looked for Billy. She knew she'd be looking for him for the rest of the school year. *Maybe I should move his desk closer to mine. I want him right under my nose all the time. If he complains to his father, so be it. Dr. Miller can just—*

"Wow, are you ever deep in thought, Ms. Dahm!" a voice teased from behind her.

Jacoba turned around. "Ms. Ko! Happy Monday! How are things in second grade?"

Judy Ko came alongside Jacoba. She was twenty years younger, twenty pounds lighter, and two or three inches shorter.

"Today things are good in second grade. How are you?"

Jacoba didn't answer. They both looked out over the children playing all around them.

"Really, Ms. D, how are you?" The other teacher looked at Jacoba and then out over the play area again. "I know it was rough for me, for my class, when Sam Rigby's mother died in January. I can't imagine how hard it would have been if Sam had died."

If only you knew, Jacoba thought. *If only you knew how complicated this has all become.*

Suddenly a lively game of chase enveloped the teachers.

"Hey, I am not home base!" Ms. Ko yelled as several children crowded against her. "Okay, friends, time to get back to work!" She blew two short tweets on the whistle around her neck and started to walk back to the sidewalk.

Jacoba's students came running from all directions to line up in front of her. Sweaty and out of breath, Christopher slid into place and waited for Jacoba to give him the nod. Nod given, Jacoba watched as the line reentered the building. She started to count the children: *One, two, three . . . Christopher, Jake, Maddie. Four, five, six . . . Lillian, Ernesto, Jean. Seven, eight, nine, ten . . . Elizabeth, Stephanie, Judy, Diane.* Now they were all inside the cooler, darker hallway. *Eleven, twelve, thirteen, fourteen . . . Amy, Sophie, Leo, Carlos. Fifteen . . . Adam. Sixteen . . . Billy Barnes. Things are never going to be the same again.*

Simon looked up when he heard Richard's voice coming from the precinct hallway.

"Oh, no, Elizabeth, that's not how I answered it!" Richard's lament carried loud and clear into the line of office carrels.

"Richard, I'm sure you did your best. Let it go.

Time to shift gears and move on to the next good thing."

Simon smiled to himself. What would they do without Elizabeth? She faithfully sat in front of her computer and found things out for the rest of them. And when she wasn't on an information safari, she was encouraging someone.

Richard came and stood next to Simon's desk, class notes in hand. "Oh, man, Detective Roe, I think I really screwed up."

"So I heard." Simon tried to keep a straight face. "Like Elizabeth said, I'm sure you did your best. That's all you can do." The phone rang, saving him from having to say more.

"Detective Roe speaking. How may I help you?" He listened to the response. "Mr. Hirsch! May I put you on speaker phone? Then Officer Barclay can be part of our conversation."

"Yes, certainly. My wife, Naomi, is here with me, so I'll put you on speaker phone on my end too."

Simon hit the speaker button on the phone's console as Richard took the chair next to him.

"Can you hear me, Mr. Hirsch?"

"Loud and clear," Neil Hirsch's voice sounded into the room.

"So, Mr. Hirsch, did you talk to your son?" Simon reached for a pen and the notepad on his desktop.

"Yes. Last night Jake told me that he, his sister,

and Jeremy Davis had met a lady named Miss Sally in the park. Max is Miss Sally's dog."

Naomi Hirsch picked up the narrative. "The kids promised this Miss Sally they'd keep her and the dog a secret. A secret," she repeated. "That's very concerning to us."

Simon and Richard exchanged looks.

"Jake told me Miss Sally said she and Max needed their privacy to do their work in the park," Neil added.

Naomi's voice came through the phone speaker again. "Detective Roe, Neil and I wondered if she was some kind of undercover cop."

"I don't know of a Miss Sally working at this precinct." Simon looked at Richard. "Do you know of a Miss Sally working here?"

"No," Richard said.

"Mr. and Mrs. Hirsch, we'll do some checking on our end. In the meantime, I suggest if the twins ride bikes in the park, you go with them, at least until we get this cleared up."

"The twins don't go to the park during the week." Naomi's voice was decisive. "And if they want to go on Saturday or Sunday, you can be sure Neil and I will be tagging along."

"Good. Thanks for calling. We'll get back to you if we discover something you need to know."

"Thank you, Detective."

A loud click came through the speaker. Simon reached out and pressed the button on his phone.

He looked expectantly at Richard. "So, Officer Barclay, your thoughts?"

"I'm automatically suspicious of any adult who asks children to keep a secret."

"Me too."

"Who would know if there is a Miss Sally on some sort of official assignment in the park? And what about Max? The day I saw Max, I didn't see anyone else around, but someone was nearby; someone whistled and he took off."

"I'll check to see if we have anything undercover going on in the park."

"A park ranger might have noticed Max."

"Does the park even have rangers?" Simon looked at Richard.

"I've never seen rangers in all the times I've biked or jogged there."

"Well! That makes me wonder who runs the park. I never thought about that before—is it a city park, a state park, or is it federally run?"

"Maybe Miss Sally works for the FBI!"

Simon laughed. "The FBI undercover in Grandburg? I don't think so. But you know who can answer our questions about the park? Marvin Artz, over in City Hall. He runs the Offices of Parks, Recreation, and Cemeteries." He rocked back in his chair. "Let's walk over and see what we can find out."

They took the stairs down to the first floor, crossed the lobby, and exited onto the sidewalk. They both warmed up quickly as they walked up

Center Street and passed The Cat's Meow Bookstore. City Hall was across the street on their right, a two-story dark-red brick building surrounded by large, black-limbed oak trees. They crossed Center Street and took the short sidewalk to the entrance. Richard opened the door for Simon, letting out a delicious rush of cool air. They stepped through the metal detectors into the high-ceilinged lobby. Simon took the lead as they crossed the highly polished terrazzo floor.

"Stairs okay?" Simon asked Richard.

"Sure."

The farther down the stairs they went, the cooler it got. Once they'd reached the basement, Simon led the way down a quiet corridor past a bank of elevators. Fluorescent lighting hummed overhead.

"Marvin Artz's office is right—"

The office door ahead of them opened abruptly, and a tall, heavyset man dressed in a three-piece suit hurried into the hallway.

"Excuse me," the man said into the air without looking at Simon or Richard. He rushed to the stairwell and started a rapid ascent.

"Man on a mission," Richard said.

Well, Simon thought, *I wonder what William Barnes was doing down here?*

The men entered a spacious office. Three desks were equally spaced along the length of it. The middle desktop held a telephone, a computer monitor and keyboard, a printer, and a large cardboard blotter. A row of filing cabinets rested against the far wall behind it. High windows ran all along that wall. A short man stood with his back to them in front of a large oak map case. His wire-rimmed glasses rested high on his head, gray hair swept back in a ponytail. He wore a dark shirt with a sweater over it and light khaki pants. Two long, thin map rolls rested against his shoulder. He turned around when Simon closed the door.

"Morning, Marvin! Got a minute for a few questions?"

"Well! Detective Roe, good to see you! I'll be right with you after I've put these maps away."

"I wonder how old this building is," Richard said to Simon. "This room reminds me of my grandmother's basement. And it has that same damp feel."

Marvin joined them. "This building was built in 1855."

"Wow! That would make it over a hundred and fifty years old!"

"It's had a few face-lifts over the years. The 1920 fire damaged the brick on the north and west sides. On a sunny day you can see the color difference between the 1855 bricks and the newer ones."

"I never thought of something from 1920 as being newer." Richard laughed.

Marvin looked at Simon. "So, Detective Roe, is this young man your new partner?"

"Marvin Artz, meet Richard Barclay."

Simon continued as the two men shook hands,

"He's on loan from Tilden College. He's in the advanced police academy internship program over there. Marvin, we're working on a case that involves the park. We need background information about it and are hoping you can fill us in on the who, what, when, where, and why."

"Well, I guess I put those maps away too soon." Marvin turned back to the map cabinet. As he pulled open a wide drawer he looked back over his shoulder. "The gentleman who left right before you came in was asking about the park too."

So Dar's rumor might be true! Simon thought.

Marvin carried two long, thin paper tubes to the middle desk. He scooted the computer's keyboard to one side and unrolled one of the maps. Richard and Simon helped hold the edges down.

"This map dates back to the late 1800s. See anything familiar?" Marvin asked.

"I recognize the river," Simon said as he surveyed the drawing in front of him.

"Look at all the forest," Richard said in amazement. "And the town is small—just a few streets."

"In the 1800s, the forested area belonged to an indigenous tribe," Marvin said. "In 1900, the tribe was cheated out of the land by a local businessman who then cut down trees from the edge of town all the way past what is now the park's second scenic overlook." Marvin drew an imaginary loop in the air just above the map with his finger.

Simon looked at Marvin and back down at the map.

"When the businessman died in 1928, his son donated the land to the federal government to be set aside as a park. Thanks to the New Deal in the '30s, the park really took shape. Here, we need the other map." Marvin carefully rolled up the first map and unrolled the second.

"Okay, I recognize more than the river on this one," Simon said.

"Much of the land along the river was reforested. The perimeter road went in where the logging road had been." Marvin's finger hovered over each place as he named it. "The scenic overlooks were already well established, as was the Prayer Trail. The jogging trail was created along with cabins and a modest campground."

"Groups from states to our south started Civil War reenactments on the park's north edge. The cemetery, chapel, and gift shop were added later, after World War II. Park rangers managed it all."

"So the park is run by the feds," Richard said.

"Ah, no," Marvin answered. "When the national economy tanked thirty years ago, the feds offered the town council the opportunity to purchase the park at a pittance. The council jumped at the chance. Now it's run by a small corporation here in Grandburg."

"So that's why I've never seen park rangers on duty there," Richard said.

"Right. After several instances of vandalism a few years ago, the corporation hired a security firm to patrol the perimeter road and picnic areas. They patrol three or four times a day from April through November. From December through March, they patrol if the snow isn't too deep on the roadway. No plow service."

"I know Al Barfield runs the camping office and the gift shop," Simon said.

"He's been the manager for years. He handles the camping schedules, supervises the volunteers who keep the gift shop going, and is the go-to person if there's a reenactment being planned."

"And what about cutting the grass, cleaning the picnic areas, garbage removal, things like that?" Richard asked.

"The last I heard the corporation had hired Lisa's Lawn and Landscape to cut the grass. The city waste service visits the park several times a week to police picnic areas and empty trash cans."

"We keep talking about the park, little p. Doesn't it have a more official name? Seems like it should, but I've never heard one," Richard said.

"Good question, Officer. No, the park doesn't have an official name or title. That was one of the stipulations of the 1928 donation."

"How odd!"

"Marvin, do you know anything about a Miss Sally working at the park?" Simon asked. "She's been seen there with a dog."

"Miss Sally? Sally's back? With Max! Well, what do you know!"

"Then there is a Miss Sally working in the park!" Simon had a moment of enlightenment. "Does she work for Mr. Barfield?"

"Oh, no, Sally isn't on staff at the park."

"Marvin, if Miss Sally is working at the park how can she *not* be on staff there?"

Marvin looked down at the map in front of him. "You need another piece of the park's history to understand what she's doing there." He looked at Simon and Richard. "The Fire of 1920 is well documented and remembered in Grandburg. But do either of you know about the fire that happened twenty years before that one?"

Both men shook their heads.

"As unfortunate as the 1920 fire was, the one that happened in October of 1900 was a much more profound tragedy."

"What happened?" Simon asked.

"The Native American village on the river just north of town was burned to the ground."

"Someone deliberately burned it? Who?" Simon pressed.

"Why?" Richard added.

"Roger Rinien did it. He was the person who cheated the tribe out of land they'd called home for over one hundred years. And when they refused to move, he and the local sheriff burned the village down."

"I've lived in Grandburg all my life," Richard said, "and I've never heard any of this!"

Simon nodded at Richard. "It's news to me too."

"This is where your Miss Sally comes in," Marvin said. "She and her husband, Eric, camped at the park, looking for evidence of the Native American centuries-long presence there. Eric's dream was to see the land returned to the tribe. But after Eric died, I didn't think Sally would come back. I guess I was wrong!"

"Marvin, some children met Sally in the park, and she told them to keep her presence there a secret."

"That makes no sense to me," Marvin said. "People who knew Eric and Sally knew why they were there, what they were looking for. It was never a secret."

"Maybe she finally discovered something—and needs more time to figure out what to do about it," Simon said to Marvin and Richard.

"Mr. Artz," Richard asked curiously, "how do you know all this about the tribe and the fire?"

"My great-grandfather told the story to my grandfather, who told it to my father, who told it to me. My great-grandfather was the chief of the tribe when the village was burned, their land stolen, in 1900."

Jake rolled over in his bed and looked toward the window. He knew he had another fifteen minutes before he would hear his dad's footsteps coming up the stairs followed by sharp raps on his door. Jake liked mornings. Maddie did not. If Jake didn't hear his sister moving around in her room once Dad had gone back downstairs, he would go and wake her up.

Jake piled his pillows high and leaned against them. He replayed last night's conversation with his dad over and over in his mind. He knew he'd said too much. He'd seen the change on his dad's face when he'd let Miss Sally's name slip. And now he didn't know what to do. He wished again he'd never drawn that picture. He wished again his best friend, well, second best friend after Maddie, hadn't died. He wished he could go back in time and change things. He thought about the latest story Ms. Dahm was reading to them after lunch, *A Wrinkle in Time*. That's what he needed: a tesseract, a wrinkle in time. He'd tesser back to the Thursday afternoon before everything had unraveled, and he would stop Jeremy from riding his bike in the park.

When the three of them had ridden home from school that fateful Thursday, he hadn't known Jeremy needed saving. But Miss Sally and Max were a different story. He knew they were in danger of being discovered because of his picture, his words. He had to do something about that. He needed to talk to Maddie. She always helped him think.

He threw his sheet back and swung his legs over the side of the bed. The soft carpet squished under his toes. He was pulling clothes out of his closet when he heard his dad coming upstairs.

"Up and at 'em, son!"

"Okay, Dad," Jake called back. When he heard his dad start back downstairs, he hurried to Maddie's room and knocked as he opened the door.

"Maddie? I want to ask you something," he said as he stepped into the dark room.

"I'm awake. I'm awake," a sleepy voice came from under the mound of covers on the bed.

Jake walked over and stood at the bed's edge. Maddie's long, curly brown hair was all he could see of his sister. Maddie rolled over and yawned.

"Okay, Jake," she said without opening her eyes. "What is it?"

"Maddie, I said too much to Dad about Miss Sally and Max. I need to warn Miss Sally that her secret is out. Dad, and maybe the police, know about her now." He sat down on Maddie's bed. "I wish I'd never drawn that picture!"

Maddie sat up and looked at her brother. "But Jake, we haven't seen Miss Sally since late last summer."

"I know, but we've seen Max since then. We saw Max a few weekends ago. Max and Miss Sally are always together. She has to be there, somewhere in the park. I have to warn her, Maddie. I have to warn her today."

"And how are you going to get to the park on a school day?"

Their conversation was interrupted when their mother called out from downstairs, "Jake, Maddie, breakfast!"

"We'll talk about this later," Maddie said firmly. "Don't do anything until we've talked some more. Promise me!"

"Okay, I promise."

The next opportunity for conversation did not come until morning recess after music class. Jake followed Maddie out onto the playground, and the two of them met by the big tree where the teachers usually stood. Several of Jake's friends called to him from the field where they were organizing a quick soccer game. He waved them off and turned to his sister.

"I've made up my mind, Maddie. I'm going to ride to the park after school today. I'm sure I can get to the park and back again without Mom or Dad knowing."

"Jake, if you do that you'll be breaking the no-going-to-the-park-alone rule. And you'll be keeping something from Mom and Dad. That's the same as lying." She looked accusingly at him. "Another rule broken."

"And if I don't go, I'll be breaking one of the rules, too, the one about keeping promises. I promised Miss Sally I wouldn't tell anyone else about her. I gave her my word. All three of us did. If she is discovered, it will be my fault. I have to do something."

Maddie didn't say anything for a moment. Then she looked solemnly at her brother. "I see your point," she said.

Their conversation was interrupted by the sound of a whistle tweeting. They turned to see Ms. Dahm waving the class to her side. They hurried to take their place in line. Maddie chatted away during lunch, but Jake didn't keep up his end of the conversation.

Jake didn't say much during the ride home either. His mother eyed him with some concern.

"You okay, buddy?" she asked him as he carried his backpack into the house. "You're pretty quiet this afternoon."

"Yup, Mom, I'm okay. Just thinking."

"How much homework do you have?" his mother asked.

"Not much. A math sheet, some spelling words, and I need to read at least one chapter in my book."

"Maddie, same assignment for you?"

"I've already finished the math sheet," Maddie said in a superior tone. "And I am planning to read several chapters in my book."

Mrs. Hirsch put her keys on the kitchen counter and hung her purse on the chair. "Tell you what," she said to the twins, "after you've had a snack, change clothes and go for a bike ride. If you're back in an hour or so, you'll still have plenty of time for homework."

Jake couldn't believe his ears. All that worrying about how to pull off a Monday bike ride to the park and here his mother was, practically inviting him to do what he needed to do. He grabbed a banana and a couple peanut butter cookies. He ate them quickly and ran upstairs to change clothes, leaving Maddie at the kitchen table eating an apple. When he came back down the kitchen was empty.

"Mom," he yelled. "I'm leaving! See you later!"

He pulled his helmet off its hook and walked with quick strides to the garage. He mounted his bike and sat with his hands on the handlebars, contemplating his route, when a noise behind him caused him to turn around. Maddie was standing there, helmet in hand.

"You weren't going to leave without me, were you?" She put on her helmet and pulled her bike from where it leaned against the wall.

"You're coming with me? What about the rules?"

"I don't want you to go alone."

"Thanks," Jake said.

"And like you said, I made the promise to Miss Sally too."

They wheeled their bikes out of the garage onto the driveway. Once their helmets were on, they started pedaling up Connor Avenue. When they got to Jeremy's corner they slowed a little and saluted. Then they picked up the pedaling pace until they came to the intersection of Connor and Clay Street. They walked their bikes across and hopped back on, taking the bike path to the pedestrian bridge. When they got to the bridge there were no pedestrians in sight, so they pedaled across instead of walking their bikes. They entered the park, rode past the empty guard hut, and turned north on the perimeter road.

The temperature dropped at least five degrees as they rounded the shady curve past the first scenic overlook. Jake stopped under the sign for the Indian Prayer Trail. Maddie coasted to a stop beside him, and she steadied herself with both feet on the ground.

"Why are you stopping?" she asked, a little out of breath.

"Dad said that's where they found Jeremy's body." Jake pointed down the hill. They could just make out the jogging trail. Maddie was silent. Jake looked at his sister. "Maddie, why do you think Jeremy rode his bike down the Prayer Trail? Why didn't he tell us what he was going to do?"

Maddie shook her head. "Maybe he didn't tell us because he knew we'd do our best to talk him out of it." She looked at the tall grass growing at the edge of the gravel shoulder. A pine-and-river-scented breeze blew past them, scattering leaves and dust. "Okay, Jake, we have about fifteen, twenty minutes before we have to head back home. Where are we going to look for Miss Sally?"

"Last summer Jeremy and I found Miss Sally's special place. I'm hoping I can find it again."

"You never told me that!" Maddie looked accusingly at her brother.

"We promised each other we wouldn't tell anyone. I wanted to tell you, but . . ."

"Yeah, I know, a promise is a promise." Maddie looked far from convinced.

"Maddie, I'm sorry, but I gave my word. Dad says—"

"I know what Dad says," Maddie interrupted impatiently. "Come on, let's go."

When they got to the second scenic overlook, two cars were parked by the picnic tables. Jake led the way to the opposite end of the parking lot and dismounted. He walked his bike along the boxwood hedge at the top of the slope. He could see muddy river water far below. He went through a break in the hedge, Maddie close behind. They propped their bikes against a tall pine tree and Jake started to descend the grassy slope, his eyes studying the ground ahead of him. Maddie took a few hesitant steps away from her bike.

"Jake," she called. "What are you doing? Looking for snakes?"

"I'm looking for the path," he called back. "There's a path that leads all the way down to the river. Jeremy and I found it when we were chasing Max." Ten steps later he yelled, "Found it! Come on, Maddie!"

Jake waited impatiently for her to catch up with him. "There's another path that goes off this one," he said when she came alongside him. "That path leads to Miss Sally's spot." He started walking again, head down, scanning the path edges, hoping to see a break. But they made it all the way down to the water's edge without finding a second pathway. They stood together and watched the brown water flow rapidly past them.

"See that?" Jake pointed to the roiling breakers in the middle of the river. "The water's so deep right now the sandbar is underwater."

Maddie was first to see the snake glide through the water a few feet to their left. "Snake! Run!"

The twins ran back up the trail with Maddie in the lead. After putting a safe distance between himself and the snake, Jake slowed down, looking again for the other path. Suddenly he called out to his sister.

"Hey! Maddie! I found it!" He pulled an armload of brush out of the way to reveal another path that led sharply down toward the water again. The overgrowth along the path was thick and tall. The trees ahead grew more closely together and created deep shade.

Maddie came to Jake's side and looked past him into the woods. "Are you sure this is it, Jake? It doesn't look like anyone has walked here in a long time."

Jake nodded. "Yup. This is it. I remember how it felt like we were walking into a leafy green tunnel when Jeremy and I were here."

He took a few steps into the woods and motioned for the reluctant Maddie to follow. They had only walked a few yards before the path beneath their feet became very soggy. Jake stopped abruptly and Maddie, who had been watching the ground, banged into him.

"Hey! Watch out!"

"Sorry!"

The twins looked ahead and saw a broad wet expanse where there was usually dry land.

"Come on, Jake. Let's go back. This place gives me the creeps."

"Okay," Jake said.

"Where do you think Miss Sally is now?" Maddie asked as they ascended the slope on the way back to their bikes.

"Some place higher, for sure, if she's staying close to the river. Or maybe she's moved some place deeper inside the park, some place joggers or walkers or runners or other campers won't find her."

"Do you think there even is such a place in the park? Is the park that big?" Maddie asked Jake as they got back to their bikes. "I've never thought about that before. How big the park is, I mean."

"Mr. Barfield says you could get lost in the middle of the park if you weren't careful."

"Mr. Barfield probably says that so you boys stay where he wants you to stay," Maddie said.

"Maybe," Jake answered. Then they both heard the City Hall clock chime the hour. "We better head back, Maddie."

They pedaled out of the overlook parking lot and back onto the perimeter road. The ride was easier on the way back; the gradual decline and gentle curves created a pleasant increase in speed and air flow. The twins rolled back into their driveway at almost the same time that their dad's car came down Connor Avenue. Mr. Hirsch got out of his car as the twins were taking off their helmets.

"Good bike ride?" Mr. Hirsch asked as he reached into the backseat of the car to retrieve his briefcase.

"Excellent!" Jake answered.

He and his sister hurried out of the garage and into the house. Jake followed Maddie upstairs, glad they'd not been asked where they'd been, glad he'd tried to right the wrong he'd committed, sorry they hadn't found Miss Sally.

In his bedroom he took his homework pad out of his backpack and flipped to today's assignment page. He reached into the bag, pulled out the math sheet, spelling workbook, and library book, and piled them on his desk. He needed a pencil. He dug deeper into the backpack and found one, sat down at his desk, and reached for the math sheet. But the unfinished business in the park kept him from the first multiplication problem. He twirled the pencil between his fingers.

"If we couldn't find Miss Sally, then maybe nobody else will either. And the next time we meet Max in the park, we'll follow him to Miss Sally and warn her. That's all I know to do." He twirled the pencil into its writing position, and feeling both cheered and relieved, set to work on math.

Chapter Twelve

Jonathan took a sip of his latte and made a face when the cold dregs at the bottom of the cup hit his tastebuds. He checked the time in the lower corner of his computer screen: 10:30. The coffee shop tables around him were empty now, but he knew they wouldn't stay that way much longer.

Paper's due at noon. I have an hour and a half left, he thought. *I could get another coffee and work on it a little more, or I could send it now and be done with it.*

He leaned back in the chair and stretched. He watched several students come in and line up at the counter to place their orders. Reluctantly he brought his eyes back to the page on his computer screen. Snatches of conversation fell on his ears, competing with the words in front of him. A burst of laughter came from the table to his left, distracting him further. It was the mouthwatering crunch of a potato chip that finally pushed him over the edge.

That's it! I'm done.

With a few quick keystrokes he emailed his paper to Dr. Summit. His sense of satisfaction quadrupled when he realized he had just given himself the gift of time.

Ahhhh! Ninety minutes until study group meets. Ninety wonderful, unexpected, unclaimed, unassigned minutes! He picked up his empty coffee cup. *First things first—more coffee.*

A few minutes later, fresh-brewed latte in hand, he sat back down, packed away his computer, and pulled a slim, multicolored brochure out of his backpack.

"Good morning, Jonathan Rigby," a woman spoke right over his head. He looked up and recognized the smile, the curly brown hair, and the dangling earrings.

"Mary! Good morning!"

Mary pulled out a chair and sat across from Jonathan. "Got any more of those great chocolate chip cookies?"

"I wish!" Jonathan took a sip of his coffee and looked across the table at Mary. She looked back at him. "So, Mary, a couple more days and the semester will be over. Got any plans for the summer?" He folded his hands on top of the brochure.

"I'm in the middle of an internship your dad's set up at Rinien House," Mary said. "Goes through the summer, but I'm enjoying my time there, so it's fine with me. What about you? What are your summer plans?"

"I'm not sure what I'm going to do. Maybe take some classes . . . or do something else."

Mary checked her watch. "Oh, gotta go. Choir practice starts in five minutes!" She got up, pushed in her chair, and picked up her coffee. "See you later, Jonathan. Glad we could chat."

He watched her walk away and wave to friends as she passed another table. Then she pushed through the coffee shop doors and was gone. He lifted his hands off the brochure and looked down. He had memorized the faces of the men who smiled up at him from the glossy cover. Jonathan flipped the pamphlet open, lifted it off the tabletop, and read the heading. *Is God calling you to a life of service? Spend six weeks this summer in discernment at—*

"Hi, son. Get that paper finished?"

Jonathan jerked up and stared into his father's face. Shock catapulted him out of his seat. He jammed the brochure into his backpack. "Yes, Dad, all done. Gotta go." He zipped shut the backpack and grabbed his coffee. "Choir practice!" he shot over his shoulder as he made a beeline for the exit.

"Choir practice?" his father called after him, mystified.

Jonathan turned back just long enough to give his father a single wave. He pushed the door open and stepped out onto the sidewalk. Humidity and bright sunlight hit him all at once.

Choir practice? How dumb was that? Hope that fib doesn't come back to bite me.

He walked fast and didn't stop until he came to his favorite bench by the lake. He sat down, glad for the shade, and dropped his backpack at his feet. He looked out over the still water. The brochure called to him, so he pulled it out of his backpack and smoothed it out on the bench boards. Then he flipped it over and pondered the phone number listed on the back.

Just call, he told himself. He could hear his mother's voice in his head. *You're gathering information. Calling doesn't commit you to anything. It's just a step in the process.*

He pulled out his phone and punched in the numbers. After only two rings someone came on the line.

"St. Gregory's. Father Mike speaking. How may I help you?"

Father Mike? Jonathan couldn't believe it. "Father Mike! This is Jonathan Rigby."

"Jonathan, what a delightful surprise! What can I do for you today?"

"I've been looking at the brochure about the summer discernment program. I'm thinking about attending."

"Wonderful! Would you like to drop by for a chat about it?"

Jonathan looked out over the water. Breeze fingers rearranged his hair. Would a talk with Father Mike take him deeper than he wanted to go right now? What would his mother have said? *You're gathering information. It's just a step in the process.* He grinned.

"Yes," Jonathan said. "Yes, I'd like that, Father Mike. When could I come?" He pulled out his calendar and fished a pen out of a side pocket. As he opened the calendar in his lap, he heard pages turning on the other end of the line.

"How about tomorrow afternoon, say around one?"

Tomorrow? So soon? Jonathan stifled his inner resistance. "Okay, yes, I'll be there."

"Good. See you then, Jonathan. Blessings on your day."

Tomorrow. Well. How about that? Leaves rustled above his head. A blue jay flew out, landed on the sidewalk just beyond his feet, pecked at the cement, and then flew off. He put the calendar away, stood up, slung the backpack over his shoulder, and started back toward the main campus.

"Hope I can get the car tomorrow. Otherwise it will be a toasty walk to St. Gregory's and back."

Jacoba walked back to her desk after the last fourth grader had left for the day. She surveyed the disorder in front of her. It was never a good sign when she couldn't see the wood surface of her desktop. When she'd tried to uncover her buried lesson-plan book earlier in the day, stacks of math and language arts papers had slid into each other. One of her students had left a crayon portrait with "I love you" scrawled across it in her chair. Jacoba picked up the portrait and gave the crayon teacher an appraising stare.

"I wish my hair looked half this good!"

The loudspeaker's sharp click startled her.

"Good afternoon." Dr. Miller's voice bounced

off the walls of the empty classroom. "Faculty meeting in the library in ten minutes." *Click.*

"Faculty meeting?" Jacoba spoke to the portrait. "I completely forgot." She added the drawing to the paper avalanche on her desk.

"Ten minutes. Okay," she said to herself, "I'll do a quick restack, and then check my box on my way to the library." She began sorting papers. She decided she'd grade the spelling and math at home. She clipped them together and slid them into her canvas bag along with her empty purple plastic water bottle. Then she retrieved her purse from deep in the back of the bottom desk drawer. Purse and bag in hand, she walked out of her classroom and up the hall toward the teacher's lounge. When she got closer, two other teachers came out. One of them held the door open for her.

She walked across the room to the boxes on the far wall. Hers was the third box on the second row. She reached into the cubby hole and pulled out a thin stack of papers. She dropped items into the canvas bag one at a time: the June edition of the school newsletter, two magazine subscription flyers, and a long white envelope with her name written on it. The envelope had been in her box for a week. She knew what was in it: her contract for the next school year. She took a step back and scanned the rest of the mailboxes. She saw telltale lines of white in at least seven other boxes. She knew why she hadn't signed and returned hers. She readily admitted to herself that she was being passive-aggressive. She was pretty sure she wasn't alone.

Oh, for the days of Cassie Elliot. During her tenure as principal, contracts had come out mid-March, not mid-May. Cassie sat down with each teacher before anything was signed. Cassie Elliot had run a tight ship, but she was always in conversation with her people, always open to someone else's perspective. Dr. Miller's "my way or the highway" approach had turned much of the faculty against him in short order.

Jacoba retraced her steps, exited the lounge, and walked quickly down the hall. She joined the line of people entering the library, and put her things down on the familiar round table where she always sat during staff meetings. A low murmur of voices surrounded her as other staff members took their places. Dr. Miller hadn't arrived yet, so she retrieved the purple water bottle from her bag and went to refill it from the bubbler in the corner. When she came back, Judy Ko was sitting in the chair next to hers. Lisa Warren was next to Judy, and Coach Hilby sat opposite Jacoba.

"Hello, everyone," Jacoba said as she sat down and scooted her chair forward. The others were all studying the meeting agenda that had been placed on the table while she was getting water. The eyes that met hers were not happy. She pulled her copy of the agenda closer just as Dr. Miller walked briskly past their table and up to the microphone.

"Testing, one two three," he spoke into the mic.

"Can everyone hear me?" Conversation in the room ceased. He continued. "You should each have an agenda. If you don't have one, raise your hand and Mrs. Globe will give you one."

Three hands went up. Mrs. Globe made her way around the tables to deliver agendas. Judy reached over and pointed to two lines on Jacoba's agenda. Jacoba read the lines and looked back at Judy, a quizzical expression on her face. Dr. Miller's voice boomed out over the tables again, calling them all to attention.

"Let's get started. We have a lot to cover this afternoon."

Jacoba stared across the room at Dr. Miller. This wasn't how Cassie Elliot had run meetings. Cassie had always started with a joke, usually a bad joke that had made folks cringe and laugh. And meeting agendas had never held surprises. Well, they had never held *unpleasant* surprises. Dr. Miller's agendas, on the other hand, were regularly salted with them.

An hour later, Dr. Miller adjourned the meeting and hurried out. Tension hovered over the tables. Group after group exited the library with little or no conversation, faces grim. Coach Hilby stood up, shoved his chair hard against the table, and walked out. Lisa got up and hurried out right behind him. Judy slung her purse strap over her shoulder, looked at Jacoba, and mouthed the words "parking lot." Jacoba nodded, picked up her purse and canvas bag, and followed Judy out of the library and outside into the sultry afternoon.

They walked down the sidewalk to the parking lot and stashed their belongings in their cars. Jacoba rolled down her windows to let the heat escape and waited on the sidewalk under the shade of an oak tree for Judy.

"I can't believe that guy!" Judy spit out the words after slamming her car door. "How can you stand there so calmly, Jacoba? If I were you, I'd be having a fit!" She came into the shade and stood next to her friend.

"It hasn't hit me yet," Jacoba said. "But it will." She shook her head slowly back and forth.

"Poor Lisa. She was crying, I think." Judy turned her gaze back toward the building. "What a way for her to find out her position has been cut to part time. It isn't right to treat people the way Dr. Miller does. Do I ever wish Cassie hadn't retired."

"You and me both," said Jacoba.

The two women were silent for a moment. Several other teachers came down the sidewalk and stopped when they got to Jacoba and Judy.

"Think Cassie would come back if we begged hard enough?" Mrs. Hoffman, the first-grade teacher, asked wistfully as she stood next to Jacoba.

"I feel sorry for Barb Globe," said Miss Winston, the art teacher. "She has to deal with him all day, every day."

"Jacoba, did you know he was going to ask you

to move up with your class and teach fifth grade next year?" Mrs. Hoffman asked.

Jacoba shook her head. She looked past the first-grade teacher and saw the principal coming down the sidewalk in their direction.

"Heads up. Here comes Dr. Miller."

The women abruptly dispersed. Jacoba heard the double beep of one car door opener after another. She got into her car and put the key in the ignition. Engine engaged, she put up the car windows, turned on the car's radio and the AC. Dr. Miller walked to the spot of shade on the sidewalk in front of her car and stopped. Jacoba could see him standing there out of the corner of her eye.

No, I am not talking to you, she thought angrily. *I can't handle another word from you today.*

She shifted into reverse without looking up, and then, instead of using the rearview mirror, she looked over her shoulder to check for oncoming cars. No one was behind her. She quickly pulled out of her parking place and, without a backward glance, drove the remaining few yards to the exit. She turned onto Ridley Street and headed home.

Later that evening Jacoba sat on her screened porch, math and spelling papers untouched on the little table next to her lounge chair. A steady breeze kept the porch comfortable. She looked out into her backyard, hoping to see a firefly or two. Weariness weighed down her arms, her legs. Even her hands and fingers felt heavy. *I'm always tired at the end of the school year,* she reminded herself. But on the heels of that thought came her recognition that this tired was different. This tired was deeper, darker. It sapped her energy and sabotaged her concentration.

This tired hadn't been part of life last fall. By Thanksgiving she, her students, and the schedule were all in sync. December had been so much fun. Jacoba smiled at the memory of the precious Christmas gifts the children had given her. *I needed most of Christmas vacation to write thank-you notes.*

But then came January. The Rigbys' car accident, Sarah Rigby's death. Mrs. Rigby had been Jacoba's room mother nine years ago when Jonathan Rigby was in her class. She had volunteered in her room for several years after that. Jacoba had come to consider her a friend. She was looking forward to maybe even having Sarah as room mother again, when Sam got to fourth grade. Sarah's death cast a shadow over January, and the shadow hadn't gone away.

Classroom life in February, March, and April had been unremarkable. But things were not copacetic outside the four walls of her classroom. She'd not opened the teacher's lounge door on the sound of laughter in months. As a matter of fact, the lounge was often empty these days. Teachers went in to check their boxes, refill their coffee cups, and leave again.

Then came Jeremy Davis's death. Sorrow surged in Jacoba as she looked out beyond the porch screen. *Why did he ride down that Prayer Trail? Surely, surely that wasn't my fault.* Tears rolled down Jacoba's cheeks as she wrapped her arms around her knees.

And today. Dr. Miller's first announcement had been an irritating inconvenience: all classrooms were to be emptied of everything except the furniture by end of the last day of school. *Jacoba, you can do it. It will take some planning, but with Mrs. Pratt's help, you'll get it done.*

Dr. Miller's second announcement disclosing cutbacks and changes for the next school year had sent shockwaves across the room. Jacoba couldn't believe her ears when he had announced his intension to move her up with her fourth-grade class to be their fifth-grade teacher. *Dr. Miller had me right in front of him in his office yesterday. Why didn't he tell me then about the teaching change? And the audacity of that man! Not to ask, but to tell, all of us what to do, how things will be.*

Anger and anxiety roller-skated hand in hand through Jacoba's brain. *Another year with Billy, knowing what I know now? And without any support from Dr. Miller? No way. It's all just too much.*

Chapter Thirteen

Unrested and unsettled, Jacoba hurried into the school building on Wednesday morning and headed straight to her classroom. She flipped on the lights, dropped her canvas bag in her chair, and pulled out her lesson plan.

I can do this today, she told herself with all the confidence she could muster. *I can do this today.* But discouragement chimed in. *Yes, but what about tomorrow, and the day after that?* Jacoba closed her eyes and took several deep breaths. *I can do this today. I choose to stay in the now. Now I'm fine. Wednesdays are good days. Everything is going to be okay.*

The tinny reverberations of slammed locker doors echoed up and down the hallway. Suddenly three giggling girls burst into the room and dashed toward their desks.

"Ladies! No running!"

Wednesdays are good days. Everything is going to be okay.

Several more students came through the door, smiled in her direction, walked to their seats, and began pulling assignment pads and worksheets out of their backpacks. Friends greeted friends between rows and across the room. When the five-minute warning bell rang, Jacoba started a quick head count. A triple rap on the classroom door startled her, and she turned to see Billy and his mother march into the room. Billy headed toward his desk, his bookbag catching and releasing the corner of his mother's skirt.

"Good morning," Jacoba said, years of practice putting warmth into her words and a smile on her face. Billy's mother returned her smile.

"Good morning. I've brought cupcakes." Mrs. Barnes walked over and put them on Jacoba's desk. "It's Billy's birthday today."

Jacoba's eyebrows went up when she saw the bakery logo on the trays. She'd ordered the same extravagantly frosted treats from Mary's Muffins when she'd hosted her book club last month. Those gourmet cupcakes had put a dent in her grocery budget, but, oh, were they ever worth it. The memory of the delectable, creamy, sweet icing made her mouth water.

"We'll certainly enjoy these. Thank you, Mrs. Barnes."

The final bell rang, and the sharp click of the public address system came on. Jacoba moved to the front of her desk and faced her class. An expectant hush settled over the room.

"All right, everyone, let's get ready for the Pledge of Allegiance and the morning announcements."

"I'll just say goodbye to Billy," Mrs. Barnes said.

Billy glared at his mother as she came up the aisle. When she stopped at his desk and bent over to speak to him, he leaned as far away from her as he could without falling out of his chair. Mrs. Barnes straightened and headed for the door, her long skirt swishing around her ankles.

Jacoba felt a strong surge of compassion for Mrs. Barnes. *Oh, Billy,* she thought. *That's no way to treat your mother.*

When lunchtime came Jacoba picked up the cupcakes and headed out the door with her class. Once they'd gotten to the cafeteria she walked down the line and stood in front of Billy.

"So, Billy, ready to pass out cupcakes once everyone is sitting down?"

"Not really," he said defiantly. Children in line on either side of Billy turned to look at him.

"Do you have a different idea?"

Billy shot her an insolent look, and Jacoba was sorry she'd asked. She shifted to Plan B.

"Sophie," she called up to the front of the line, "since you're line leader today, would you help me pass out Billy's cupcakes?"

Fifteen minutes later, children seated and cupcakes distributed, Jacoba eyed the large clock on the cafeteria wall. She had just enough time to dash to the teacher's lounge to enjoy her cupcake, and check her box and her phone for messages. Last stop, the ladies room, and then she'd pick up her students again.

She opened the door on an empty teacher's lounge and crossed to the mailboxes. Nothing there. Good. She sat down at the rectangular table in the center of the room, slung her purse on the back of the chair, and pulled out her cell phone. A text from Marty popped up on the screen.

BIG NEWS! COME ASAP! PREPARE 2B SHOCKED!

Jacoba grinned. She wondered what the big news was this time. She texted back OK with a thumbs-up emoji and slid her phone back in her purse. Then she looked reverently at the cupcake in front of her. She was sorry she didn't have more time to savor it. She blissfully consumed the frosting and then went to work on the cake. She had just taken the last delectable bite when Barb Globe came through the door.

"Oh, good, you're here." Barb sat across from her, clipboard in hand. "I have a question for you from Dr. Miller." She gave Jacoba a nervous smile. "Remember, I am only the messenger." She looked past Jacoba's head to the mailboxes. "Please don't kill the messenger."

Jacoba started to laugh. "Well, that sounds rather ominous, Barb! What's the question? Make it quick. My lunch break is over."

Barb turned her attention from mailboxes to clipboard. "Since you haven't turned in your contract, Dr. Miller wants to know if you're coming back. And he wants to know by tomorrow morning."

The words stunned Jacoba. She looked across the table in disbelief. "What? Barb!"

Barb didn't look up. "Please don't make me say it again," she pleaded softly.

"Barb!" Jacoba went from stunned to incredulous. "I don't believe this!" She rose from the chair, snatched the empty cupcake liner, slung her purse strap over her shoulder, and headed for the door.

"Jacoba," Barb called after her, voice trembling, "Jacoba, I'm sorry."

Jacoba turned halfway around to deliver an angry retort, but remembered just in time that poor Barb Globe was, indeed, only the messenger. She jerked the door open and marched angrily toward her classroom. Halfway there she stopped and did an abrupt about-face. Her students were still in the lunchroom. She raced to the cafeteria, where she found her forlorn fourth graders in line against the south wall.

"Sorry I'm late," Jacoba said to the parent volunteer chatting with the girls. "Thank you for watching them."

"No problem, Ms. Dahm." The volunteer looked at her more closely. "Everything okay?"

"Yes." She forced a smile and turned to her students. "Okay, friends, short time on the playground and then back to work."

Jacoba headed out of the cafeteria, her class following obediently behind her. Once they were out of the building, some of the children charged toward the swings. Others just slowed their walk and continued their conversations. Sophie came and stood next to Jacoba.

"Poor cupcake," she said sympathetically, her eyes on Jacoba's hand.

Jacoba followed Sophie's gaze to her left hand, where the edges of the silver cupcake liner peeked out.

"Poor cupcake," Jacoba echoed. She walked over to the garbage bin, uncurled stiff fingers from around the wrapper, and threw it in. Did she have time to walk a couple laps around the playground? No. She saw fifth and sixth graders coming out of the side door, heading in her direction. Fourth-grade time on the playground was over.

"Time's up, friends," she called across the grass. *Time's up,* she repeated to herself. *Tomorrow morning . . . I have to decide by tomorrow morning.*

When the school day ended Jacoba shoved three more sets of papers into her canvas bag alongside the two sets left over from the day before. With a strong sense of déjà vu, she grabbed the canvas handles and lifted the bag off her chair. She thought about Marty's text, glad for an excuse not to go right home. A short time later she pulled out of the school parking lot onto Creston and considered her route to the antique mall. She could take River Street through downtown, or she could take Cherry Street and drive along the southern edge of the park.

The park, she thought. *I need the peace.*

A few minutes later she turned onto Cherry Street and travelled along the park's tree-lined verge. When the car passed under the pedestrian bridge, she caught sight of rotating bicycle tires and thought of Jeremy. Winding Creek came into view, running parallel to Cherry Street, water barely visible from her vantage point.

At the large sign for the public beach and boat ramp she put on her blinker. Seconds later she steered into the alley behind the two-story yellow-and-beige-brick antique mall. She parked under the turquoise BEHIND THE TIMES sign, got out, and headed to the concrete retaining wall on the river side of the alley. She always looked to see how high the water was when she parked in back. The Grand had come over the wall only once in all her summers at the antique mall, but that single event had provoked a perpetual paranoia in her. This afternoon she was pleased to see several hundred yards of dry ground between wall and latte-colored river.

Jacoba wasn't pleased when the delivery door knob turned easily in her hand before she'd inserted her key. She had talked to Marty over and over again about the importance of keeping that door locked. Marty hadn't disagreed, but unless Jacoba was there, the door stayed unlocked during the day. Jacoba slid her key back in her purse, entered the backroom, and locked the door behind her. As her eyes adjusted to the dim interior, her nose told her where she was. Lemon furniture polish and northern woods potpourri mingled with the aroma of musty inventory to create that unmistakable fragrance, Essence of Old. She walked to the gently swaying beaded curtain that separated the workspace from the mall's spacious main floor and passed through to the well-lit interior.

Women's voices came to her from the front. She headed in that direction, looking to see what had changed since she'd last been there. She passed several rows of dining room tables, ornate chairs, and cedar chests. With a twinge of disappointment, she discovered the pine kitchen table she'd had her eye on was gone. A tall cherry bureau and matching vanity stood in its place.

You should have gotten it when you saw it, she chastised herself. *You shouldn't have waited.*

She looked above the furniture to the paintings hung in multiple groupings on the wall. Nothing new there. She turned around to the tall glass bric-a-brac cabinets in the center of the room. Not being a fan of bric-a-brac, she started to walk away when a flash of scarlet iridescence caught her eye. She stepped forward for a better look. On the bottom shelf of the last cabinet she discovered a taco shell–shaped dish with an unmistakable amber sparkle.

"Leave it to you to find the one new piece of red carnival glass in the whole mall." Marty came and stood beside her. "How about a cup of coffee?" Without waiting for Jacoba's answer she headed to the café area behind the cashier counter. "It's been busy today. I didn't even have time to eat lunch!"

Lunch. Jacoba's mind left its happy place.

"Whoa, serious expression there." Marty

looked at Jacoba as she poured herself some coffee. "What's going on?"

Jacoba pulled out a bentwood café chair and sat down at a small, round, oak pedestal table. "Before I tell you my news, I want to hear your news."

Marty gestured with the carafe. "Want some?"

"No, thanks," Jacoba said. "So, what's your big news?"

Marty joined Jacoba at the table and took a sip of her coffee. "Mmmm. The elixir of life! Are you sure you don't want some?"

"No, Marty, really, I don't want any. Thank you," Jacoba said, exasperation mounting. "Tell me your news!"

Marty put both hands around her coffee. "You know that big antique mall over in the next county? The one with all the glassware, and high-end furniture, and vintage clothing?"

"Oh, yes, I found one of my favorite pieces of carnival glass there."

"Well," Marty paused for effect, "that mall is closing at the end of June!"

"No way! Are you sure?"

"I'm absolutely sure. Two dealers from over there were waiting for me when I got here this morning. Apparently the owner decided to retire, and no one was interested in taking over the business."

"Wow! Marty, there must have been at least fifty booths in that mall."

"More like one hundred. And now all those

dealers have to find a new home for their treasures." Marty grinned and sipped her coffee. "The two who were here this morning rented the last available space in the balcony without even going upstairs to look at it. I think we are about to experience a tsunami of dealers from over there. So, Jacoba, we need more booth space. Where could we put more booths in here?"

Jacoba let her eyes travel around the first floor. Then she looked up to the blue sky and clouds beyond the three large skylights high overhead. Her eyes shifted to the iron-railed balcony that ran along the four exterior walls of the building. She followed the square, brick balcony support columns down to the main floor, where they passed through the wood flooring into the basement.

"Remind me again how old this building is."

"Well, according to my grandmother, the original building was a combination furniture store and carpentry workshop. What we are sitting in now was rebuilt after the 1920 fire. In the fire, the roof caved in and took the second floor with it. Marty looked up into the wide expanse overhead. "Whoever thought of putting in those big skylights and a balcony in place of a solid second floor was a genius!"

The cowbell over the front door clanged. Marty got up. "Bet that's Sandy with the mail. I've got a couple letters to give her. Make yourself a cup of decaf," she urged. "Be thinking of where we could put more booths." She headed to the front.

More booths. Hmmmm.

Jacoba looked around. Five high-shelved booths filled the north wall. Waist-high glass cases held vintage jewelry in the front corner. Seven low-shelved booths were set up in front of furniture and paintings. She walked over to the balcony staircase. Had the staircase survived the fire? She looked at the weathered treads. So many feet had taken these steps over the years.

Jacoba started the steep climb to the top, her eyes on the wall, her hand on the railing. Marty had hung small- to medium-sized portraits, some oil paintings, and some old photographs, all the way up to the balcony. Halfway to the top, she paused long enough to gaze into the serious face of an older woman with deep-set eyes and auburn hair piled high on top of her head. The woman wore a tailored blouse with a frilly collar and many tiny pleats.

"Boy, would that have been an ironing nightmare!"

The gentleman in the next picture stared into Jacoba's face with wide eyes and dimples that reminded her of Santa Claus. His voluminous beard and bountiful head of hair covered the photo all the way to the top and sides of the round, gilt picture frame. Not for the first time Jacoba wondered who these people were who lined the stairway, and how their portraits had come to rest in an antique mall.

Warmer, heavier air engulfed her when she

stepped out onto the balcony. The cowbell clanged again, and she looked over the wrought-iron railing to the floor below. She could see the top of Marty's head. The mail carrier's bag disappeared through the front door. Feeling a little dizzy, Jacoba stepped back, regained her equilibrium, and started walking the balcony course. The floor creaked under her feet as she passed one booth after another. Shelves of old books gave way to tables of dishes and glassware, which flowed into bedspreads, tablecloths, and mannequins wearing fancy dinner jackets. When she got back to where she'd started, she took one last look across the balcony expanse before carefully making her way downstairs. Marty was waiting for her at the bottom step.

"Well? Got any ideas?"

"I think the balcony will have to stay as it is. The fire marshal is already unhappy with the narrow aisle and only one exit up there."

"That's what I thought too." The women went back to the café area and sat down.

"But I do see some possibilities on the main floor," Jacoba continued. "For instance, if we move the furniture closer together, do more table/chair stacking, we would free up enough space for another booth or two. And if we moved the jewelry cases under the front windows, the empty corner would be perfect for another booth, maybe two."

Marty was nodding in agreement. "I'll call

Strong Men Moving first thing tomorrow morning and get the guys over here. What else?"

"I know you like the front entrance to be nice and open. The fire marshal does too. But that's another possible place for a couple display cases or some low shelves."

Marty looked doubtfully at Jacoba. "I don't know. I really do like the way Behind the Times looks with the entryway uncluttered." She took a deep breath and let it out slowly. "Even if we did rearrange furniture and display cases, that only gives us five or six additional rentable spaces. I'm thinking we'll have a lot more than five or six dealers coming from the other mall."

"Say, Marty, what about the basement?" Jacoba asked suddenly.

"Oh, Jacoba, the basement's a mess," Marty said woefully. "There are corners down there where Bob won't even go."

"Then it must be bad!" Jacoba grinned. "I didn't think Bob was afraid of anything."

"Oh! I almost forgot!" Marty jumped up from her chair. "I have something else to run by you." She hurried around the corner of the checkout counter and came back waving a sheet of typing paper. She handed it to Jacoba.

"'Looking for new hands to handle old stuff.'" Jacoba looked across at Marty. "Clever!" She looked back to the page and continued reading. "'Assistant wanted for up to twenty hours each week during June, July, and August at Behind the

Times Antique Mall. Work hours are flexible. Work responsibilities would include lifting, carrying, sorting, and general schlepping.'" Jacoba burst out laughing. "Schlepping? What a great word! And it certainly describes what we do!"

"I'm getting too old to move boxes and put up bookshelves. Time for a younger generation of helping hands to join us."

"I'm with you on that!" Jacoba read the next lines. "'Interested? Drop by Behind the Times during business hours.'" She looked at Marty. "Good idea. Have people come, no appointment. Saves you all those phone interruptions and no-shows."

"That's what I thought. One less step in the process."

Jacoba handed the flyer back to Marty. "So, where are you planning to post this?"

"I hadn't thought that far."

"How about putting one up on the Tilden coffee shop job board. And if you don't get any response from there, put an ad in the paper."

"Yes! Of course!" Marty gave her friend a shrewd look. "You have such good ideas. Sure you don't want to become my business partner?"

"I value our friendship too much for that," Jacoba said, no smile on her face.

"Well, I know better than to press. But I'm leaving the offer on the table," Marty said obstinately. "So, Jacoba, how soon before you are here every day?" Marty looked expectantly at her friend.

"The last day of school will be the first

Thursday in June. I can start on the following Monday."

"Wonderful! But will that leave you enough time to pack up your classroom after your students are gone? I'm anxious for you to start, but it doesn't have to be that tight."

"All the packing has to be done by the last day of school—Dr. Miller let us know at staff meeting yesterday."

"Oh, Jacoba, you're so organized you'll get it done." Marty looked at her friend. "But I can see by the look on your face that there's more."

Jacoba recounted what else had happened at yesterday's staff meeting. "I went home mad, and I didn't sleep well. I got through this morning okay, but then Barb Globe asked me if I was coming back next year—Dr. Miller wants to know." She could feel her blood pressure rising all over again. "And Dr. Miller wants to know by tomorrow morning."

"Oh my," Marty said softly. "Jacoba, you have had one heck of a May."

Chimes sounded suddenly from several different areas of the main floor.

"Four thirty already, almost closing time," Jacoba said, changing the subject. "I'll get going so you can put this place to bed."

"Bob's taking me to Marcellino's for dinner. Why don't you come with us?"

"Thank you for the invitation, but no, I should go home. I have a lot to think about."

"You know what I think about you and your shoulds," Marty said sternly.

"Yes, I do." Jacoba looked at Marty, a twinkle in her eye. "I should do better."

Marty laughed. "Jacoba Dahm, you are hopeless! Hopeless! All the more reason to keep praying for you."

Jacoba got up. "Prayers appreciated." She looked out into the mall. "And think about putting some booths in the basement. I bet there's untapped potential down there!"

Jacoba walked through the storeroom and out the back entrance to her car. She drove past the park again, but she was too preoccupied with the decision she had to make to give the green space more than a passing glance. Once home, she hefted the canvas bag of classwork out of the backseat, carried it into the stuffy, coffee-scented kitchen, and deposited it on the woven seat of a ladder-backed chair. She unlocked and opened the sliding glass door to the porch. Cooler air wafted into the room. She went back to the kitchen table and looked woefully at the bulging canvas bag across from her as she sat down.

"How did I get this far behind? Really, Jacoba," she chastised herself, "you should have planned better."

Jacoba looked from the bag to the peaceful shade of neighborhood trees beyond the kitchen window. She remembered Marty's admonishment not thirty minutes before. "I know, Marty, I know: stop should-ing myself."

Her eyes lingered over the leafy canopy beyond her window, a new thought taking shape in her mind. "Have I asked myself what I really, truly want? Am I listening beyond the should, or am I stopping and letting the shoulds have the last word?"

Her growling stomach demanded attention, momentarily overriding her considerations. She took a jar of peanut butter out of the pantry, a sleeve of crackers out of the freezer, and brought them back to the table. After retrieving a knife and plate, she sat down again. As she reached for a cracker her eyes fell on the paper-crammed canvas bag. "That's going to take me hours to do." She put the cracker back down. "Dr. Miller, the changes at school, Jeremy, Billy . . . Why do I keep pushing myself? I don't want to do this anymore."

She looked out the kitchen window to the trees and said it again, a little louder.

"I don't want to do this anymore."

A new sentence bubbled up from deep within her.

"I don't have to do this anymore."

Relief and astonishment flooded her being.

"I don't want to. I don't have to."

She sat back in her chair and put both hands on the table edge. "I'm not going to sign my contract. I'm going to give myself a chance to recover from this year. I'm going to give myself time to think about what I should do next—no! Not what I *should* do. What I *want* to do."

She looked at the peanut butter and crackers in front of her, suddenly the hungriest she'd been in a while. "I wonder if it's too late to join Marty and Bob at Marcellino's?" She pulled out her phone. She couldn't wait to tell Marty what she'd decided.

Chapter Fourteen

Jonathan sat on a bench close to the edge of the lagoon, where modest amounts of windblown fountain spray hit him with refreshing coolness. From this vantage point he had a clear view of his dad's parked car beside Preston Hall.

"If I'm walking to St. Gregory's, I need to leave now," he said to himself. "But I don't want to walk." He fingered the car keys in his pocket. "I want to drive."

Suddenly an overabundance of spray necessitated a hasty move farther down the bench. He rubbed his wet watch crystal against his blue jeans.

Just take the car, Temptation whispered in his ear. *Just take the car. Your father has office hours this afternoon. He won't even notice it's gone.*

Jonathan frowned.

Okay, you want the car? Go ask.

After another liberal dousing from the fountain, he moved to a different bench. He couldn't see the car anymore, but he could see Preston Hall's entrance.

Suddenly the front doors opened, and his father started down the steps. He was off the bench and calling out to his dad as another sentence came to mind. *And what are you going to say if he wants to know why you want the car?*

"Dad! Dad!"

"Hi, son." Solomon stopped on the sidewalk and waited as Jonathan jogged across the street.

"Dad, can I use the car?"

Solomon hesitated, but then to Jonathan's relief he gave his permission. "Just be back by three. Sam's counselling session is at three thirty."

"Thanks."

Jonathan swung his backpack over his shoulder, pulled the car keys out of his pocket, and tried to appear nonchalant as he walked to the car. He unlocked the door and tossed his belongings into the back. He got in, fastened his seatbelt, and put the key into the ignition. He checked the time. He'd get to St. Gregory's early, but he didn't care.

Less than ten minutes later, Jonathan pulled into the large parking lot between the church and rectory. He had it entirely to himself and drove slowly down the rows, trying to decide which space to take. He finally parked as far away from the street as he could get. He checked the time again.

Fifteen minutes until my appointment. Well, I'll just sit here and wait.

But it wasn't long before the car's interior became unbearably warm. He got out of the car, slammed the door, and hit the lock button on his key fob. He walked a few feet to an island of shade under a large maple. He felt foolish standing with only a tree for company in the middle of an empty parking lot. He turned toward the old stone church.

If it's open, I could pray until right before one.

He walked across the parking lot and took the three wide cement steps up to the arched, wood-paneled doors. The knob turned easily in his hand, and he stepped into the shadowed narthex. He let the door close behind him and moved farther into the space as his eyes adjusted to the dimness.

The last time he'd been in the narthex was for his mother's funeral. He remembered Mr. Billingsley escorting him, his father, and Sam into the sanctuary, down the middle aisle. They had joined Uncle Mark and Aunt Marilyn on the front row. It had been so strange to sit with these people, his family, and not have his mother present among them. Deep sadness had engulfed him.

It was during Father Mike's benediction that Jonathan had glanced over at his dad and witnessed his father's angry expression. His father's ire had been lurking just below the surface ever since.

A siren wail brought Jonathan abruptly back to the present. *Probably an ambulance headed up the street to the hospital,* he thought.

But the sound didn't recede. Instead, it got louder and louder. Finally, it was so loud Jonathan was sure it was right outside. He opened the door and looked into the parking lot just in time to see a fire truck pull in close to the rectory. He spotted a thin line of smoke rising from behind it. He exited the church and ran back to his car, wondering if he should move it. But once there he could see plenty of space between his car and the fire truck. Jonathan winced as several of the rectory smoke detectors started to shriek. Two firefighters crossed his line of sight as they raced toward the smoke. Seconds later the rectory's front door opened, and Jonathan recognized Father Mike's tall form amidst several other adults as they hurried down the front steps. They came across the rectory lawn to stand with him.

"Father Mike! What's happening?"

"Jonathan! Lots of smoke in the rectory." Father Mike pushed his black-framed glasses farther up his nose. He looked toward the gray-black cloud rising above the building and back to the people standing with him. "Are we all here?"

"Where's Father Frank?" someone asked in alarm.

Concern rippled through the group. Father Mike immediately turned and sprinted back toward the rectory's front door only to be stopped by two firefighters. At the same moment, two other firefighters rounded the back corner of the rectory, an occupied kitchen chair expertly balanced between them. A stocky man slumped in the seat, his white-haired head bowed.

"Oh, no!"

"Father Frank!"

The firefighters made their way over to them and carefully lowered the chair to the grass. The elderly priest raised his head and looked up into the faces of his coworkers with a weak grin.

"I'm okay," he said hoarsely, and then started to cough. One of the firefighters placed an oxygen mask over his nose and mouth.

"The EMTs are on their way," one of the firefighters said to Father Mike.

An ambulance pulled into the parking lot as he finished speaking. Father Frank was moved to a gurney and gave the group a thumbs-up as he was loaded into the back of the ambulance.

"I'll go with him, Father Mike," one of the women volunteered.

"Thank you, Sue," Father Mike said. "He shouldn't be by himself."

The ambulance pulled out onto River Street to make the sixty-second trip to the hospital. Another firefighter came up to Father Mike.

"Father Mike, the fire's out."

"Thank goodness! Do you know what happened?"

"Looks like a kitchen towel and a couple potholders were too close to the stove. Chili boiled over into the gas flames, and the towel and potholders caught fire. It could have been a lot worse. You'll have to replace the cabinets again, but I think the stove and the floor are okay this time around."

"Thanks for coming to our rescue," Father Mike said, shaking the other man's hand. "I thought we'd made enough changes so this wouldn't happen again. Guess I was wrong."

As the firefighter walked away, another woman

Jonathan swung his gaze away from Father Mike to the blue sky overhead and wondered how much he should say, how much he wanted to say.

"How does your dad feel about you considering the priesthood?"

Jonathan looked down at his hands. "He's not happy about it. He wants me to finish my four years at Tilden before he'll even talk to me again about going into the priesthood." He looked up at Father Mike. "But my mom was all for it. She was going to help me persuade Dad."

Father Mike looked sympathetically in Jonathan's direction. "Hard place to be in," was all he said.

"Tell me more about the summer discernment program," Jonathan said.

"It's a six-week full-immersion experience to give men considering the priesthood a clear picture of what being a priest is like."

"And at the end of the six weeks, I'd know if I was supposed to be a priest, right?" Jonathan looked expectantly at Father Mike.

Father Mike smiled and shook his head. "Ah, no, Jonathan. The discernment program is just the beginning of a lot of serious prayer and pondering—months, even years of it."

"Months or years? I thought I'd know right away!" Jonathan's shoulders sank in disappointment. Father Mike looked at him, a smile still lurking around the edges of his mouth. "Well, I can't go anyway," Jonathan said almost to himself.

"Dad said no . . . and I can't leave Sam. Not right now." He sighed and looked glumly across the parking lot to the car. "And speaking of Sam, I'd better head back to school. He has a counselling appointment this afternoon."

"Jonathan, ask the Lord to show you what's on the table for you now, today." Father Mike gave him an encouraging look. "What's to be done this week, this month, this summer? What does God want you to do now?"

"I'll do that." Jonathan tried to sound appreciative. "Thanks, Father Mike."

"You're welcome, Jonathan. And one more thought." Father Mike looked earnestly at him. "The Rigby world has been mightily rocked by your mother's death. Moving through that kind of loss takes time—for you, for Sam, and for your dad. There may not be room in your dad's mind and heart right now for the idea of you becoming a priest. But given time, I think that will change."

Oh, Father Mike. Dad. Should I bring up what he said? Should I talk about it at all? Jonathan looked at his watch, and the decision was made for him.

"It's after two thirty, I'd better get back."

They both stood up. "I'll be praying for you, your dad, and Sam. If you want to talk again, just call."

"Thanks, Father Mike."

Jonathan got back in the car, turned the AC on full blast, and headed out of the parking lot onto River Street.

Okay, God, what do You want me to do now?

It was as quiet inside his head as outside. He considered his route back to Tilden. *I have enough time to take River Street all the way to Remembrance.* He pulled into traffic and cruised along with other cars in front of and behind his.

Cars . . . A car . . . I need my own car. Jonathan sat up straighter and gripped the steering wheel. *Having a car would mean I could go to church when I wanted to. Having a car would open up the possibilities of taking classes at night or earlier in the morning. Whoa! Lord! Is this what You want me to do now? Get a car?*

Thoughts ricocheted off the wall of his brain. *How am I going to pay for a car . . . and gas . . . and insurance?*

He stopped for the red light at the corner of Remembrance and Cherry Street, the campus to his right. *I'll get a job. I'm not going to ask Dad for anything. I'm going to give him time, like Father Mike said.*

Jonathan felt bright sunlight shining in his mind, his heart, after a long string of gray days. *Thanks, Lord . . . thanks.* He parked the car behind Preston Hall and checked the time: 2:55.

"Five minutes," he said to himself. "I can check the job board and be back here in five minutes."

He jogged across the parking lot, rapid-marched along the sidewalk, and expertly dodged several students coming out of the coffee shop as he hurried in. He maneuvered between empty tables to get to the large bulletin board hung on the wall near the restrooms. He stopped in front of it, a little out of breath, and looked up expectantly. He stepped back and looked again. The board was empty. A cloud of disappointment threatened to diminish the interior light of hope.

"Hi, Jonathan! Here for coffee?"

Jonathan turned to face a stooped young man who was pushing a mop and bucket toward the restroom doors. Water sloshed around the edges of the bucket, leaving a small trail of drips in its wake. "Well, hi, Henry! How are you? I haven't seen you in a while."

Henry brushed long, blond bangs out of his eyes with a stiff-fingered repeating motion. "They changed my schedule. I work more hours now," he said proudly as he used the mop handle to steady himself. "But I don't work every day. That would be too much for me." He blinked and looked hard into Jonathan's face. "Your face isn't happy. Are you sad?"

"I was hoping to find some jobs on the job board. But it's empty." Jonathan looked back at the board.

"Oh, yes," said Henry. "The office lady took everything down this morning."

"Oh, no," Jonathan groaned.

"Don't worry, Jonathan," Henry said gleefully, "the job board always fills back up again. I've been here a long time. I know that for sure. Just come back tomorrow or the next day, and you'll see."

"Thank you, Henry. I'll come back tomorrow."

"I have to mop the restroom floors now. See you later!"

Jonathan looked longingly at the board one more time and then headed back to the car. Just after he had opened the car door his father came around the corner of Preston Hall, briefcase in hand.

"Get your errands run, Jon? Ready to pick up Sam?" Solomon started to put his briefcase in the backseat but thought the better of it. "Let's put our stuff in the trunk, shall we? Then Sam can stretch out if he wants to."

Jonathan grabbed his backpack, came around the back of the car, and unlocked the trunk. They set their things on top of a pile of winter blankets.

"You want to drive?" his dad asked, eyeing the car keys in Jonathan's hand.

"Sure," Jonathan said.

As he slowly pulled out of the parking lot and headed for Tilden's main entrance, Jonathan threw a fleeting glance in the direction of the coffee shop. He suddenly remembered a quote from his freshman lit class.

As Violet Fane would say, "All things come to those who wait." Argh, Lord! Waiting, being patient—not two of my favorite things! But I will do my best to be patient and faithful, and pay attention to now.

Bright sunlight broke out in his mind and heart again.

Chapter Fifteen

Late Wednesday afternoon Simon looked with great satisfaction at his empty inbox. He'd not seen the bottom of it since mid-March. He triumphantly closed the folder in front of him and bent over to open the file drawer. His sense of triumph slipped a bit when he opened it and realized there wasn't room for one more file, no matter how slim. He sat back in his desk chair and drummed his fingers on the arms. It was time to update all the file drawers in his corner of the office. With a sudden flash of inspiration, he said to himself, "This is a job for an intern!" He grinned. "Surely this would fit under some subcategory of the curriculum."

He pivoted his chair around. "Hmmm." He stared critically at the row of four-drawer filing cabinets along the wall behind him. "I wonder where I put the internship folder?"

Richard's voice in the hallway pulled Simon's attention in a different direction. "Come right this way, Mrs. Barnes. Detective Roe will help you."

Simon stood up and met them at the door.

"Detective Roe, this is Ursula Barnes. She's here to file a missing persons report. She's worried about her mother."

Mrs. Barnes crossed the threshold into the office, her purse held tightly under one arm. Simon put out his hand to shake hers. Her hand was cold in his.

"Come sit down and tell us what's going on."

Simon led the way to his cubicle. They both sat down, and with a few mouse clicks he opened a new screen on his computer. He looked at Ursula, inviting her to begin.

"My mother, Sally Groegan, left town almost two weeks ago to visit her sister, Beatrice. At least that's what we thought she did." She opened her purse, pulled out a photo, and handed it to Simon. He took it and set the photo down next to the monitor.

Ursula sat forward on the edge of the chair. She pushed her hair away from her face, the bracelets on her wrists jangling. "Aunt Beatrice lives a couple hundred miles north of Byington. Mother has made that trip so many times over the years she could drive it blindfolded." Her voice cracked and tears trickled down her cheeks. "I called Aunt Beatrice this afternoon to find out when Mother was coming back. That's when I found out she wasn't there, hadn't been there. Aunt Beatrice said she didn't know anything about my mother coming for a visit."

"Where does your mother live?" he asked, his eyes back on the computer screen.

"She has an apartment at Brockway Retirement Village. I've called management there already. They haven't seen Mother in a couple weeks. They thought she'd gone to visit my Aunt Beatrice too."

Ursula looked tearfully at Simon. "Where could she be?"

"She lives alone?"

"Yes, my father died several years ago."

"Does your mother have a cell phone?"

"Yes." She recited the number to Simon. "I've called multiple times. She never set up her voice mail, so I couldn't leave her a message."

Simon asked Ursula about her mother's car, and filled out a separate form to start a search for it.

"Has your mother ever done this before—disappeared unexpectedly?"

"No, never! We always know where Mother is!"

Something about the way Ursula said the last sentence made Simon feel sorry for Sally Groegan.

"Mrs. Barnes, I think searching your mother's apartment would be a good place for us to start. I'd like to do that now with your permission."

"Yes, of course, absolutely. I have a key. I'll let you in."

They both stood up. Richard came around the corner of the partition.

"Officer Barclay and I will meet you at the apartment. Please don't go in until we get there." Simon's tone was firm but not unkind.

Richard walked Ursula to the door and returned to Simon's desk. Simon picked up Sally Groegan's picture and slid it in his pocket.

"Ever driven through the Village, Mr. Barclay?"

"No, sir."

"It's quite the place. Patio homes, condos, and

an apartment building. All levels of senior living, from independent to nursing care, available on the same campus. Dar and I have talked about moving there—not anytime soon, of course," he added hastily.

A few minutes later Richard pulled out of the police parking garage with Simon on the passenger side. Their car was first at stop signs and traffic lights. Grandburg's version of the evening rush hour was over. The sun, low on the horizon, glimmered in the car's rear window as they headed east on Cherry.

"Just stay on Cherry," Simon said to Richard. "The turn for Brockway will come up in about five minutes. The Village is just beyond the Brockway Heights subdivision."

"Got it," Richard said.

When they drove past the stone marker for Brockway Heights, Simon looked wistfully toward home, silently lamenting no supper in his immediate future. His stomach gurgled.

"We're coming up on the turn," he said.

Richard flicked on the turn signal and started to slow down.

"The apartment building is at the back of the property."

Richard turned off Brockway, his foot on the brake. They drove through a neighborhood of patio homes and condos, and then they passed between several three-story buildings. "Assisted living units and memory care," Simon said.

Richard slowed even more when he saw a couple golf carts and several pedestrians waiting at crosswalks. A five-story yellow-brick apartment building loomed ahead of them. It backed up to a rusted barbed-wire fence and a long row of evergreen trees. A sparsely occupied parking lot surrounded the building on three sides. Plowed fields hugged the horizon beyond the trees.

Simon spotted Mrs. Barnes standing next to her car. "There she is."

"This is where Mother usually parks," Ursula said when they joined her. She turned and pointed toward the apartment building. "That patio with the hummingbird feeders belongs to her apartment."

They walked to the side door of the building, where Ursula punched in a code on a keypad. They heard a loud click, and Richard stepped forward to hold the door open for Simon and Ursula. The carpeted hallway in front of them was bright, the air fresh and cool. Ursula's pace quickened as she approached her mother's apartment door. She put the key in the lock, but before she could unlock it and open the door, Simon intervened.

"Mrs. Barnes, let us go in first."

Ursula stepped back from the door and nodded, her eyes wide.

Simon unlocked the door and gently pushed it open. "Please wait here." He stepped into the room with Richard right behind him. The air was stale. A lamp suddenly came on in the corner, startling them.

"Must be on a timer," Richard said.

The living room walls were painted a creamy yellow that blended well with the beige carpet. A deep-cushioned couch and a recliner were arranged around a low coffee table. Built-in bookshelves lined the wall behind the couch. A galley kitchen was just to their left, and at the far end of the room they could make out sliding glass doors going out to the patio. Two doors on another wall were partially open. They each took a door.

"Bedroom," Simon called out. "No one here."

"Bathroom," Richard called out. "No one here."

Simon went back to the front door and invited Ursula into the apartment. "How does it look to you, Mrs. Barnes?" he asked, his hands open.

Ursula turned slowly, taking in the living room, the kitchen, the sliding glass doors, the bedroom, and the bathroom. She looked up at the bookshelves and down on the coffee table.

"Well, it looks like it always looks." She turned to Simon. "It looks like it does when she's here. Where could she be?" She sat in the recliner and held her head in her hands.

Simon walked to the couch and looked at the materials on the coffee table. "You said your mother told you she was going to visit your aunt. Did she talk to you about any other trips she was considering or planning to take?"

"Oh, no! My mother is not the adventurous type. My father was the adventurous one of the two. He was always planning something."

Simon scooped up several brochures from the coffee table and handed them to Ursula.

She read the top three covers aloud. "New York City, the Bahamas, San Francisco." She looked in horror at Simon. "Mother alone in one of these places? Can this get any worse?"

"Mrs. Barnes, let's not assume anything right now," Simon said quickly. He started to say something else but a cheery voice broke in from the hallway.

"Hey, Miss Sally! You're back! I'm so glad! We were worried—oh!" a woman in her midthirties wearing light-green slacks and a rainbow-colored sweater stepped into the room.

Ursula stood up. "Rachel, this is Detective Roe and Officer Barclay."

The young woman reached out to shake hands with Simon and Richard. "I'm Rachel Graveling, the activities director here." She turned to Ursula. "You must be worried sick."

Simon handed Rachel his card. "If you think of anything that might help us locate Mrs. Groegan, please give me a call."

"Yes, certainly." Rachel took the card and walked back out into the hallway.

"Mrs. Barnes, I'd like you to look around in your mother's bedroom and bathroom," Simon directed. "Take a good look in her closet, her dresser drawers, to see if anything is missing."

Ursula got up and went into the bedroom.

Simon turned to Richard. "Mr. Barclay, let's take a look in the kitchen."

Simon went right to the refrigerator and pulled open the door. "Not much here," he said. "Some bottled water on the bottom shelf; butter, salad dressing, and barbecue sauce in the door." He straightened up. "More accurately, a family-size bottle of barbecue sauce."

He closed the door and opened the freezer. "Three frozen dinners, a pint of butter-pecan ice cream way in the back. Nothing else." He closed the freezer door and turned around.

Richard was bending down to retrieve a small dish on the floor near the refrigerator.

"For a cat?" Richard asked. He picked up a second matching dish.

"Or a dog," Simon came up beside him.

Ursula appeared at the kitchen door. "My mother's good clothes are hanging in the closet, but several pairs of casual slacks and shirts are missing. Her travel bag of toiletries and makeup is gone. So is the flashlight she always keeps by her bed."

"Mrs. Barnes," Simon pointed to the dishes Richard held, "does your mother have a dog or a cat?"

"Oh, yes, a dog. Max."

Simon and Richard looked at each other. Before Ursula could say any more, her cell phone started ringing. She checked the screen. "Excuse me, it's my husband." She moved toward the living room.

"William? I'm at Mother's apartment with the police."

"Max, Miss Sally," Simon whispered, "I think Ursula's mother might be—"

"—in the park!" Richard finished with a little too much enthusiasm.

Simon put up a warning finger. Ursula's side of the phone conversation could be heard from the living room.

"I'm sorry, William," Ursula said. "Yes, but . . . okay, I'm coming right now. I'm sorry." Ursula came back into their line of vision, phone in hand. "I have to go. My son's birthday dinner. They're all waiting for me." She shrugged her shoulders and looked helplessly around the room.

"That's all right, Mrs. Barnes. We're done here," Simon said reassuringly.

Simon and Richard followed Ursula out into the hallway, and they walked the short distance back to the sidewalk with her in the lead. Simon caught up with her.

"You'll be hearing from one of us in the next couple days, Mrs. Barnes."

Ursula nodded distractedly, hurried to her car, got in, and was pulling out of the parking place before Simon or Richard had opened their car doors.

"Park next?" Richard asked as they fastened their seatbelts.

"Yes!"

"Why the subterfuge? Why not tell her daughter she was going to the park?"

"With any luck, we'll soon hear the answer directly from Sally Groegan."

Richard kept the car's forward motion at a slow crawl as they drove back through Brockway Village, but as soon as the car turned onto Brockway Road, he accelerated.

"We still have plenty of daylight left. Let's grab something to eat on our way to the park," Simon said as his gurgling stomach progressed to a loud growl.

"Sounds good to me. We'll drive right by Burgers at the Strip."

"Oh, nice! I haven't had a burger in weeks." *And I wonder how many steps it will take to work off a burger?*

Richard turned off Brockway onto Cherry, travelled west for a few minutes, and turned north onto Creston Street. The park's tree line loomed large and shadowy on their left.

"Home sweet home," Richard said as they approached the Park View.

"And burgers, sweet burgers," Simon said with satisfaction. "I'd have a hard time living right across the street from that place, Mr. Barclay."

They joined the line of cars creeping toward the drive-thru windows. "I ate here often when I first moved into the Park View. But I discovered even a good burger lost its allure when one had too many."

"Too many good burgers? I didn't think that

was possible. But maybe that's my problem!" Simon laughed.

Order given, burgers received, they turned back onto Creston and headed for the park's main entrance. Simon opened his bag and reached in for a french fry.

"How do they do it?" He consumed one and reached for another. "Like I said, it's a good thing I don't live right across the street."

"Picnic tables by the Welcome Center okay?"

"Yes," Simon looked out the window. "If we eat fast, we'll have enough light to search the camping lots. The back parking lot is lit at night, but the overlook lots aren't."

Richard drove slowly through the open park gates and past the deserted guard hut. "Looks like we've got the place to ourselves."

"It's May, school is still in session. Come June, this place will be buzzing on a Wednesday."

They sat down at a picnic table and took out their food. The breeze grabbed at their napkins and threatened to send their takeout bags airborne. Simon regretted having to eat quickly. He wanted to savor every forbidden morsel. They both finished in short order, gathered their trash, and tossed it into the large can at the end of the row of tables.

"Okay, Mr. Barclay, let's see what we can see."

Richard switched on the car's low beams as they traveled through the deep shade on the perimeter road. In just a couple minutes they arrived at the small parking area for cabin occupants. There were only two cars there. Neither one matched the car Ursula Barnes had described.

"The road to the section for RVs and tents is right over there." Simon pointed.

Richard slowly steered the car onto the gravel road at the far end of the parking lot. The stones popped and crackled under the tires. Foliage came up close to the road's edge, opening every two hundred yards or so to reveal camp sites.

"The camp sites are spread wide apart," Simon said. "And they alternate on both sides of the road so campers have their privacy."

They didn't see any RVs, and the only tent they saw was at the site closest to the bathhouse. A car parked near the tent had an out-of-state license plate. Eventually the gravel road T-boned into the paved perimeter road again. Richard looked inquiringly at Simon.

"Turn right, Mr. Barclay. That will take us back to the gift shop and the Welcome Center."

Richard slowed down as they passed the Welcome Center parking area again and then the gift shop. No cars. They came to the chapel and cemetery next. The little white-clapboard chapel was set back several yards from the road. All its windows were dark. Richard switched from low beams to high. There was no longer enough daylight to make out the rows of grave markers in the cemetery.

They continued along the perimeter road

through a dense stand of trees to the back-entrance parking lot. The streetlights' brightness hit their eyes all at once. No cars there either. Richard stopped just beyond one of the streetlights.

"Well, Mr. Barclay, the overlook parking lots are the only places left to check."

"The car's probably not there, but I'll sleep better tonight if we look."

"My thought exactly," Simon said approvingly. "Anything at the office you'll need before tomorrow?"

"Nope."

"Good. Let's get this done and go home."

Forty minutes later they pulled up in front of the Park View, and Richard got out of the car. Simon came around from the passenger's side and slid into the driver's seat.

"See you in the morning, Mr. Barclay. I'll be here at around eight thirty to pick you up."

"Night!"

Richard watched the car pull away from the entrance and back onto Creston. He walked into the deserted lobby and checked his mailbox before starting up the stairs. On the third-floor landing he pulled the door open and started down his quiet hallway, grateful for the silence.

"I'm coming, Ethel," he said as he reached his door, key in hand. He'd unlocked the deadbolt and inserted the key into the doorknob when a baby's wail filled the air.

"Oh, no," he muttered in frustration. He turned

the doorknob and stepped into his apartment only to jump back in surprise as a furry gray bullet shot past him into the corridor.

"Ethel!" he yelled.

The cat raced along the hallway and slipped expertly through the gently closing door to the stairwell. Richard ran to the landing door, opened it, and stopped. Had Ethel gone up or down?

Think! Think like a cat! Which way would I go? Up or down? Down! I'd go down! Much less work!

Richard took the stairs in double time. The second-story landing door was shut, so he kept moving, hoping he'd see Ethel standing by the closed door to the lobby. He looked over the railing. No cat. When he got to the bottom, he looked under the stairs. No gray-striped feline. He turned around and raced back up. A little out of breath he stopped at his third-floor landing.

Maybe she's run back to the apartment.

He jogged down the hallway to his open apartment door, went in, and flipped on the lights. "Ethel! Ethel? Here, kitty, kitty, kitty!"

He checked under his bed. No cat. He ran back out into the hallway. Ethel must have gone up the stairs, not down. He ran through the landing door and started up the stairs. He hoped he'd find her at the top, her escape thwarted by a closed door to the fourth-floor hallway. All he could see when he reached the top of the staircase was the glowing red exit sign. He felt around for a light switch, found it, and turned on the stairwell's ceiling light.

His heart sank. The door to the fourth floor was open just wide enough for a cat to get through. There was a large sign on the door: PRIVATE RESIDENCE, AUTHORIZED PERSONNEL ONLY.

"Oh, Ethel! Really! Now what do I do?" Richard walked over to the door. A small kickstand held it open. He flipped it up with the toe of his shoe and pushed the door open. Unfortunately, the light from the landing didn't travel far down the passageway. "Ethel? Ethel!" he called softly. "Here, kitty, kitty! Here, Ethel!"

He took several tentative steps farther into the corridor, unable to see much of anything. He stopped. He heard music. Jazz. He crept toward the sound. "Ethel? Ethel? Are you here?" He could see a thin line of light just ahead. After a few more steps, he could see the outline of a door, an open door, open just enough for Ethel to pass through.

"Well, I've got to get Ethel back. That means knocking on the door and invading someone's privacy . . . maybe the building owner's privacy." He sighed. "Oh, Ethel."

The music stopped, then started again.

"Okay, here goes." He knocked on the door and spoke into the crack. "Hello? Good evening? Excuse me, I'm so sorry to intrude . . . I'm Richard Barclay. I live on the third floor. I think my cat is in your apartment . . . Hello?"

No answer. He knocked again with more energy. The door swung open, and his jaw dropped. The room in front of him, painted a magnolia white, was the length of three or four apartments. A bank of large windows faced the park. A studio upright piano stood in one corner with a tall potted fichus tree next to it. Nearby, sofas arranged in a U-shape sat in front of a glass-topped coffee table. At the other end of the room Richard saw an open kitchen with a low breakfast bar.

"This has got to be the owner's apartment," he said to himself. He took two hesitant steps into the room. A Van Gogh print hung on the wall to his immediate left. It was one of his favorites, a café terrace in the evening with that incredible Van Gogh sky.

"Hello?" he said again, louder.

Movement near the kitchen caught his eye, and he turned in that direction. An African American man wearing blue pajamas and cradling a cat walked toward him.

"Lose something, Mr. Barclay?" James Brown grinned across the space. "Close the door, and I'll put her down."

Richard pushed the door shut and met James in the middle of the room. "I am so sorry. She got out when I unlocked my door." Ethel strolled between them, clearly at home in the space. "Mr. Brown, this is a wonderful apartment."

"Thank you. I like it. Been my home for quite a while now."

"I just assumed the building owner lived up here."

"He does," James said, an amused expression on his face.

"Please tell him I'm so sorry for this intrusion. I'll do my best to see that it doesn't happen again." He looked earnestly at James. "I don't want the owner of the building mad at me!"

"Oh, I don't think you have anything to worry about, Mr. Barclay." James gave Richard a meaningful look.

Richard looked back, puzzled, and then, the light dawned. "Oh, man. Oh, man! Mr. Brown, it never occurred to me that the building manager might also be—"

"—the building owner!" they said in unison and started to laugh.

"Only a handful of the residents know I'm more than the manager. I want it to stay that way," James said sternly. "I enjoy my working relationship with Park View tenants. I don't want that to change."

"Got it! Not a word from me. I promise. And I don't think we have to worry about Ethel." They laughed again. "Mr. Brown, I am sorry about Ethel's intrusion, but I'm glad to know who's living over my head. I never hear you, by the way."

"I don't wear shoes up here. And I do my best not to drop things, but that does happen once in a while."

"Well, Ethel, time to go home." Richard scooped up the cat. "Long day today. Long day tomorrow. See you in the morning, Mr. Brown. I'll do my best to keep a straight face when I pass your office door!"

Chapter Sixteen

At 8:30 Thursday morning, Simon arrived at the Park View and found Richard waiting for him under the awning. "Ready for another fun-packed day, Mr. Barclay?" he asked as Richard got in and slammed the car door.

"Absolutely." Richard reached for his seatbelt.

"No crying baby during the night?" Simon checked traffic flow and eased onto Creston for the short trip to the park.

"No, thank goodness."

Simon glanced at Richard's face. "You look a bit like the cat who swallowed the canary, Mr. Barclay. Has something besides a baby-free night planted that grin on your face?"

Richard laughed. "Ethel escaped when I got home. Ran to the stairwell and disappeared."

"Uh-oh! I'm assuming this story has a happy ending, since you're grinning."

"Yes, it does. I found her safe and sound. All is well. There's more to the story, but I can't say any more."

Simon chuckled. "I'll try not to let my imagination run away with me."

He pulled up in front of the park's gift shop and parked. Traffic sounds from Clay Street, Creston, and Remembrance Road blended to create a low, murmuring rumble. As they got out of the car, Simon looked across the parking lot into the trees and then up at the darkening sky. "Bet we get some rain today." He pointed away from the car. "The camping office is behind the gift shop."

When they rounded the side of red-brick building, the traffic noise receded and sounds of the woods took its place: leaves rustled in the breeze, birds called back and forth, squirrels chattered. Richard pulled open the camping office screen door, and Simon walked in ahead of him. The small space was bisected by a long, high counter; a ceiling fan whirled lazily overhead.

"Mr. Barfield, good morning!" Simon walked to the counter.

"Detective Roe! Good morning." Mr. Barfield shook hands with Simon and then with Richard. "I'm guessing you aren't here to book a cabin. How can I help you?"

Simon took the photo of Sally Groegan out of his pocket and laid it on the counter. "Have you seen this woman?"

Mr. Barfield pulled the picture toward him and nodded immediately. "Oh, sure. That's Sally Groegan. She's in cabin number five. Is everything okay? She's such a nice lady." He handed the picture back to Simon.

"We just want to check in with her," Simon said. "What's the best way to get to the cabins from here?"

"I'll show you." Mr. Barfield came around the

far side of the counter and grabbed a walking stick in the corner by the door. He led them down the sidewalk toward the trees for a few yards, where they saw a wide, mulched path ahead of them. "Here you go," he said. "Follow that north. It eventually dead-ends into the cabins. Shouldn't take you more than five, ten minutes."

"Thank you, Mr. Barfield."

Simon and Richard stepped onto the path and started walking.

"If she's here, where was her car last night?" Richard asked.

"Good question."

As they traveled the path's steady incline, a few unexpected dips and turns kept them paying close attention to their feet. Several minutes later another path crossed theirs. A slight breeze lifted tree limbs, blew leaves across the path in front of them. Deep shade gave the path a cave-like quality A signpost was set in the ground next to the path, its arrow for the cabins pointing due north. Underneath the arrow a smaller sign read, "You're almost there!" The path turned again, and they came to a large mowed area. Along its edge, five well-spaced cabins were set back in the trees. Each cabin had its own small patio with a grill and picnic table.

They moved across the grass to the nearest cabin and stepped onto a narrow sidewalk that ran alongside it. They spotted a large metal number five above the cabin door.

"Good morning," Simon called out. "Mrs. Groegan? Are you home?"

No answer.

He stepped up to the cabin door and knocked. "Mrs. Groegan?"

A door slammed nearby and the men turned toward the sound.

"May I help you?" A short, heavyset woman dressed in a long skirt and short-sleeved T-shirt stopped within a few yards of them. Her gray-streaked hair was pulled back in a ponytail. She stared curiously at them.

"I'm Detective Roe. This is my associate, Officer Barclay. We're looking for Mrs. Groegan."

"Jane Watson." She took a few steps closer to Simon and put out her hand to shake his. "You just missed her. She and Max are out on their morning roam."

"Do you have any idea how long she'll be gone, Ms. Watson?"

"Nope, sorry. Sometimes Sally and Max are gone a long time. Sometimes they're back in an hour."

Simon took out his card and handed it to the woman.

"Don't have my reading glasses on," she said as she squinted, brought the card closer to her face and then farther away.

"My name and phone number are there. We'd appreciate it if you'd give it to Mrs. Groegan when she and Max get back. Tell her we'd like to talk to her."

"Sure, of course."

Simon and Richard waited to speak until they were sure she was out of earshot.

"Even if we split up, it would take a while to cover all the places Mrs. Groegan and Max could walk," Richard said.

"Agreed, Mr. Barclay. Let's look around, and then head back to the office to wait for Mrs. Groegan to call us."

They followed the sidewalk around the cabin to two empty parking places.

"I wonder why Mrs. Groegan hasn't parked her car by her cabin?"

"We'll have to ask her when she calls us back."

Thunder rumbled in the distance. Simon looked up. "I hope Mrs. Groegan took an umbrella with her." They didn't waste any time walking back to their parked car.

"I'm going to leave a card with Mr. Barfield," Simon said to Richard. "Just in case he sees Mrs. Groegan again."

Richard had buckled in when Simon returned. A few large raindrops hit the windshield as Simon slid into the driver's seat and closed the car door. He pulled out of the parking lot and turned onto the perimeter road. As they cruised past the chapel and the cemetery, more raindrops spattered the windshield. When they reached the back entrance Simon turned left onto Park Road. He'd stopped for the yellow light at the corner of Park and

Cherry when he suddenly bent over the steering wheel and peered up.

"Mr. Barclay! I see someone with a dog on the pedestrian bridge!" The light turned green. "I'll pull into the hospital parking lot. We'll be able to see our walker when he or she gets to the other side."

Simon turned into the lot and parked the car facing Main Street. They'd barely unbuckled their seatbelts when a woman hurried past them on the other side of the street, dog in the lead.

"Let's go," Simon said.

They got out of their car as the woman and dog crossed to their side of the street. Lightning flashed and thunder rolled. The sprinkle progressed to a full-fledged downpour. Dog and walker started to run toward the hospital parking garage. So did Simon and Richard.

Dog and walker disappeared into the shadows of the first level. Simon and Richard entered at the same place less than a minute later and stopped next to a dusty pickup truck. Rain fell in sheets, pounding the pavement beyond them. The tires of passing cars hissed on the blacktop. Simon took several steps deeper into the garage. Suddenly a woman's voice shouted frantically from higher up in the garage. "Wait! Stop! That's my car!"

Both men ran up the incline in the direction of the shouting. They rounded the corner to the second level when a tow truck roared past them. The truck's brake lights flashed at the exit as the crossing arm swung up. Within seconds the truck disappeared into the rain.

They resumed the jog uphill. A minute or two later, at the far end of the third level, they spotted someone sitting on the garage floor, arms around a small dog. They'd only walked a few feet in that direction when the dog saw them. He stood up and gave a couple short barks, tail wagging. The person on the ground got up slowly and pulled the dog close.

"I'm Detective Roe, this is Officer Barclay. We're with the Grandburg Police Department."

"Police? Thank goodness! My car was just towed away!"

"Sally Groegan?" Simon asked. She looked so much like her picture that he didn't need her answer, but he asked anyway.

"Yes, I'm Sally Groegan." She looked from Simon to Richard, puzzled. "How do you know who I am?"

Simon pulled her picture out of his pocket. "Your daughter has asked us to look for you."

"Ursula . . . Oh, no!" She looked from the photo to Simon, and then to the empty space where her car had been. "Oh, no!" She looked down at the dog. Oh, Max." She shook her head, closed her eyes for a second, opened them again, and looked squarely at Simon. "So, am I under arrest?" She said it calmly but Simon was aware of how close to tears she was.

"No, no, Mrs. Groegan. We just wanted to find you." He gave her a sympathetic smile.

"Why did they tow my car?"

"I'm afraid that's our fault," said Simon. "When your daughter filed a missing persons report yesterday, we put out an APB on your car."

"The good news is," Richard interjected, "your car isn't far from here. The impoundment lot is only a couple blocks away."

They walked back down to street level. The rain had stopped. Steam rose from the pavement in wispy fingers.

"Our car's around the corner in front of the hospital." Simon pointed ahead of where they stood.

When they reached the car, Richard opened the rear door for Mrs. Groegan and Max. "Well, friend, do you smell Ethel?" Richard said as the dog sniffed the cuff of his pants. "May I pet him?" he asked Mrs. Groegan.

"Of course! He's wet, though, sorry about that," she said.

"No worries," said Simon. "The inside of this car has seen a lot worse."

Simon started the engine and turned on the air conditioner. Richard buckled himself in and turned to the backseat. "Mrs. Groegan, were you in the park with Max a couple Fridays ago?"

"A couple Fridays ago. Hmmm, let me think." She looked down at Max, avoiding Richard's eyes.

"I was on the jogging trail when a dog who

looked just like Max ran in front of me," Richard continued. "Does Max come when you whistle?"

"Yes, he does." Sally looked out the window at the passing scenery.

Simon pulled up to a tall chain-link fence and stopped the car. He looked at Richard, eyebrows raised. He could tell by the look on his face that they were connecting the same dots.

"All right, Mrs. Groegan," Simon said, "Let's get your car back."

"I'll hold on to Max," Richard volunteered when they'd gotten out of the car. He took the leash Mrs. Groegan handed him.

Simon led the way through the open gate into the impoundment lot. Sally's car was already being offloaded from the tow truck bed.

"Hey, Armondo!" Simon headed toward a man in blue jeans and a short-sleeved blue shirt, clipboard in hand, standing to one side of the slow-moving car.

"Detective! What brings you here?" The man lowered the clipboard and walked over to shake his hand.

"I'm chasing that car." Simon pointed to the car that had now come to a stop near them. "How merciful are you feeling today?"

"Merciful?" Armondo looked suspiciously at Simon and then behind him at Mrs. Groegan. "Don't tell me this is her car."

"I'm afraid so. She was in the parking garage when the tow truck went right past her."

"I yelled, but the driver kept going," Mrs. Groegan said.

Armondo shook his head. "Well, I'm sorry to hear that, but found is found."

"Yes, found is found." Simon looked calmly at Armondo. "The car is off the truck, but it's not officially parked on the lot yet."

A young man in a plaid shirt and blue jeans got out of the tow truck and slammed the door. He came around the side, pulled earbuds out of both ears, and nodded to them.

"Hmmm." Armondo looked at Simon first and then down at the papers on his clipboard. "Well," he looked over at Mrs. Groegan, "if you can prove this is your car, I'll just charge you for the tow. I've got a staff to pay," he said to Simon defensively. "These guys don't work for free."

"Thanks, Armondo," Simon said. "Mrs. Groegan, got your car keys?"

Mrs. Groegan reached deep into her purse and came up with a black key fob. She pressed the red alarm button and her car sprang to life with lights flashing and horn honking.

"Guess that's all I need," Armondo said. "If you'll come this way, we'll settle up on the tow. Won't take a minute."

Simon followed a few feet behind as Armondo and Mrs. Groegan walked to the towing office. Richard and Max brought up the rear. Armondo and Mrs. Groegan went inside but Simon, Richard, and Max stayed outside. Simon spotted two rusty folding chairs propped against the front of the office under the overhang. After checking to make sure the chairs were dry, he unfolded one for Richard and one for himself.

"So, Mr. Barclay, what do you think?"

"I think Mrs. Groegan knows more than she's saying." Richard looked down at the dog. "Max, I sure wish you could talk."

Mrs. Groegan came back through the door at that moment. Max jerked the leash out of Richard's hand and dashed to her side.

"Whoa, Max!"

"I've got him," Mrs. Groegan laughed. "Max, I'm right here. I wouldn't leave you." She picked up his leash and wrapped it twice around her hand.

"Glad this worked out so well," Simon said. "Mrs. Groegan, could we have a little more of your time? Officer Barclay and I have a couple more questions."

"Oh, yes, of course."

"I'll go see if Armondo has another folding chair." Richard disappeared into the hut, reappearing shortly with chair in hand. He opened the chair next to Mrs. Groegan, who looked at the brown seat with obvious misgivings.

"Oh, wait—" Richard darted back inside and came out again with several sheets of paper towels. He put them down on Mrs. Groegan's chair. "Voila!"

Mrs. Groegan smiled and sat down, but didn't

lean back. Richard returned to his place next to Simon. Max yawned and stretched out next to her chair.

"About your car. Why did you park in the hospital parking garage instead of by your cabin?"

"I didn't want my daughter, or anyone else for that matter, to spot my car at the park. Ursula would have a fit if she knew I was staying in a cabin by myself."

"Have you been doing this for a while then?" Richard asked.

"For two or three years." She looked matter-of-factly at the men. "My husband, Eric, was passionate about bringing to light an injustice that happened on park land a long time ago. After he died, I decided to continue what we'd started together. I feel close to him when I'm in the park, in cabin number five."

She reached down and ran her hand across Max's curly coat.

"When I lived north of Byington, keeping the park trips a secret was easy. I'd park in the hospital parking garage and move the car periodically so it wouldn't get towed. But last year Ursula insisted I move to Brockway Village. I tried visiting the park without staying in the cabin. But it just wasn't the same."

Simon nodded. "I'm sure it wasn't."

"I've managed to keep a very low profile at the park. That's easier to do in the spring and the fall, harder to do in the summer." She looked down at

Max, who slept contentedly at her feet. "Sometimes Max and I cross paths with children riding bikes on the perimeter road or the jogging trail."

"Speaking of that," Richard said, "do you remember meeting some children in the park and telling them to keep you and Max a secret?"

"Oh, goodness." Mrs. Groegan looked embarrassed. "It sounds so silly when you say it out loud like that. Yes, I remember. Maybe last September or October."

"Mrs. Groegan, when we were on our way here, I asked if you and Max were in the park two Fridays ago. You didn't answer. Were you in the park then?"

"I . . . yes," she said quietly. "Yes." She looked out into the car lot.

"Where you there on Thursday?"

Sally sighed. "I guess I should tell you. Actually, it would be a relief to tell you. Yes, I was in the park two Thursday evenings ago. Max and I were taking a late evening walk when Max found the body of a little boy in deep grass near the jogging trail. I knew right away he was dead. I couldn't stand the thought of his family not knowing where he was, not knowing what had happened to him. So I moved him to the jogging trail. His bike too. I was sure someone would find him there . . . find him quickly."

"And you were right," Simon said. "Did you move the body by yourself?"

"Yes, I did," Mrs. Groegan answered matter-of-factly. "I'm stronger than I look."

Simon and Richard both suppressed the urge to grin.

"Mrs. Groegan, moving a body is a felony. Did you know that?"

She looked in surprise at the men. "A felony? No! All I could think about was his family, worrying, not knowing. He looked about the same age as my grandson, Billy." The expression on her face lengthened with guilt. "And now I've put Ursula through that."

The tow truck driver came out of the hut and gave them a fleeting look of curiosity. They watched him climb into the cab and drive out the gate.

"I can understand wanting to keep your daughter in the dark. But not to report a little boy's death and then move the body . . ." Simon looked quietly at Sally. "Is there something else going on, something besides your daughter discovering your whereabouts?"

Sally didn't answer. Simon and Richard waited. One minute flowed into two, into three.

"Mrs. Groegan?"

She looked at them both, distress evident in her wide-eyed expression and the way she held her mouth. "My son-in-law wants to build condos on the land my husband, Eric, was sure belongs to a Native American tribe. When Eric died, my son-in-law thought Eric's search for the truth died with him. He would be furious if he found out I was in the park. I'm afraid he'd take his anger out on my daughter and grandson."

"Have you found anything?" Richard asked.

"No. I'm close to giving up, but it meant so much to Eric. Sometimes I feel like I'm being torn in two." She looked at Simon and Richard. "So, what happens now?"

"I think Officer Barclay and I have all the information we need." Simon looked encouragingly at Mrs. Groegan. "We can call your daughter and let her know you're safe. Or you can make the call yourself."

"I'll call Ursula when I get home this afternoon. That gives me a couple hours to think about what I want to say." Sally got to her feet. "Let's go, Max. It's time to face the music."

At the sound of his name, Max jumped up, barked twice, and wagged his tail. Richard took the chair back inside as Simon and Sally walked toward their cars.

"Thanks again for getting my car back for me," Sally said. She opened the door to the backseat for Max, who jumped in and sat patiently as she clipped the doggie seatbelt to his harness. "I'm sorry for all the trouble I've caused. I'm remembering that poem I learned in elementary school. 'Oh, what a tangled web we weave.'" She looked sheepishly at Simon.

"Glad we could help, Mrs. Groegan. I hope your conversation with your daughter goes well." He closed Mrs. Groegan's car door and waved as she exited the lot.

"So, now what?" Richard asked as he and Simon got in their car and started the short drive back to the precinct.

"We take Mrs. Groegan's name off the missing persons list and make sure the APB on her car has been cancelled. She says she's going to call her daughter this afternoon, and I think she will."

"What about the fact that she moved Jeremy Davis's body?"

"I'll have a conversation with the DA about that. The extenuating circumstances may make a difference."

Simon swung into the police parking garage and pulled the car into his usual parking space. He switched off the car's ignition and left the keys dangling from the steering column. Neither he nor Richard reached for a door handle.

"Now we know who moved Jeremy Davis's body, but I'd still like to know why Jeremy road down the Prayer Trail in the first place." Simon looked at Richard. "I'm thinking that's one mystery we'll never solve."

Jacoba pulled into the alley behind the antique store and parked in her usual place. She checked the river first and then walked to the back entrance. Unlocked. *Yes, this is Grandburg, after all, certainly*

not the crime capital of the world. But still. When I'm working here, that door will be locked.

"Hello? Marty?" She pushed aside the beaded curtain and looked to the checkout area. She didn't see her friend or anyone else. "Marty?" she called more loudly. She took several steps into the main room and stopped. Suddenly a loud, prolonged rumble came from beneath the floorboards. Marty's voice came next, repeatedly uttering her one and only bad word. Jacoba hurried to the wide stairway to the basement.

"Marty?" she yelled down the stairs. "Are you all right?"

An exasperated Marty answered immediately from down below. "Yes, yes, I'm okay. But I've made a huge mess. I need some help."

Jacoba came down to the bottom step. Four glittery blue Christmas balls rolled to the stairs and came to a stop at her feet. A sea of cardboard boxes covered the basement floor between her and her friend.

"Oh, my!" She started laughing.

In the light from the naked bulb hanging from the ceiling, Jacoba could see that several of the boxes had burst open, their contents strewn across the hardpacked dirt floor. Dust motes danced in the air.

"What happened?"

Marty pointed to the box tipped sideways at her feet. "I started an avalanche when I pulled it out. I didn't realize it was one of the shelf supports." She looked back at the shadowed brick wall where the makeshift shelves had been. "Hey, Jacoba! A door!" She moved closer for a better look. "At least I think it's a door."

"Hang on, I'm coming over." Jacoba made her way slowly toward Marty. "These boxes look really old."

"Some boxes of my grandmother's stuff are down here." Marty gave the muddled mess a discouraged look. "Hopefully not in this pile."

Jacoba picked up a piece of newspaper and held it up to the light. "September 7, 1922. Wow!" As her eyes became better adjusted to the dimness, she could see brickwork framing the door on either side, and a brick arch over the top. She leaned down and lifted the bottom corner of one of the few intact cartons in front of the door. "This thing is heavy. I wonder what's in here?"

"We need a flashlight," Marty said. "I keep one down here somewhere." She disappeared into the basement recesses for a moment. "Here we go." She came back to Jacoba's side and shone a bright flashlight beam on the area in front of them. "This door is definitely smaller than the other doors in the building." She slowly outlined the wooden door frame with the flashlight beam and swung the beam down one side. "I see a knob and a keyhole. If there's a room behind there, it's under the street." Marty shone the beam upward along the basement's exterior wall to make her point. "Look, the windows are sidewalk level."

Jacoba followed the light as it moved from one dirt-smeared windowpane to another. Tires and hubcaps flashed by as a car drove past on the street.

"Think you could reach the doorknob?"

Jacoba was reaching for the knob when they both heard the cowbell over the front door clang.

"Customer!" Marty announced. "Race you!"

Jacoba whirled around and picked her way back across the cluttered floor. She just missed crushing one of the Christmas balls at the edge of the bottom step. She pounded up the stairs ahead of Marty, but when she reached the top step Marty pushed past her.

"Hey!"

The front door had already closed when Marty made it to the counter just ahead of Jacoba.

"That must have been Sandy. Here's the mail." Marty sifted quickly through a stack of envelopes, her eyes tracking on the return addresses. "Excellent, excellent, good, good, oh!" She pulled the letter opener from the pencil cup on the counter and slit open a legal-sized envelope. After extracting the contents, she waved the sheets of paper at Jacoba. "This is another application for booth space!" she exclaimed.

"But Marty, there aren't any more spaces!"

"Your suggestion about booths in the basement got me thinking. I've already called Ron at Beacon Electric. He's coming out on Monday to see what can be done about improving the lighting down there. I know it's a mess right now, but I'm sure we could get it shipshape if we could see what we were doing."

"We need a clever name for that area," Jacoba said, getting into the spirit of the new endeavor. "We'll need to pick up some of the stuff—make a path for Ron."

"I'm so glad to hear you say 'we.'" Marty looked down at the application and saw brown smudges from her fingers along one edge. "I'd better wash my hands."

"Me too," Jacoba said. "We've touched stuff that hasn't been touched in a very long time!"

They walked together to the sink in the workroom. Marty let the water run a few seconds before wetting her hands and pumping a generous amount of soap foam on her palms. Jacoba followed right behind her.

"Much better," said Marty. She took two paper towels to dry her hands and handed two more to Jacoba. They threw their paper towels away in the round metal can next to the sink and walked back to the café area.

"So, Jacoba, I've thought about you off and on all day. What did Dr. Miller say when you told him you weren't coming back?"

"He didn't say anything. He wasn't there." Jacoba looked at her friend. "When I got to school this morning, I found out he was attending a regional principals conference for the rest of the week. So, I wrote 'I'm not returning' across the top of the contract, gave it to Barb, and spent the rest of the day enjoying my fourth graders."

Clocks started chiming the four o'clock hour from several corners of the store.

"Decision made, intentions declared, mission accomplished. How do you feel now?" Marty asked.

"I feel relieved," Jacoba said. "I feel lighter, inside and out."

"I'm glad," Marty said softly.

"I'll have the whole summer to figure out what's next. I'm looking forward to being back here." Jacoba sat up suddenly in her chair. "Marty, abrupt change of subject—that door downstairs! I'm so curious!"

"I know, I—"

The cowbell clanged. Both women got up and headed toward the front of the store. A tall, thin woman with long black hair walked up to the counter. Her generously applied makeup, complete with bright-red lipstick, gave the impression she was just starting her day. The sequins on her jeans and T-shirt sparkled in the afternoon sun shining through the skylights.

"Hi, I'm Tiffany Clark. I'd like to talk to someone about renting booth space."

"Certainly, Tiffany. I'm Marty Blankenship, the owner of Behind the Times, and this is my manager, Jacoba Dahm."

Jacoba looked sideways at Marty, eyebrows raised, but didn't correct her.

"How much room might you need?" Marty led Tiffany over to the café area. "We have several options."

Jacoba raised her eyebrows at Marty again as they sat down.

"You aren't planning to close your doors anytime soon?" Tiffany looked anxiously from Marty to Jacoba and back to Marty.

"Oh my goodness, no! Absolutely not. Behind the Times is here to stay."

Tiffany looked relieved. "Good," she said. "Change is hard for me. I'm just not as flexible as I used to be."

Jacoba felt a sudden kinship with this woman. *Change isn't easy for me either. How flexible am I?* she thought. *I'm about to find out, ready or not.*

"Marty, I'm going to head home. Tiffany, I hope to see you again soon."

"Oh, say, Jacoba, I haven't had time to do anything with the Help Wanted flyer."

"I can take it over to Tilden, but not until Saturday morning."

"That would work just fine. Thanks! It's on the desk in the workroom." She turned back to Tiffany. "So, tell me about your treasures. What will you be bringing to Behind the Times?"

Jacoba walked down the aisle and through the beaded curtain to the workroom. The desk on the other side was littered with several invoices and yesterday's newspaper. She found the flyer under the Sports section. As she walked back out into the alley and got into her car, she considered taking the flyer to Tilden now.

"No," she said decisively. "No, time to go home." Once she'd turned onto Cherry Street, she glanced at the side of the building and counted basement windows.

"One, two, three—I'm driving over whatever's behind that door right now!" She wondered how big the underground space was. "It must be deep, since it hasn't caved in when cars have driven over it." She looked toward the park and noticed how close Winding Creek came to the street's edge.

She drove by the hospital and passed under the pedestrian bridge. She stopped as the light turned red on the corner of Cherry and Clay Street. As the car idled, she thought about the newspaper she'd found on the basement floor. What had the date been? September something, 1922. Was Cherry Street even here then? She looked out the driver-side window to the park. She was suddenly struck by how little she really knew about Grandburg's past.

"Home again, home again," she said to herself a few minutes later as she pulled into her driveway. She retrieved her bulging canvas bag, slammed the car door, and walked up the steps. But when she inserted her key into the door's lock, the little door in the antique mall basement came back to mind. *Ahhhh, a mystery. Nice!*

Chapter Seventeen

Solomon turned slowly into the driveway of Rinien House and let the car coast to a stop behind a second vehicle, a Tilden parking sticker on its bumper.

Good. Mary's here.

"We've found something in the attic," she'd told him excitedly earlier in the week. "And we'd rather show you than tell you about it!"

A blue jay scolded him on his walk up the driveway. The Saturday-morning air was cool, the sky clear. Solomon took his time, appreciating the manicured lawn and taking in the view of the house. Ancient oak trees shaded the two-story colonial residence. Two red-brick chimneys, one on either side of the house, extended above the blue-gray shingled roof.

So many windows, Solomon thought, counting four on the first floor, four identical ones directly above those, and three attic dormers. He'd only been inside Rinien House once. Ms. Polding had given him the grand tour and a very good cup of tea.

The first-floor sunroom protruded unexpectedly from the north side of the house like a builder's afterthought. Square-trimmed boxwood bushes lined the stone foundation from one end of the house to the other. He was still a few feet from the red front door when it opened.

"Dr. Rigby! Good morning!" Rinien Polding greeted him warmly. "Welcome to Rinien House." She opened the door wider, and Mary Pritchard came into view next to her.

"Good morning!" Solomon stepped into the high-ceilinged front hall. The air of old house settled all around him with a quiet calm that matched the morning.

"I'd offer you tea, but I'm sure you'd rather get right to the reason for your visit." Rinien looked teasingly at Solomon.

"Well, I have to say Mary's announcement has certainly piqued my curiosity. I'm anxious to see what you've found." Anticipation and hopefulness, pleasant internal intoxications he hadn't experienced in a while, bubbled up unexpectedly.

"All right then. To the attic! Mary," Rinien commanded, "lead the way."

Mary headed purposefully toward the wide staircase. Solomon waited for Rinien to go ahead of him, but she remained in place.

"Go ahead, Dr. Rigby," she said. "It takes me a little longer to get upstairs now than it used to. I'll be right behind you."

Solomon headed upstairs, the broad oak banister smooth under his hand.

"The stairs to the attic are at the end of this corridor," Mary said when he joined her at the top.

They walked to a narrow door, and when Mary

opened it, Solomon saw another staircase, this one much steeper, disappearing into the dark. Mary flipped a switch next to the door, and a single bulb came on high overhead. Another door, closed, was visible now at the top of the stairs.

"I'm glad for the handrail," Mary said over her shoulder as she started up. She climbed with a slow, cautious step. "I worry about Ms. Polding on these stairs."

Mary threw her weight against the attic door, and it popped open. Solomon realized almost too late that he was taller than the door frame. He ducked and took a few more steps into the A-frame room before he could straighten up. Bright light streamed through the three dormer windows. He could see a distinct aisle down the attic's center. Solomon looked around with a mixture of awe and curiosity at the sheet-shrouded furniture, several steamer trunks, lamps, lampshades, and many, many boxes.

"How in the world did you decide where to start?"

Mary cast a proprietary eye over her domain. She took a couple steps down the row and pointed. "Ms. Polding told me to start with that steamer trunk, and I just kept moving to my right."

"And that's how we found what we found," Rinien's matter-of-fact voice came from behind them. The rubber tip of her cane made a muffled rhythmic knock on the floorboards as she walked over to join them. "See the middle dormer window? I'm sure my grandmother, Rachel Rinien, painted there. You don't have to look hard to see all kinds of paint splatters on the rug," she added in mild disapproval. "That does not happen in my studio."

"You're an artist, Ms. Polding?" Solomon asked.

"Yes. I do portraits mostly."

They walked forward to the edge of a well-worn India rug. Solomon noticed an empty easel set up on one corner of it.

"Mary, is there a chair close by? I'd like to sit down."

Solomon looked at Rinien with concern and offered his arm for support.

Mary hurried back down the aisle, whipped a ladder-back chair out from under a sheet, and swung it around just behind Rinien.

"Thank you," Rinien said. She released Solomon's arm and winced as she sank into the seat. "Carry on, Mary!"

Mary walked across the rug to the dormer sill. She reached below it, and Solomon heard the clinking of metal rings on a rod as she slid a curtain aside to reveal two widely spaced shelves. He could make out the tops of several paint brushes in two tin cans, rags, some tubes of paint, and two oblong tin containers.

"Supplies for oil painting, including turpentine," Rinien said as Mary held up one of the tin cans. "Show Dr. Rigby the paintings." She settled back in her chair, an expectant grin on her face.

Mary closed the curtains and stepped away from the shelves. She reached along the left side of the dormer and pulled out a canvas with dimensions no bigger than a sheet of paper. She held the canvas edges between the palms of her hands and turned to show it to them.

A young girl stared at Solomon from the canvas. Black hair, straight and long, framed a face with high cheekbones, brown eyes open wide, and a broad nose. Her lips were set in a defiant line. A thin, beaded band encircled her head. He wasn't sure if she was angry or happy, but the energy that radiated from her eyes kept him staring back.

"My grandmother was born in Rinien House in 1889. She grew up here, married, moved away, and was widowed just a few years after her marriage. She and her young son, Daniel Polding, my father, moved back to Rinien House in 1919. She died in the house in 1965."

Rinien stopped for a moment to catch her breath. "I have seventeen of her journals from 1899 to 1963. I found them right after I moved back to the house in 1990, but I've only recently read through them all. I'm doing a lot more sitting than I used to do," she said with quiet regret. "Her journal entries for November of 1900 were all about losing a friend, a Native American friend, whose village north of Grandburg was torched.

Deliberately." She stopped and looked to Mary, who continued the narrative.

"Ms. Polding thought the fire was a young girl's fantasy, and maybe the friend was a figment of her imagination too. But then I found this." Mary set the portrait on the easel.

"Mary and I think she was the friend my grandmother wrote about in her journals," Rinien said. "And there's more. Mary, show Dr. Rigby the larger painting."

Mary retrieved another canvas from the right side of the dormer and held it in front of her.

Solomon stepped closer to take in the detail. "Houses, a church, people on a street, dogs. I see the river! Is that the second scenic overlook? I recognize the rock formation!" He looked quizzically at Mary and Rinien. "There was a village there?"

"Yes," Rinien said. "A Native American village—Grandma Rachel's friend's home."

"I've been to that spot in the park many times," Solomon said. "There isn't any sign of a village ever being there." He turned back to the painting. "Mother Nature does quick work of reclaiming what's hers. And in this case, she's had an overabundance of time."

"According to my grandmother, the tribe had lived on that site for over a hundred years. She wrote multiple entries about a fire being deliberately set in October of 1900 to drive the people away." Rinien's mouth trembled. "After the fire she never saw her friend again."

Solomon gazed soberly at the painting of the village. He lifted the canvas out of Mary's hands for a closer look. "A church, complete with steeple and cross, right in the middle. What kind of church would it have been?" I wonder what denominations were around here in 1900?"

"St. Gregory's was here," Rinien said promptly. "I know because it celebrated its one hundred fiftieth anniversary in 1990, when I turned fifty. My father had died, and I'd just moved back to Grandburg."

"I go to the Episcopal church on Connor Avenue," Mary said. "It's old, but I don't think it's been around as long as St. Gregory's."

Solomon set the village canvas next to the young girl's portrait. "Your grandmother was an excellent artist," he said to Rinien. "The people and dogs are so real I almost expect them to start moving. And your grandmother's friend looks like she's on the verge of saying something to us."

"There's one more painting you should see," Rinien said, her expression sober. "Mary, show him Roger."

Mary went back to the middle dormer. She picked up a canvas hidden in the shadows. It was another small one, the size of a coffee table book. She handed it to Solomon.

He found himself looking at an overweight, be-whiskered gentleman wearing a fancy-collared shirt under a checkered waistcoat. The man's attention was focused on an open pocket watch held in his left hand. The right hand held a cigar just beyond his face.

"Meet Roger Rinien, my great-grandfather and Rachel's father. Roger Rinien built this house in 1885. My grandmother was convinced her father was behind the village burning. Dr. Rigby, I want you to find out if that's what happened." Rinien spoke with the most energy she'd shown all morning. "And if you discover a wrong was done, I want to do everything in my power to make it right."

Solomon's eyes widened; his eyebrows arched. The joy of the hunt woke deep within him after months of slumber. It stretched, yawned, and straightened, alert to grand potential. He handed Roger Rinien's portrait back to Mary, and she leaned it against one leg of the easel. He picked up the painting of the village and took it to the window to take advantage of the light.

"We need to establish there was a village at the overlook. I think a good place to start would be the church. Records of births, deaths, baptisms, and weddings would have been kept there." He put the painting back on the easel.

"But wouldn't the records have been destroyed when the village burned?" Mary asked.

"That depends on where they were kept." Solomon's mind shifted into high gear. "The church—that's the place to start," he said again, almost to himself. The joy of the hunt carried him easily to the next step. "Since St. Gregory's was around in 1900, there might be information about the church or the village in St. Gregory's archives. I'll stop by the rectory on my way back to campus and make some enquiries."

"Wonderful," Rinien said, beaming. She stood up. "Mary, let's bring Grandma Rachel's friend and the village downstairs and put them in the parlor." She looked severely in the direction of Roger Rinien's portrait. "But you, Roger Rinien, are staying up here."

Thirty minutes later, after another excellent cup of tea, Solomon got up to leave.

"Ms. Polding, may I take a picture of your grandmother's paintings?"

"Of course."

Solomon pulled his phone out of his pocket and snapped photos of the Indian girl and the village. When Rinien and Mary escorted him to the front door he felt like he was being launched on an adventure, sent out on a mission. Thoughts tumbled over each other in his mind as he walked back to his car. He'd been a student of American history for a long time, but this was the first time American history had appeared right in his own backyard. Well, almost in his backyard. The village would have been a twenty-to-thirty-minute walk from his house on Madison Street.

What would that walk have looked like, one hundred years ago?

The joy of the hunt further energized Solomon's

speculations as he got into his car and headed up Connor Street toward St. Gregory's.

Why would Roger Rinien have wanted that particular piece of land? How did Roger Rinien make his money in the first place? Rinien House is certainly a testament to big bucks. Was Roger the first Rinien in Grandburg, or had others come before him? I'm sure Ms. Polding would know more about that.

Solomon turned left onto River Street and pulled up in front of the rectory. The moment he looked ahead at the rectory's front porch, the joy of the hunt collided with his months-old dolor and spiritual malcontent.

What am I doing here?

"Dr. Rigby, good to see you! It's been a while," a familiar voice came from behind him on the sidewalk. Solomon instantly assumed his professor persona and turned to face the voice.

"Father Lewis. How are you?" He reached out to shake the priest's hand. The joy of the hunt snatched grief and anger, shoved them into a box, slammed the lid, and sat on it.

"Please, call me Father Mike."

Solomon didn't answer. Father Mike appeared not to notice.

"So, Dr. Rigby, what brings you to the rectory on a Saturday?"

"I'm on a fact-finding mission," Solomon said. "I'm researching a village that was located just north of Grandburg in the 1800s. There was a church there, and I'm hoping to find a connection between that congregation and St. Gregory's."

"Do you know the name of the village or of the church? Was the congregation Catholic?"

"All unknown," Solomon said in his best professor voice.

"Sounds like a mystery," Father Mike said approvingly. "My kind of thing. If the congregation was Catholic, we might find something in the archives." He checked his watch. "I have an hour before Saturday confessions. Want to take a look?"

Solomon couldn't say yes fast enough.

Father Mike led the way across the parking lot to the church, but much to Solomon's relief didn't take the front steps up to the narthex. Instead, they walked together around the side of the building to another door. Father Mike pulled it open, and Solomon stepped past him into a hallway with stairs directly to his right.

"This way, Dr. Rigby."

Father Mike led the way downstairs to the church basement. The staircase ended in a large well-lit space. Long tables with chairs occupied the center of the room. Father Mike walked past the tables to a glass-windowed door. The sign on the door read:

ARCHIVES
AUTHORIZED PERSONNEL ONLY
PLEASE KEEP DOOR CLOSED

Father Mike reached into his pants pocket and pulled out a ring holding several keys. "One of these should get us in," he said. The first and second key didn't fit. But the third key did, the lock clicked, and he opened the door.

The space was dark, the air cool. Father Mike flipped on the overhead lighting to reveal metal file cabinets of varying sizes all along one wall. Solomon noticed there were no windows. Metal shelves stood against another wall with five neat rows of burgundy-colored volumes. Father Mike headed toward those.

"You said 1800s, right?" Father Mike started to reach for a book midway on the third shelf but stopped abruptly. "Oops, almost forgot. We need to wear gloves if we're going to touch these. Father Frank's rule, and a good one!" He got gloves for them both from a small cardboard box at the end of the shelf. Gloves on, he reached for the volume again, and opened it.

"Okay, we're in the right section. This is a register of statistics for St. Gregory, August through December 1860. Look at that penmanship." He showed Solomon the page. "Nobody writes like that anymore."

Solomon chose a volume a bit farther down the row. The men sat across from each other at a small workstation next to the copier. Solomon opened the heavy cardboard cover and looked at the title page.

"This one is for January to June 1870." He

carefully turned pages, scanning the list of names of deceased parishioners written with many loops and swirls.

Winter, deaths, Sarah . . . The joy of the hunt felt the lid bump. Grief and anger wanted out.

"I'm going to try another one," Solomon said after a few more pages. He got up and pulled a different journal off the shelf. "1899, minutes of St. Gregory council meetings," he said as he came back to the table. The room was quiet for a few minutes, the silence broken only by the soft sound of pages turning.

Suddenly Solomon spoke. "Father Lewis, listen to this." He ran his gloved finger under the peacock-blue ink as he read aloud. "'The roof of the chapel in the woods was damaged in last month's storm. Temporary repairs were made. St. Gregory's will share the cost of additional repairs.'" He looked at Father Mike. "I think the village was located where the park's second scenic overlook is now. In the 1800s there would have been a lot of woods there. Makes sense to call a church in that location the chapel in the woods." He turned more pages. "Here it is again, 'The chapel in the woods needs new altar cloths.'"

Father Mike replaced the volume he'd taken and chose one right next to the gap where Solomon's had been. "Budget and expenditures, 1899," he said after he'd opened the book. He sat down and turned pages slowly. "Well, isn't this interesting! An entire page dedicated to the chapel in the woods' finances. This chapel was no small operation. It looks like it was a mission of St. Gregory's." "Why weren't these people worshiping here, in our sanctuary? The second scenic outlook isn't that far away!"

Solomon's eyes met Father Mike's across the table. The joy of the hunt pressed him to bring Father Mike into his confidence. "Let me tell you a story," he said. He recounted what he knew about the village, the fire of 1900, Rachel Rinien's journals, and the three paintings in the attic of Rinien House. He showed Father Mike the photos on his phone.

"And bravo to Ms. Polding for wanting to right this wrong!" Father Mike said when Solomon finished. Did you know any of the other members of her family?"

"No, she was the only one left when Sarah and I moved here. Jonathan was a toddler—1991." The joy of the hunt felt the box lid pressing up hard against it, grief and anger demanding air. Memories flashed across Solomon's mind at lightning speed. Sarah, Jon, their then-new house on Madison Street. The joy of the hunt was holding on for dear life when Father Mike came to the rescue.

"Dr. Rigby, I'm intrigued by all this. I'd be happy to look for other references to the chapel."

"I appreciate the offer," Solomon said, "but—"

Father Mike looked at his watch. "Uh-oh, I should be in the sanctuary now!" He got up swiftly from his chair and laughed. "It's never good when the confessor has to confess first!"

The men reshelved the books, pushed in their chairs, and tossed their gloves in the trash can by the copier. They hurried to the door, and Solomon turned off the light. Father Mike relocked the door, and tested the knob just to be sure it was secure.

"What do you say, Dr. Rigby?" Father Mike asked as they crossed the carpet and hustled back up the stairs. "Helping you would give me a legitimate excuse to spend a bit more time in the archives, which I would love. And," he added wryly, "the justice angle fits in nicely with my calling."

Solomon laughed. "Okay, yes, I'd appreciate any help you can give."

"I'll check in with you next week, whether I find anything or not. Please tell Sam and Jonathan I said hello."

They shook hands and parted ways. Father Mike dashed in the direction of the sanctuary. Solomon darted across the parking lot to his car and got in. After he'd texted Jonathan, *I'm coming!* he started the car.

This has been a good day. I can't wait to tell Sarah—

Instantly the joy of the hunt was catapulted off the box by a deep surge of emotions from within.

Sarah. Sarah's not here anymore.

The pain peaked and gurgled down again. The joy of the hunt sat up, a bruised, quiet presence in Solomon's mind. Grief and anger sat next to it. The confluence of energies brought tears to his eyes, but to his surprise, didn't overwhelm him.

His car joined the line at the red light on Clay and Remembrance. The light changed, and he crossed to campus. He spotted Jonathan sitting on a bench in the shade behind Preston Hall, head down, a book open in his lap. Love for his son swooped in and overshadowed his other emotions. And then, after months of desuetude, gratitude joined love to flow over, under, around, and through them all. Solomon threaded his bow with his first arrow prayer since Sarah's death and let it fly.

Thank you, Lord, for my boys, for my work.

"Hi, son," he called out the window as he pulled into the parking place nearest the bench where Jonathan sat. "Sorry I'm late. It's been a very interesting day."

Chapter Eighteen

Jacoba stepped onto her front porch and closed the door behind her. She made sure she'd locked it and faced the bright Saturday morning, glad to be able to take a walk and think. She patted her jeans pockets one more time, reassured by the shapes of the house key and her phone. She rolled Marty's flyer into a cone and started out.

The walk to Tilden would take her through the north edge of her neighborhood and then, if she wanted to, she could take the shortcut through the college apartments to the main campus. As she walked along the sidewalk, she heard the City Hall clock tart to chime. Ten o'clock. She reached the edge of the apartment complex and stood there for a moment. The three rectangular red-brick buildings angled out in front of her with a walkway snaking between them. Several students, backpacks in hand, moved ahead of her in the same direction she was traveling. She smiled as she watched heads go down, almost in unison, eyes on cell phones.

She was glad hers hadn't rung yet this morning. She pulled her phone out of her pocket to silence the ringer. She wanted to escape the growing chorus of voices reacting to her contract decision. By Friday morning the news was out. Friday afternoon Mrs. Pratt had been waiting outside her classroom door with tears in her eyes.

"I am so sorry you are leaving," she'd said quietly. "This has been my Lillian's best year."

Judy Ko and Lisa Warren had detained her in the parking lot for a lengthy conversation. Friday evening two other teachers had called, and that conversation had kept her up past her bedtime.

Jacoba stopped at the edge of Remembrance Road and joined the students who were waiting to cross, their heads still bent over their phones. The traffic light turned red, and they moved en masse to the other side. Heads came up momentarily, they chose what direction to take, and heads went back down again. Jacoba started the short walk to the coffee shop. Just as she caught her reflection in the coffee shop windows, she heard a voice call out behind her.

"Ms. D! Ms. D!"

A tall, curly-haired young man in blue jeans joined her reflection in the glass. She turned around to face him, wondering who this was.

"Ms. D! It's me, Jon, Jonathan Rigby!"

"Oh, my goodness, Jon! What a lovely surprise!" She searched Jonathan's face, trying to find the fourth grader she'd known nine years before. She caught glimpses of the younger version in his eyes and mouth. "Are you a student here at Tilden?" she asked.

"Yes, finishing up my freshman year," Jonathan replied proudly.

Several people walked past them and entered the coffee shop. "Jonathan, do you have time for a cup of coffee? I'd love to hear how you're doing, what your plans are."

"I'd like that," Jonathan said. "I'm meeting my study group in the library in," he looked at his watch, "forty-five minutes. One more exam to go."

"Perfect! Come on."

Jonathan stepped ahead and held the door open for Jacoba. They walked up to the counter, and he pulled out his wallet. "Ms. D, let me buy your coffee. I'm trying to fill up my card to get a free one. If I buy two cups at once, I get double credit."

Jacoba laughed. "Sure. I'll be happy to help you toward your goal."

Coffees in hand, they moved to a table near the windows at the front of the shop.

"I need cream and sugar. Can I get anything for you?" Jonathan asked.

"Just a packet of sugar, thanks," Jacoba said as she slid out her chair. She pulled her phone out of her pocket and laid it on the table. She sat down, and after checking to make sure the table surface was dry, she set the flyer next to the napkin dispenser.

"Here you go," Jonathan said as he handed her a stirring stick, and a sugar packet.

"Such service," Jacoba said approvingly. She tore the sugar packet open and carefully poured its contents into her coffee. As she stirred, she looked across the table at Jonathan. "So, Jon, talk to me. I can't believe you are in college now!"

Jonathan opened two creamers and added their contents to his coffee. Then he opened three sugar packets, poured those in, and vigorously stirred the light-brown liquid in his cup. "I'm really enjoying my classes here," he said after he'd taken a sip. "And for the most part, I like my professors."

"I'm so sorry about what happened to your mom." Jacoba put both hands around her coffee and looked sympathetically at Jonathan. "I can't imagine how hard losing her must have been, must still be . . ."

"Missing Mom doesn't go away, but I'm doing okay. It's not constantly on my mind the way it was right after the accident."

"I see your little brother on the playground almost every day," Jacoba said.

"Yeah, Sam. He's doing okay too. Sometimes he's a bit of a pest, but for the most part, we're good." Jonathan grinned across the table, and Jacoba smiled back.

"I'm sure you are an awesome big brother," she said. "And your father? Is he still teaching American History here?"

"Yup," said Jonathan. He took a sip of coffee and looked out the window.

Jacoba couldn't miss the sudden chill in the air. She changed the subject. "So, do you have any ideas about what you want to be when you grow up? You were one sharp fourth grader."

Jonathan didn't answer.

"Sorry, Jon, force of habit," Jacoba said. "I always wonder what my students will grow up to be!"

"Actually, I'm glad you asked." Jonathan picked up the coffee stirrer next to his cup and put his elbows on the table. "I loved all the things we did in your room: the story after lunch, the mailboxes, the sky-watching charts we filled out in our backyards at night. When my mom did those with me, we talked about God. That's when I first thought about becoming a priest."

Jacoba sat back in her chair. She hadn't expected this. She didn't know what to say. Silence settled between them again. She noticed Jonathan didn't seem bothered at all by the lag in conversation.

"My mom was all for it," Jonathan said after a moment or two. "I really miss her, and I miss her support."

"I'm sure you do, Jon," Jacoba said softly.

Suddenly a repeating beep erupted from Jonathan's side of the table and caused Jacoba to jump.

"Oh, sorry! That's my ten-minute warning for meeting with my study group. Guess I better get going."

"Thank you for the coffee. I'm so glad you saw me on the sidewalk!" Jacoba reached for her phone and the flyer. "Jon, can you point me in the direction of the job board? I want to post this." She held up the paper cylinder.

"It's right over there, by the restrooms. Looking for someone to grade papers?" he joked.

"Now there's an idea," Jacoba laughed. "No, my friend, Marty Blankenship, owns the antique store downtown, and she's looking for some part-time help. Know anybody who might be interested?"

"Yes, me!"

"You're kidding!"

"I'm definitely interested. But," he added regretfully, "I don't know anything about antiques."

"Oh, no worries there. Marty's looking for someone who can lift and carry inventory. You don't have to know what you're moving; you just have to be careful moving it! Think you might be able to stop by the store for an interview today?"

"Yes! I'll be done with my study group by twelve thirty. I could be there at around one."

"Excellent! You know where Behind the Times is, right?"

"On the corner of Cherry and High Market?"

"Yes. Oh, this is so great! No need to post this." She stuck the flyer in her pocket. "I have a pretty good idea how your interview will go."

Jonathan lifted his backpack and slung it over one shoulder. "One o'clock, Marty Blankenship. Got it. Thanks, Ms. D."

Jacoba watched Jonathan leave the coffee shop and break into a run on the sidewalk. In a few seconds he was no longer in her line of vision. She sat back and took a sip of coffee. She hardly noticed the cooled liquid as she swallowed. She was reaching back in her memory for Jonathan's fourth-grade year. She smiled to herself when she thought about the things he remembered, especially the chart and the fact that Jonathan's mother had done the assignment with him.

And now he's thinking about becoming a priest. Isn't that something!

Still savoring the conversation, she got up, threw away her almost empty coffee cup, and started the walk home. She waited until she'd gotten past the apartments to call Marty.

"Behind the Times, Marty Blankenship speaking."

"Exciting News, Jacoba Dahm speaking!"

Marty laughed on the other end of the line.

"Marty, I'm sending you a job applicant. Jonathan Rigby. He's a former student of mine. He'll be there at one. You are going to love him!"

"Great! Can't wait to meet him. Oh, sorry, Jacoba, line forming on my end. Gotta go!"

Jacoba grinned as she slipped her phone into her pocket. She headed east on the sidewalk along Cherry Street. Cars zipped past her, creating a refreshing breeze. She briefly considered showing up at the store during Jonathan's interview, but immediately decided against it. Marty needed to make up her mind about Jonathan without undue pressure from a highly biased associate.

"And I am highly biased," Jacoba said to herself

as she crossed Cherry at a four-way stop and turned south. A car honked at her and the driver waved. Jacoba recognized a parent of one of her fourth graders. She smiled and waved back. She reached the corner of her street and started down the uneven sidewalk. Tree roots had broken through the concrete in several places, making foot traffic difficult. Jacoba decided to skirt one particularly damaged section of pavement altogether and stepped into the grassy lawn that ran alongside it just a few feet from her own driveway. She looked in the direction of the little house she called home and sighed. Several stacks of papers awaited her on her kitchen table.

That's something I will not miss, she thought. *The never-ending job of grading papers.*

Jonathan hurried along the sidewalk that passed under the pedestrian bridge on Cherry Street. He'd had a hard time participating in the study group. All he could think about was the job opportunity. He'd hoped to get the car for the trip to the antique mall, but it hadn't been parked where he and his dad had left it earlier in the morning. So he was walking.

The hospital rose ahead on his left. The antique mall was two corners after this one. A man with a large teddy bear and balloons disappeared through the hospital's double doors as Jonathan walked along the north side of the building. He looked toward the park. The lot near the park's back entrance was full. He could see three runners moving together along the jogging trail. Once he'd passed the medical arts building, he saw Behind the Times on the corner of the next block. He crossed High Market Street and stopped in front of the store's large plate-glass windows. Beyond the glass he could see rows of furniture, shelves of dishes and glassware, and people moving up and down the aisles.

His initial excitement about the possibility of part-time employment took a nosedive. Doubts mingled with the aromas of fresh-baked bread and oregano from the Italian restaurant a few yards away.

What am I doing here? Jonathan asked himself. *I've never had a real job.* He looked through the window again at the glassware. *What if I break something that's worth more than what I make in a week, or a month?*

"Excuse me, excuse me!"

Jonathan turned around and saw a hand truck piled high with liquor boxes. A woman peered at him over the top box.

"Could you please hold the door for me?"

Jonathan quickly moved to the front door and pulled it open, the cowbell clanging over his head. The woman struggled to get the hand truck over the sill, the boxes tipping precariously.

"Here, let me. You hold the door." Jonathan

switched places with the woman. He rested one hand firmly on the top box and slowly swung the hand truck around. He went backward through the door into the mall's entryway.

"They go right this way."

Jonathan followed the bouncing ponytail down a wide aisle. He noticed the sparkling sequins on her shirt and jeans. His mom would have loved those. A tiny wave of grief lapped around the edges of his heart. He looked at the woman again. He was pretty sure she was much older than his mother. For some reason that made him feel better. He brought the cart through a beaded curtain to a little workroom.

"Just park them right here. I can do the rest. Thank you again."

Jonathan walked slowly back up to the front of the store, intrigued by all the merchandise that surrounded him. Dulcimer music played softly in the background. When the woman behind the checkout counter finished with the customer she was helping, Jonathan stepped forward.

"My name is Jonathan Rigby. I'm here for an interview with Marty Blankenship."

"Oh, Jonathan! I'm Marty Blankenship. I saw you come in, and I thought you were with Crystal." Marty came around the corner of the counter and shook Jonathan's hand. "Congratulations! You just passed one of the tests for working here: you successfully moved a hand truck full of boxes from point A to point B." She stepped into the aisle ahead of Jonathan. "I need to stay close to the front. Busy day today."

Jonathan followed her the short distance to the café area. He sat down when she did. He felt his confidence wavering again.

"So, Jonathan, did you bring a résumé?"

"I don't have a résumé." He looked down at his empty hands. "And I've never had a job." He could feel the heat rise in his face. His cheeks must be turning red.

The woman in the other chair shifted a bit. "Ever mow grass in your neighborhood?"

"Oh, yes! I mow several lawns."

"And what about housesitting, or dogsitting, or babysitting?"

"I have a younger brother, Sam. I've been his babysitter lots of times, but we don't call it babysitting, we call it brother-sitting."

Marty laughed. "Brother-sitting. I like that. What about volunteering?"

Jonathan thought for a minute. "I helped stock shelves at the food bank twice last winter. And my entire senior year, I was part of a group of students who visited Grancy's Daycare once a week and read to preschoolers."

"Nice!"

The cowbell clanged.

"Customer. I'll be right back. Everyone who comes in that door gets a personal greeting!"

Marty walked quickly to the front. Jonathan took a couple deep breaths. He wasn't at all sure how the interview was going. At least he'd had an answer for each of Mrs. Blankenship's questions. The dulcimer music stopped and after about ten seconds began again. Jonathan thought he recognized the tune, but he wasn't sure. Taking another deep breath, he was aware of a subtle fragrance all around him. He had no idea what it was. What if Mrs. Blankenship asked him to identify it?

He glanced up and noticed the balcony area for the first time. He leaned back to get a better look. Someone was moving high above him along the balcony railing. "I wonder how you get up there?"

Sunlight suddenly came streaming through the skylights. Jonathan looked away from the glare, and his gaze fell on the worn oak surface of the table in front of him. He ran his hand along the rounded edge.

"It's beautiful, isn't it?" Marty sat back down next to him. "We found it downstairs a few years ago when we put in the new furnace. And that brings me to the next part of your interview." She looked expectantly at Jonathan. "You've already demonstrated your skill at using a hand truck. Now I want to see what you can do with the mess in the basement."

Jonathan followed Marty across the main floor. She turned and disappeared behind a large, square brick column. When he came around the column, he discovered two sets of stairs: one going up and the other going down. Marty was already halfway down the stairs.

"It will take me a second to get to the light," Marty said. "Be careful. The stairs are steep."

Jonathan took his time. With each step down he noticed the air was cooler. He'd just reached the bottom step when he heard glass shattering.

"Shoot! I wonder what I just broke?"

Jonathan heard the raspy *ka-ching* of a pull chain, and light splashed out into the space. He could see a jumble of cardboard boxes and other objects strewn haphazardly across the floor. Marty picked her way carefully back to his side.

"Your assignment is to clear a path from here," she pointed to the ground where they stood, "all the way to the other stairs on the west end of the basement." She pointed into the dark recesses beyond them. "Got an electrician coming Monday morning, and he needs to be able to walk down here. I'll bring you a broom and a dustpan for the broken glass." She started back up the stairs.

Jonathan stepped into the basement and looked in the direction the path was supposed to go. "Makes the most sense to start where I can see what I'm doing," he said to himself.

He'd already moved three boxes when Marty came back down the stairs with the broom and dustpan. "Here you go, Jonathan," she said as she leaned the broom against the wall and put the dustpan next to it. "And if you find gold, we split it fifty-fifty!"

Jonathan laughed.

Marty headed back up the stairs.

After lugging two more boxes out of the circle of light, Jonathan could see bare floor and a fistful of glass shards. He got the broom, swept the glass out of his way, and reached for another box. When he lifted it a glass chimney rolled past his feet. He put the box next to the others and turned back to retrieve the chimney.

"I wonder if the lantern this belongs to is down here somewhere?" He stepped carefully, looking down between boxes, but it was too dark to see. He turned back into the light and reached for another box.

"Whoa, feels like a box of rocks!" Jonathan barely lifted it off the ground before letting it fall back. The lid slid to one side. "Well, what do you know! It is a box of rocks! Why would there be a box of rocks down here?" He remembered Mrs. Blankenship's words. "I wonder what gold looks like?" He reached into the box and pulled out a rock. It was heavy in his hands. Dirt fell away from it as he held it closer to the light. It looked like the rocks in his backyard.

He put it back, readjusted the lid, and started to push the box across the floor with both hands. With some stops and starts he slid it over to the growing line just beyond the staircase. In the next ten minutes he discovered four more boxes of rocks. Once he'd pushed them over to join the others, he stood up to survey his progress.

The floor was clear from the bottom step to the other side of the lit section of the basement.

Jonathan stared in the direction of the stairs Mrs. Blankenship had indicated were at the far end of the room. He couldn't see anything. It suddenly occurred to him that there must be a door at the top of those stairs and opening it would let light into that end of the basement.

He walked under the lightbulb and stopped at the edge of its circle of influence. He took a tentative step forward, and then another, and another. After about ten steps he was standing in deep gloom. He held his hand in front of his face. He could barely see it. He looked back to the cleared floor space. It was an island in an ocean of dark. He turned back around and started to slide his feet forward, one foot at a time. He was suddenly aware of the sweet smell of lumber mixed with the damp mustiness of basement. It reminded him of junior high shop class. The toe of his shoe hit something solid, and he reached down to touch it. His fingers slid across the tread of a stair step and bumped into the hard plastic of a flashlight barrel.

"Yes!"

He picked up the flashlight and turned it on. A beam of light shot out into the dark. He aimed it on wide treads leading right up to the basement ceiling.

"Aha! A trapdoor!" Jonathan walked up the steps until the trapdoor was just above him. If he sat under the door, he could use the upper part of his body to push it open.

His first push against the wooden panel was

tentative. He wanted to get some idea of what he was up against. The panel didn't budge. He pushed harder. The panel still didn't budge.

"I wonder if there's something on top of it?"

He took a deep breath and tried again. Did the panel move? He wasn't sure. He scooted down one step so he could add his leg muscles to the push. He gritted his teeth and tried a fourth time. Suddenly the panel came unstuck, swung open, and hit the floor above Jonathan's head with a deafening bang. Light poured in all around him.

"What was that?" Jonathan heard Marty's startled voice close by. "Is everybody okay?'

Jonathan stood up and found himself eye level with the legs of several chairs and the bottom of a beaded curtain. "I did it," he called out guiltily. "I made the noise." He reached the top step and climbed into the room where Marty was standing.

Her astonishment gave way almost immediately to laughter. "My husband has tried to open that trapdoor for years," she said in awe as she looked down into the hole behind Jonathan. "I didn't expect you to get this far this fast!"

"I still have a lot to do," Jonathan said. "I was just hoping to get more light down there."

"Great idea," Marty said.

Jonathan sat on the edge of the hole in the floor and dangled his legs until his feet hit a step. He stood up, carefully turned around, and started going backward down the stairs. The trapdoor allowed enough light into the space to make his descent easier. He retrieved the flashlight along the way.

Once he was back on the basement floor, he pointed the light under and behind the stairs, revealing the stone and mortar foundation. *I wonder how old this building is?* The sweet aroma of cut lumber floated past him again, but he didn't see wood or woodworking equipment anywhere.

He walked back and stood under the bulb hanging from the ceiling. His curiosity got the better of him, and he kept the flashlight on. He trained the beam along the wall on the north side of the building. He could make out brick arches, a small wooden door, and farther down a coal delivery chute. He traced watermarks on the stone all the way to the front of the store, where the basement floor sloped up abruptly. He started walking toward the front, but debris on the floor stopped him before he got far. Stacks of furniture piled up ahead of him—tables, chairs, a couple file cabinets, and boxes, many boxes, imploded or sagging or their contents spilling out onto the floor.

He retraced his steps and stopped just beyond the hanging lightbulb, where he set aside the flashlight. The next box he lifted was light, the lid tightly fastened. Faded handwriting was scrawled on one side of the box, but he couldn't make out the words. The box after that one was much heavier. When Jonathan lifted it, the contents shifted.

"Feels like books," he said. The same illegible

handwriting covered one side. He carried both boxes over to the others.

The third box had handholds. He put his hand into the slots and lifted it off the floor. Without warning the bottom of the box gave way, and the contents came pouring out. Jonathan looked down on a mound of brown file folders covering his shoes. He flipped the box upside down so the snugly fitting lid was now the box bottom. He set it on the ground, picked up a few folders at a time, and started to stack them in the box. Once the folders were back together again, he shoved the box across the floor to join the others. Two more boxes and a partial Christmas tree later, he was done. He stood back and surveyed his work. The way was clear now for one person, maybe two, to get from one staircase to the other.

Marty appeared at the top of the stairs nearest him. "Nice job!" she said as she came down the steps. "This is great! The electrician should be able to make something work down here. Now let's go upstairs and finish our conversation."

Jonathan followed her up, and they sat at the round oak table again.

"As far as I'm concerned, you're hired." Marty reached for a sheet of paper in the center of the table. "I just need your contact information and a couple references. Once I've checked those, I'll call you in for a scheduling/orientation meeting. You'll be hearing from me midweek at the latest."

Jonathan wrote down his address and phone

number. *Two references. Well, Ms. Dahm will be one. Who for the other? Father Mike. Yes, Father Mike.*

Jonathan handed Marty the information and headed for the front door. He was ready for the sound of the cowbell this time. He crossed High Market, checked his watch, and started to walk a little faster. He was supposed to meet his dad for the drive home soon. An interior spark of optimism warmed and energized him. He started whistling "Dona nobis Pacem" as he headed back to campus.

Thanks, Lord. Thanks for showing me what I can do now.

Chapter Nineteen

Jacoba listened to the rise and fall of child-chatter beyond her desk. As long as it stayed at this level she wasn't going to say anything. She wanted the last afternoon with her fourth graders to end on a high note.

Mrs. Pratt came and stood next to her, an empty cardboard box in hand. Her auburn bangs stuck to her forehead, and a dark line of moisture marked the neck and underarms of her red T-shirt. "Back cabinets are empty, boxes labeled for whoever teaches fourth grade next year," she said. "Your desk drawers are next. And then we're done!"

"Great!" Jacoba looked down at the last of the paperwork for the front office. "I'm almost finished here. Give me a couple more minutes, and then we can go through the drawers together."

"Good. I could use a water break," Mrs. Pratt said. She put the box on the floor. "Think one will be enough, or should I get another one?"

"Why don't you get another one, just to be on the safe side."

Mrs. Pratt headed toward the hallway. Lillian intercepted her, gave her a hug, and ran back to her seat. Jacoba rechecked the page and filled in the last blank.

"Sophie, would you please take this to Dr. Miller's office? Mrs. Globe is waiting for it."

She looked at the clock on the far wall. The minute hand was inching closer and closer to dismissal time.

Come on, Jacoba. You're in the homestretch now. You'll get it all done. You always do.

Jacoba pulled open the center desk drawer. Pencils, pens, and paperclips jostled, jingled, and rolled around in the broad, shallow space. She did a quick assessment of the deeper desk drawers. "I can recycle some of this and take the rest home," she said to herself.

She'd started sorting and organizing the center drawer's contents when an impatient triple rap on the doorframe caused her to look up. Two burly men parked a hand truck at the door.

"We're here to move boxes," the taller one said as they walked toward her desk.

"Already?" Jacoba said in surprise. "Before dismissal?"

"Cleaning crew arrives at four. Gotta get all the boxes out, furniture stacked ahead of them."

"Okay. The boxes are in the back." Jacoba and the children watched as the men expertly maneuvered the hand truck between the rows of desks and started piling boxes onto it.

"Friends," Jacoba said, taking advantage of the momentary silence, "check in your desks and in your cubbies one more time. Make sure you aren't leaving anything behind. It will be time to go soon."

Time to go. It's all happening so fast.

Desk lids creaked up and clunked back down. Conversations resumed as children traveled over to the cubby side of the room. Mrs. Pratt reappeared with a second box and put it down beside the other one. Before Jacoba could say anything, there was another knock on the door. Barb Globe hurried over to Jacoba's desk and scooted in front of Mrs. Pratt with an apologetic smile.

"Ms. Dahm, I need your signature on these three pages, and Dr. Miller wants your answer to this question." She put the papers down in front of Jacoba. "I'll wait right here and take them back."

Lips tight, Jacoba grabbed a pen out of the open drawer. She signed where the secretary indicated and wrote a succinct sentence in a space clearly intended for paragraphs. Barb looked like she was about to comment on the brevity of Jacoba's response, but when their eyes met, she beat a hasty retreat.

"Time for speed-packing, Mrs. Pratt," Jacoba said. "I'll sort through it all later."

Mrs. Pratt knelt beside the desk and pulled open the bottom drawer. "I won't pack your purse," she laughed.

"Thank you!"

Jacoba grabbed the other box and started dumping drawer contents into it. They were closing the last drawers when the familiar click of the public address system redirected their attention.

"Good afternoon, everyone." Dr. Miller's voice

filled the room. "May I remind you: Everyone must be out of the building by three thirty, and the parking lot should be empty no later than three forty. Teachers, leave your classroom doors open, bring keys and record books to the front office. Work crews are already standing by to move in as soon as we are out of the way." The PA system clicked off but then clicked on again. "Have a wonderful summer. See you back here in the fall!"

"If you'll give me your car keys," Mrs. Pratt said, "I'll put these boxes in your trunk."

"I can carry these last two boxes out; you've helped so much already."

"No, no," Mrs. Pratt insisted. "I'm happy to do it. Lillian can go with me right now and carry one. You have been such a blessing." She put out her hand and forced a smile through her tears. "Keys, please!"

Jacoba took the car keys out of the front pocket of her purse and handed them to Mrs. Pratt. "My trunk is already full. These will have to go in the backseat. You know which car is mine?"

"Oh, yes," she answered confidently.

Jacoba looked at the clock: three minutes to dismissal. She stood up. All eyes were on her. Talking stopped. She pinched herself to stem the rising tide of tears. She forced as broad a smile as she could muster, and announced with dramatic flourish, "I'm proud of you. I'll never forget you. I now pronounce you fifth graders!"

The bell rang, and cheers echoed throughout

the building. Jacoba's students shouldered their backpacks for the last trip through this particular classroom door. Jacoba kept her composure amidst her children's hugs, thank-yous, and tears. Mrs. Pratt handed back the car keys, hugged her, and followed Lillian out the door. Billy Barnes marched past her, eyes straight ahead, bulging backpack clutched to his chest.

"Have a good summer," she repeated for the sixteenth time to his retreating back. She watched him step into the stream of children headed to the main hallway. *And may your next teacher get your number early on.*

The hallway emptied in short order. She went back to her desk, sat down, and looked at bare bulletin boards, student desks askew, and the empty milk carton mailboxes on the windowsill. The mailboxes were the only sign that she, Jacoba Dahm, had taught in this classroom.

Dr. Miller won't be pleased if they stay there.

She smirked for a moment before she chastised herself. *Jacoba Dahm, you were brought up better than that.* But she didn't get up. Instead she pulled out her phone and saw Marty had texted her.

"Stop by on your way home?" Jacoba read aloud. She texted back a thumbs-up, put her phone in her purse, and reached in her pocket for her car keys. Time to go. Out of habit she turned to grab the handles of her canvas bag, only to discover it wasn't in its usual place.

Right! Mrs. Pratt packed it. No more papers to grade!

Judy Ko called to her from the doorway. "Shall we turn in our record books together? If you're with me, I know you'll keep me from hitting anyone over the head with mine."

They both laughed.

At precisely 3:35, Jacoba backed out of her parking space and joined the mass exodus from the parking lot.

Last time.

She turned onto Salazar, then River Street, and then High Market, where downtown's afternoon energy was in evidence. To her left someone was rearranging the sandwich signs at the entrance of the Alley Cat Bar and Grille. On her right the perpendicular parking spaces in front of the new gift shop, Baa Baa Black Sheep, were all taken. She drove to the alley at the back of Behind the Times and pulled up under the mall sign. She made her mandatory river check, rolled her eyes at the not-unexpected open back door, and entered the storeroom. She was surprised by several chairs blocking her path to the glass bead curtain. She was even more surprised by the open trapdoor. She walked around the chair barricade, pushed through the beads, and started up the aisle, expecting to see Marty. The *ding-ding* of the push bell on the front counter prompted her to walk a little faster. She greeted the waiting shoppers across the counter and was searching for a receipt pad and pen when Marty materialized at her elbow.

"Jacoba! I wasn't expecting you today."

Jacoba turned a questioning eye on her friend. "But Marty, you texted me."

Marty looked back at her, confused. "I did?" Then her face lit up. "Oh, yes, I did! What's wrong with me?"

For the next few minutes Marty wrapped purchases and chatted with customers while Jacoba handled cash and receipts.

"Come on!" Marty said as they waved the last patron out the door. "I want you to see the basement. You won't believe it!"

They walked together to the stairs.

"Stay here."

Hand on the railing, Marty quickly made her way down to the basement floor. Suddenly bright light from below illuminated the worn stair treads. The pits and cracks in the brick wall that supported the handrail were visible in sharp relief.

"Come on down, Jacoba!"

When Jacoba got to the bottom step, she saw the underground room as she'd never seen it before. Four banks of tube lighting hung from the ceiling in front of her, and the resulting brightness exposed a topsy-turvy sea of boxes and other miscellaneous debris. The bright light extended all the way to the staircase at the river end of the room.

"Wow, Marty!" Jacoba stepped onto the basement floor. "This is amazing!"

"I know! I'm so excited! Once we've dealt with the mess down here, there will be room for several booths, don't you think?"

Jacoba moved farther into the basement and looked around. "Yes," she said. "Absolutely. I can't get over the difference the lights make!"

Her eyes fell on the little door set in the north wall, and she stepped over several boxes for a better look.

"Reminds me of the door to my grandmother's root cellar," Marty said, following her progress. "It was so low I had to duck to go in or out."

Jacoba reached for the doorknob. "The knob turns, but the door is shut tight." She looked back out over the newly visible space toward the river end of the basement. "And the trapdoor is open! Bob finally succeeded?"

Marty laughed. "Nope. Your Jonathan opened it on Saturday when he was here for his interview! And you can thank him for the path from one set of stairs to the other."

"No kidding! Isn't he a great kid?"

"Great young man," Marty corrected approvingly. "Yes, he is, and he starts Monday."

"Good! We'll begin our summer stints together!"

"Oh, Jacoba." Marty gave her a stricken look. "Today was your last day. I completely forgot!"

"No worries, Marty. Really," Jacoba said. "It's a relief to be done. I'm looking forward to working here, doing something completely different." The sharp *ding-ding* of the checkout counter bell summoned them back upstairs.

An hour or so later, Jacoba pulled into her

garage and turned off the ignition. She sat there for a moment, the busy day catching up with her. She got out of the car, purse and keys in hand. Her stomach growled.

Wish I'd thought to stop at Marcellino's on the way home. Quick snack first, then boxes.

She unlocked the door into the kitchen and hung her purse from the back of one of the kitchen chairs. After she'd washed her hands, she got the peanut butter jar out of the pantry, collected a sleeve of saltines from the freezer, and grabbed a plate and knife. She sat down and looked at the items in front of her. Something was missing.

Grape jelly. The last day of school calls for grape jelly.

She took the small glass jar out of the refrigerator door and sat back down. She slathered a generous knife full of peanut butter on a cracker first, and then dipped the knife into the grape mixture. When she pulled the knife back out, a little brown snake of peanut butter remained in the jelly.

"One of the benefits of living alone," Jacoba declared into the kitchen. "I'm the only one to care if I get peanut butter in the jelly." After she'd made herself five cracker snacks, she dipped the knife into the peanut butter for one more small taste.

"No one will care if I lick the knife either!"

Snack consumed, she was ready to face the boxes.

Work smarter, not harder, she thought as she let

the lid of her trunk swing up. *Where can I put these so I don't have to move them more than once?*

She looked around the garage and then back into the trunk. She reached for the Jeremy box. Yesterday, she and the children had packed all the memorial tokens they'd left on Jeremy's desk. Then they'd solemnly processed out to the parking lot and put "the Jeremy box," as they'd called it, in her trunk. She'd promised the children she would bring it to Mr. and Mrs. Davis.

I want this to stay clean and bug free. It should go in the guest room closet until I can deliver it. The rest of the boxes can stay right here in the garage until I sort through them.

Jacoba put the Jeremy box on the step by the kitchen door and went back to the trunk. She hefted the boxes out one by one and stacked them along the wall to the right of her front bumper. A few minutes later, she slammed the lid on the empty trunk and walked around to the backseat.

"Last two!" she said to herself. "And then supper, shower, and bed."

When she opened the door, she noticed something on the other side of the boxes, just out of reach. She went around to the other side of the car and discovered a scrapbook on the seat.

Oh my, oh, Mrs. Pratt!

She took it right to the kitchen table, made sure the surface was free of peanut butter and jelly, set it down, and parked herself in front of it. She read the title on the rectangular purple paisley cover,

Time with Ms. D. A short note from Mrs. Pratt was penned on the inside:

> *Thank you for opening the children's eyes to the wonders all around us. You opened the eyes of some grown-ups too! Thank you for the ways you helped us all, children and parents, grieve for Jeremy. This has been a hard spring, but what a blessing to have traveled through it with you. You will be missed.*
>
> > *Grace and peace,*
> > *Kimberly Pratt*

Tears rolled down Jacoba's cheeks as she turned the pages of the scrapbook. In drawing after drawing she recognized versions of herself either perched on her stool in front of the class with a book in her hands or standing under the big tree on the playground. She laughed out loud when Judy Ko's unmistakable black hair and trim figure appeared next to her in one of the pictures. When she got to the end she started over again, this time searching each drawing for the artist's name. She looked, smiled, and continued to the next one. Oh, how she was going to miss her little community of children.

In the last picture the artist had placed the children and Jacoba in a circle. She counted seventeen children, one with a halo over his head. *Who drew this?* She started to guess. *Maybe Jake Hirsch. Or*

Sophie. There was no signature on the front, so she turned the page over and gasped. *Billy. Billy Barnes.* She sat back in astonishment. *Billy?* Her stomach gurgled, redirecting her attention. Boxes. She needed to finish dealing with the boxes.

She took the scrapbook to the living room and put it down reverently on the coffee table. She went back out to the garage, retrieved the boxes from the backseat, and put them with the others. She brought the Jeremy box inside to the guest room, where she slid open the louvered closet doors and set it on the floor under the row of empty coat hangers.

Done.

The scrapbook on the coffee table called to her as she passed it on the way to the kitchen. She came back and flipped to the last page. Where was Billy in the drawing? It didn't take long to find him. One child sat apart from the others, not completely out of the circle, but almost. That child was as far away from Jeremy as it was possible to be. She traced the circle of children with her finger. One at a time she identified her students. She was amused by Billy's creative portrayal of each of his classmates. Sophie, one of the brightest children in the room, wore a headband made of oversized stars. Timid, shy Lillian sported bunny ears. Maddie and Jake Hirsch were dressed in identical shirts and baseball caps with coach's whistles on black cords around their necks. Jacoba followed the circle to Jeremy. Was there more than the halo to differentiate him from his classmates? Yes. Jeremy, the writer, held a pencil and pad of paper. A memory danced at the edge of her thoughts.

The poem. I forgot all about Jeremy's poem!

In her mind's eye she saw Jeremy walk up to her desk on that fateful Thursday afternoon, poem in hand, and proudly proclaim, "My best ever." What had he called it? Something long and flowery. Jacoba closed her eyes and opened them again, chagrinned.

Did I even look for it after Detective Roe and I talked about it? No, no, I didn't. I never even thought about it again.

"It doesn't matter," she said firmly to herself. "It doesn't matter. It's over. The year is done, and I'm done with it. I'm ready to do something completely different." She got up and headed to the kitchen. "Something completely, absolutely, positively, totally different."

Chapter Twenty

Simon got up from his desk and turned the fan more in his direction. July in Grandburg was not for the fainthearted. He looked to the windows along the east wall. Sunlight streamed through the blinds. Closing them now would buy him at least another half hour of cooler working conditions. As he twisted the first tilt wand, his eyes traveled up the street to City Hall. William Barnes was making his condo proposal to the city commissioners there this morning. Simon looked down at his watch. The meeting must be almost over by now.

"I was surprised he asked me to join his team instead of the realtor he used for the condos on the greens project," Dar had said earlier that morning as she had poured cornflakes into a blue glass bowl. After adding milk, she'd dipped her spoon into her cereal and stirred it thoughtfully.

"You haven't said yes, have you." Simon bit into a piece of toast. He didn't want Dar working with William Barnes after what Sally Groegan had said. But this was Dar's decision to make.

Dar scooped a spoonful of cereal, ate it, and started talking again. "I can't get past the *Times* story about the Native Americans—their land stolen, their village burned to the ground. I know it happened over one hundred years ago, but wrong is wrong." She looked pointedly across the table at Simon. "Is there a statute of limitations on justice being done?"

"Not in my book, but I am a detective, after all."

"That land should be given back to the tribe."

They finished breakfast in a companionable silence. Dar got up, took her empty bowl to the sink, and rinsed it out before she plunked it down in the dishwasher rack. She poured herself a second cup of coffee and came back to the table.

"And Sime, the park—the second scenic overlook will be gone. I shudder at the thought of condos built on that beautiful site. The perimeter road will have to be rerouted, the Prayer Trail moved." She sipped her coffee and reached for the sugar bowl. "Seriously, does Grandburg even need more high-end housing?"

Simon looked across the table at this woman he adored. "Ah, my love, you're preaching to the choir."

"I know," Dar had said softly.

Simon twisted the last tilt wand and went back to his desk. The fan breeze gently ruffled the paperwork in front of him. The justice angle made the decision clear for him. The land didn't belong to the city of Grandburg or to William Barnes; it belonged to the Native Americans.

"Good morning, Detective." Richard plunked down in the chair next to Simon's desk. "And a hot morning it is!" He turned so he was more in line with the fan.

"You're blocking my air, Mr. Barclay," Simon laughed and rolled his chair a few inches to the right. A text bell sounded. "Your phone or mine?"

Richard checked his phone. "Yours."

Simon reached for his phone on the desk blotter, read the message, and texted back. "Hold down the fort, Mr. Barclay. Mrs. Roe requests my presence for lunch. She's waiting for me in the parking garage."

"I'll do my best!" Richard gave Simon a jaunty salute and moved over to his own desk.

Simon's hand hovered reluctantly over his suitcoat. He reminded himself the walk to the car would be short, so he'd only be moderately sweaty when he got there. On his way out the door he stopped next to the fan just long enough to reorient the breeze toward Richard.

"Thanks, sir." Richard grinned back at him and powered up his computer monitor.

Simon took the stairs down to the parking garage. A humid blanket of air wrapped itself around him as soon as he opened the door to the outside. Dar's car was right by the curb. He slid into the seat, slammed the door, and turned the passenger-side air conditioner vents in his direction.

"So, how was it?" he asked as he pulled the seatbelt across his chest and lap.

"Awful." Dar pulled away from the curb and headed for the exit. "Could we go to the Alley Cat? I'm sure Barnes will be at Marcellino's."

"Sure. I haven't had my quota of Alley Cat tuna

this week!" He looked over at his wife, hoping to get a chuckle out of her, but she didn't even turn her head.

It was still early enough to find a parking place in front of the bar and grille. Simon opened the restaurant's door for Dar and followed her past the latest cat art on the entryway walls. As usual the statuesque Shantal greeted them from the hostess podium.

"Detective, Mrs. Roe! Welcome to the Alley Cat." Shantal picked up two menus and stepped in front of them. "Your usual booth, Detective?"

"Booth, Dar, or table?"

"I wish we could eat on the patio, but it's too hot." Dar looked past Shantal into the main dining room. "Could we sit at that corner table?"

"Absolutely! Right this way, please."

Simon glanced at his favorite booth as they passed it. Mezzo, the elegant Siamese guarding the space, stared accusingly at him.

"Sorry, Mezzo," Simon said under his breath. "Next time!"

When they got to their table, Simon took the seat facing into the dining room so Dar could have an unencumbered view of the Grand River. Shantal handed them each a menu.

"Your server today is Ramon. He'll be right over."

"Say, Shantal, any more visits from the chicken finger bandit?" Simon asked.

"No, not in a while." Shantal smiled at them both. "Enjoy your lunch!"

Simon gave the menu a perfunctory once-over and put it to one side. Dar took a little longer to make her choice before she closed her menu and placed it on top of his.

"Having anything with your tuna?" she asked with a hint of a smile.

"I think I'll have a small order of sweet potato fries." Simon unrolled his silverware and put the napkin in his lap.

"I'm going to have the summer greens and strawberries with poppy-seed dressing. Do I need my own sweet potato fries, or may I have a few of yours?"

"For you, I'll share."

Ramon came alongside their table, introduced himself, took their order, and headed for the kitchen.

Dar rested her chin on her hand and looked past him out the window. "Thanks for giving up your booth to sit here. I need a river recharge."

"So, the meeting was awful?"

"Yes. Awful." Dar didn't elaborate. Her eyes remained on the river, not on him.

Simon waited. He'd lived so many years with this woman that he knew silence was his best course of action. In the meantime, he observed his surroundings. The tables nearest them were still empty, but the rest of the dining area was filling up. Three women sat in the booth under Mezzo's provocative blue-eyed stare. Two men sat at the bar. Simon recognized one of them. *An arrest a while back at the Park View apartments. AJ something. Drunk and disorderly? Yes. And where's Jackie? She's always here for the lunch rush.*

Ramon brought their lunches in record time. "Your tuna, sir." He set the plate down in front of Simon. "And the summer salad for you, ma'am." With a mischievous grin he put the plate of sweet potato fries on the table equidistant between Simon and Dar. "Can I get you anything else? No? Enjoy your lunch."

When Ramon was several tables away, Simon murmured to Dar, "I wish I had a dollar for every 'enjoy your lunch' I've heard over the last month!" He reached for three sweet potato fries.

Dar bowed her head to say grace over her salad, and then nibbled a couple strawberries. When she took a long drink from her water glass, sighed deeply, and looked across the table at him, Simon knew the wait was over.

"I'm mad, Sime. And I'm sad too. The vote was five to two, even after Dr. Rigby, a professor from Tilden, presented evidence proving the village had been there." She plunged her fork into her salad and speared several layers of green. "Money won today," she said. "Money won."

Simon bit into his tuna on whole wheat without breaking eye contact.

"You could practically see the dollar signs float-ing in the air after William Barnes made his presentation. The city already made money from the land sale, and the condos would be a future source of tax revenue. Some of the downtown merchants predict the condo owners will be big spenders." She ate the lettuce on her fork. "I don't know what to think about that."

Ramon came by and added more ice water to their glasses. "Everything okay? How about some dessert? Fruit pies just came out of the oven."

Sweet potato fries, pie—just means taking more steps. Maybe I'll walk back to the office.

"I'd love a piece of blueberry pie and some coffee." Simon looked at his watch and at his wife. "I have time for dessert if you do, Dar."

"Yes! Pie and coffee. Sounds good."

Simon pushed the plate of fries in her direction, prepared to make the ultimate sacrifice of giving the woman he loved the last delectable morsels. Dar shook her head and brought her napkin to her lips.

"You eat them, Sime. I can say no if pie is coming." She took a sip of ice water. "I feel better. Nothing like a good dose of chlorophyll to brighten one's outlook."

Simon rolled his eyes. Dar caught him, and they both laughed.

"Having a wonderful listener of a husband helps too," she added.

Ramon returned with their dessert and coffee.

"Where's Jackie today?" Simon asked him. "She's usually made the rounds at least twice already."

"She's out on a catering gig," Ramon answered. He picked up their lunch plates and replaced them with generous slices of the Alley Cat's homemade blueberry pie. The thick, sweet purple filling peeked out from under the golden-brown crust. Simon's mouth watered.

"Can I get you anything else?"

"No, thank you, Ramon."

"Then I'll bring the check."

Simon and Dar ate their pie slowly, savoring every blueberry mouthful. Dar took in the view out the window for a moment. "I told Mr. Barnes I wouldn't be working with him. He wasn't happy."

"I'm sure he wasn't." Simon thought again about Sally Groegan's concerns about her son-in-law. He was glad Dar wouldn't be working with this man.

A text notification chimed at close range. They both checked their phones. Simon chuckled and showed Dar his screen. "It's Richard. He forgot his lunch."

Ramon appeared and handed Simon the black folder with the check inside.

"We're not quite done after all, Ramon. I'd like an order of chicken fingers and barbecue sauce to go!"

Chapter Twenty-One

Jacoba headed to the front of the antique mall as soon as she heard the clang of the cowbell. Jonathan greeted her from just inside, water dripping from his umbrella.

"Wow, is it ever raining!" He pointed the partially closed umbrella toward the floor. "Where can I put this?"

"Just leave it open on the mat."

Jonathan reopened the umbrella and set it at his feet.

"You didn't walk here, did you?" Jacoba asked. "That would have been one wet stroll from campus!"

"Oh, no. Dad felt sorry for me and drove me over. He'll pick me up at five." He cocked his ear toward the balcony. "Hey," he said with a touch of sarcasm, "I don't hear the sweet sound of dulcimers!"

Jacoba laughed. "No, you don't. You hear the sweet sound of smooth jazz 100.1. We're under a tornado watch and a flash flood advisory, and 100.1 gives frequent weather updates. I really hope we don't hear the sirens this afternoon."

"I'm with you on that!" Jonathan said. He came and stood next to Jacoba. "So, if you've had the radio on, you've heard about the bones at the construction site in the park."

"Oh, yes."

"My dad's pretty jazzed. That's all he talked about on the ride over here."

"I wonder if finding bones means the condo project will be put on hold? I hope so. Condos in the park." Jacoba frowned. "Makes my blood pressure rise just thinking about it."

Marty came up the aisle and joined them. "Hi, Jon," she said with none of her usual enthusiasm. She looked at Jacoba. "No sign of them. I don't understand it."

"She can't find her keys," Jacoba explained to Jonathan. "We've looked everywhere."

"Car keys?" Jonathan asked.

"No. The keys to the curio cabinets, the cash register, and the front and back doors. Fortunately I have keys to the doors, so I can lock up tonight if we can't find hers. But I don't have any of the others."

Jonathan was about to say something when the jarring weather alert signal came over the radio.

"This is the National Weather Service. A strong line of thunderstorms has formed south of the Grandburg area and is moving rapidly in a northwesterly direction. Reports of small hail and damaging winds are ahead of the line. Tornadoes are possible. Rainfall could exceed two to three inches, bringing the risk of flash flooding to low-lying areas. Stay tuned for further updates."

"We don't have to worry about the river," Jacoba said confidently. "I checked when I parked this morning. It would have to rain for days before it got high enough to flood us."

"So, Mrs. B, when was the last time you used your keys?"

Marty looked back and forth between Jonathan and Jacoba. "I really don't remember," she said helplessly. "I must have had them this morning, because I got in the building."

"Unless you didn't lock up last night," Jacoba said quietly, looking at her friend with concern.

"Of course I locked up!" Marty said indignantly. "My keys have to be here somewhere."

"Jon, why don't you look in the basement. I'll search the balcony again." Jacoba turned to Marty. "We'll find them," she reassured her quietly. "Why don't you take a coffee break. There's enough in the carafe for at least one more cup."

Marty headed for the café area, and Jonathan and Jacoba walked to the stairway. Jacoba went up, Jonathan went down. She crossed the balcony threshold to the first booth and ran her hands over the vintage linens on the table in front of her. Nothing. She looked under the table at the hardwood floor. A couple dust bunnies rolled past her feet.

"Ms. D!" Jonathan's urgent tone carried up the stairs.

Jacoba hurried down to the basement. She

looked across the now fairly organized, well-lit space. She didn't see Jonathan.

"Jon?"

"I'm back here." His voice came from somewhere behind her. She walked around the stairs toward the unlit portion of the basement. The floor slanted up abruptly, bringing floor and ceiling closer together in this part of the cellar. Jonathan was waiting for her with a flashlight in his hand. When she stood next to him, he pointed the light into the gloom behind a brick support column. A mound of blankets covered the dirt floor.

"Someone's been sleeping here," Jonathan said. "My little brother does the same thing with his blankets."

Jacoba felt the hairs stand up on her arms.

"I came back here because I smelled fresh-cut lumber. Do you smell it?"

Jacoba sniffed the air, taking a step closer to the blankets. "I do! What do you suppose that is?"

"I don't know, but I smelled it on the trapdoor side of the basement when I was making the path for the electrician."

Jacoba raised her eyebrows. "That was weeks ago! I really hope whoever's been down here hasn't been here that long." A gleam next to the blankets caught her eye, and she bent down to look. "Jon, whiskey bottle." She spotted something poking out from under the blankets. "And a takeout container. It's from the Alley Cat." She frowned in concern. "We really have to find those keys."

"Do you call the police about something like this?"

"Yes." Jacoba looked back at the blankets. "Let's find the keys. Then I'll call."

Jacoba walked back up to the balcony and resumed her search. She had progressed to the third booth when an intense clap of thunder shook the building, and the mall's lights blinked out. The tornado sirens' eerie wail filled the air, and she rushed downstairs. Jonathan met her on the first floor, flashlight in hand.

"Marty? Marty!" Jacoba called urgently.

"I'm here." Marty appeared from behind the curio cabinets and joined them. "I hate those sirens!" She put her hands over her ears.

"Come on," Jacoba said. "Basement. Lead the way, Jon."

Jonathan headed back down. Marty followed him with Jacoba bringing up the rear. He turned the flashlight beam back up the steps so Marty and Jacoba could see where they were going. They sat at the bottom, and Jonathan clicked off the flashlight.

"Well, at least the sirens aren't as loud down here," Jacoba said. She wrapped her arms around her knees. "I wonder how long this will last?"

"Please, Lord," Marty spoke into the dark, "no tornadoes. Please."

"I hope Dad and Sam are in a safe place."

Jacoba looked at the brick walls surrounding them. "We're certainly in a safe place. This building has been here a long time. It is dark, though." She laughed. "Putting lights down here was pure genius, Marty."

They'd only been sitting in the gloom for a few minutes when the sirens' wail changed from warning to all clear.

"Good!" Jacoba stood up. "I hope nothing happened. We've not had a tornado touch down in years."

"Now if the power would just come back on," Marty said.

Jonathan idly clicked on the flashlight. The beam reflected off water creeping steadily toward them on the basement floor.

"Water!" Jacoba said in alarm. "That can't be coming from the river."

"I bet it's from the creek!" Marty said.

Jonathan played the beam along the lower part of the wall on the creek side of the basement. When the light hit the little door, they could see water seeping under the threshold and rippling out into the room.

"This isn't good," Jacoba said, her anxiety rising. "Water seeks the lowest level. This basement is a lot lower than the creek bed."

"Oh, no," Marty wailed. "The booths down here will be ruined! And my grandmother's boxes are down here somewhere!" She stepped down into water. "Oh, great. I hate wet shoes."

"Jon, set the flashlight on a higher step. See if that gives us some light to work by."

Jonathan set the flashlight on the sixth step from the bottom.

"I've got to find those boxes!" Marty took a couple soggy steps farther into the room.

"Did your grandmother's boxes have weird writing on them?" Jonathan asked suddenly. "I remember seeing those when I was straightening up down here."

He headed into the darker recesses of the basement and came back carrying a medium-sized cardboard box. He brought it into the line of light for Marty to see.

"Yes, that's one of them! Jacoba, is that cursive writing?"

"Yup. Marty, wasn't your grandmother from the Netherlands?"

"Yes, her family moved here when she was a teenager."

"That's why it looks weird to you, Jon. Dutch cursive and Dutch words!"

"There are three or four more of your grandmother's boxes in the corner," Jonathan said. "I'll get them."

"Thanks, Jon."

"We'd better get moving. The water's already getting a little deeper." Jacoba rolled up her pants legs.

Jonathan brought the rest of Marty's grandmother's boxes to the first floor. Jacoba joined Marty just beyond the steps in a booth filled with breakables. They carefully pushed ceramic pieces on a middle shelf to one side to make room for plates and cups now perilously close to the water. Together they shifted the dishes to an upper shelf. Jonathan came and did the same thing on the other side of the booth.

"Wish we had some jazz to listen to!"

"Or the news. I wonder what's happening with the storm?"

"Got a joke, Ms. D? You always had a joke ready when I was in your room."

"I did?" Jacoba looked at him in surprise. "I don't remember that!"

"You did," Jonathan said. "Want to hear my favorite?"

"Sure!"

"Knock, knock."

"Who's there?" Jacoba and Marty chorused.

"Banana."

"Banana who?" the women sang out.

"Knock, knock."

"Who's there?"

"Banana."

"Banana who?" the women said a bit more forcefully.

"Knock, knock."

"Who's there?"

"Orange."

"Orange who?"

"Orange you glad I didn't say banana?" Jonathan started laughing at himself.

Jacoba and Marty groaned. The flashlight dimmed and flickered.

"Marty, don't we have more batteries in the workroom? I'll go—"

A loud bang reverberated near where they stood. Rushing water swirled and eddied around their ankles.

"The little door!" Jonathan yelled. "It's open!"

"Oh, no! Oh, no!" Marty and Jacoba scrambled to the stairs.

Jonathan sloshed over to the little door and tried to close it, but the water was streaming through it too forcefully. Jacoba grabbed the flashlight and trained the faltering beam on the place where Jonathan stood.

"Snakes! Jon, there are snakes in the water!"

Marty shrieked and ran up the stairs.

"Yaaaaaaaaa!" Jonathan bellowed as he splashed through the water and joined Jacoba on the steps.

"The trapdoor—we need to close it, and board up the opening at the top of these stairs. We don't want snakes to make it to the main floor!"

Jacoba and Jonathan charged upstairs and raced past Marty. They navigated the main aisle and pushed through the beaded curtain to the chair barrier. Jacoba grabbed one side of the trapdoor, Jonathan the other.

"One, two, three!" They heaved it up to a ninety-degree angle, then pushed the door forward. It slammed into the floor with a resounding crash.

"Done. What about the other side?" Jonathan asked.

Jacoba ran to the furniture section. She hurried down the row of dining room tables and chairs. "Could we stand a table on its end in the landing opening and push chairs against it?" she asked the others. "Would that be enough?"

"Yes," Marty said. "I think so."

"There's an old door right over there." Jonathan pointed. "Could we use that?"

It took all three of them to carry the old oak door across the showroom floor, down the first set of basement stairs, and maneuver it into place.

"This will work. It's wider and taller than the opening."

"Here." Marty pulled a chair out of the café area. "Put this against it."

Jonathan took it out of her hands and shoved it in place. "Let's put a couple more across here."

Jacoba came with another one, Marty brought a third. They stood back to admire their work. At the same moment the lights came back on, and they cheered. Several clocks chimed the half hour.

"Four thirty! What a day." Jacoba looked around the main floor.

"Power is on but not the radio station. That can't be good," Marty said. "These wet shoes are coming off. I need some coffee!"

"You and your coffee," Jacoba laughed, "I'll make some."

"Bob will know who to call about the snake-and-water-situation," Marty said. "Now where did I leave my phone?"

"I'm going to check in with Dad."

"Jon, tell your dad I can bring you home."

Jacoba took off her shoes, collected Marty's, and set them next to Jonathan's umbrella on the mat by the front door. She padded barefoot across the hardwood floor to the coffee bar to make a fresh pot of coffee. She reached for the box of sugar packets. It felt unusually heavy in her hands. She flipped the box lid back and discovered Marty's keys.

Jonathan came into the café area, and Jacoba lifted the keys out of the box for him to see.

"You found them," he said.

Jacoba nodded.

"Why would she have put them there?"

"I have no idea," Jacoba answered. "Did you reach your dad?"

"Yes. He said a tornado went right up the creek bed and into the park!"

"Was anyone hurt?"

"Nope, just did a lot of tree damage. Oh, and he said it would be great if you brought me home. He said take River Street and not Cherry. Lots of trees down along Cherry."

"Okay."

Marty joined them.

"Close your eyes and hold out your hands," Jacoba said to Marty.

"No way!" Marty answered staunchly. "Not after snake sightings!"

"I promise, no snakes."

"Okay," Marty said reluctantly.

Jacoba placed the keys in her outstretched hands.

"Oh! You found them!" Marty clutched the keys to her chest. "I am so relieved! Where were they?"

"Where we should have looked in the first place," Jacoba teased. "In the box of sugar packets."

"I left keys in a box of sugar packets? Why would I do that?" She looked down at the keys in her hands and shook her head in bewilderment.

"Let's have some coffee and regroup," Jacoba said practically. "Did you get Bob?"

"Yes, he's on his way." Marty looked around for a place to sit where the chairs had been.

Jonathan brought over two chairs from the furniture section and went back for one more. Jacoba handed the first cup of coffee to Marty.

Marty took a sip and gave a sigh of satisfaction. "Ah, the elixir of life," she said.

"We need to call the folks with booths in the basement," Jacoba said. "The mall is insured for something like this, right, Marty?"

Marty continued to sip her coffee and look in the opposite direction.

"Marty?"

"I don't know," Marty said in a small voice. "But Bob will know." She brightened. "Bob can handle it."

Jacoba was still thinking about Marty's reply after she dropped Jonathan off at his house on Madison Street. She had worked at the antique mall for quite a few summers now, and she'd been friends with Marty for even longer. She couldn't remember ever hearing Marty say, "Bob can handle it." The antique mall had always been Marty's business, Marty's pride and joy, Marty's baby. And what about the keys? Innocent mistake, or evidence of something more serious going on?

As Jacoba pulled into her driveway, her thoughts circled back to the uninvited guest in the basement. Jonathan had reminded her about that during their drive home. Was there even any point in calling the police given the current state of affairs? She hit the button for her garage door and watched with relief as it opened. Good. Power was on at her house. Her headlights illumined the garage's interior as the car rolled inside and came to a stop. The cardboard boxes next to her right bumper cast tall shadows on the garage wall. Boxes. They were going to need a lot of boxes when the water receded and the snakes were gone.

"I bet I could empty some of those and take them in tomorrow." She got out of the car and walked around to look at the collection.

"But not tonight. I'll do it first thing in the morning!"

Chapter Twenty-Two

The next morning, Jacoba backed the car out of the garage to make room for emptying boxes. She stood on her driveway for a moment and looked up and down Patterson Street. Mr. Barfield was out already, picking up limbs and twigs in his front yard. A chainsaw revved close by.

"I hope that's not coming from Verna's," she said to herself.

Jacoba slammed her car door and walked back into the garage. She set up an ancient card table and plunked a woven wastebasket next to it.

"Might as well just start with the top box and work my way down."

Jacoba lifted the lid of the box nearest her. She groaned and chuckled when she saw spiral-spined teacher's editions. "Those will have to go back." She hoisted the box off the stack and shoved it under the table. The next carton contained flash-cards and games. Jacoba took them out and stacked them on the card table. She triumphantly put the empty box aside.

"That's one!"

The next three boxes held books from her class-room library. "Hmmm. I'm not sure what I want to do with these. I wonder if Judy Ko would like to have them?" Jacoba did some cramming and rearranging, and gained another empty box.

"That's two."

A wave of nostalgia swept over her when she lifted the lid of the top box on the second stack. There was her coffee mug, the chalk holder the children had nicknamed "Peewee," and miscellaneous items from the lost-and-found drawer.

She picked up Peewee and her coffee mug. "I'm keeping you," she said. She tipped the box on its side and poured the rest of the contents onto the card table. A small red jacks ball rolled off and bounced toward the steps to the kitchen.

"I'll get you later." she said as she watched it disappear into a corner, then turned back to her work. "You're doing great, Jacoba. Second stack, second box. Let's see what's in here." She leaned forward and saw more teacher's manuals. "Oh, no! Well, I have plenty of time to return them."

She pulled the other box of teacher's editions out from under the card table.

"Good. There's room for more in here."

She wrapped her fingers around three manuals to make the transfer. When she lifted them, she discovered a spring-clipped stack of papers underneath.

"Math worksheets? How did these get here? Well, it doesn't matter now."

Jacoba unfastened the black clip and turned to the wastebasket to toss the worksheets.

"So glad I don't have to grade you," she said as

she let the sheets cascade ceremoniously from her hands. She watched them fan out in the bottom of the wastebasket. Blue-lined notebook paper with cursive writing peeked out from under printed pages of numbers. She bent down and pulled several sheets back out. Poems.

She took the wastebasket to the steps and lifted out the rest of the paper. And there it was. Jeremy's poem. The familiar handwriting brought tears to her eyes.

"I can't believe it." She took a deep breath and started reading Jeremy's poem aloud, the words echoing in the space.

> *From This Time Forward and*
> *Forevermore*
>
> *I heard the words at Grandmother's house,*
> *"From this time forward and*
> *forevermore!"*
> *I added, "No more fear!"*
> *The words in hand, the actions planned, I*
> *went right out the door.*
>
> *I'll take my words to the top of the trail*
> *To join the warrior line.*
> *I'll ride down the trail from post to post*
> *And the victory will be mine.*
>
> *I'll shout the words and move so fast*
> *Fear will lose its grip.*

It will fly off into the woods
Never to make another trip.

I'm doing it soon.
Maybe today.
"From this time forward and
forevermore!"
No more fear, hurray!

Jacoba wept.

Acknowledgments

Thank you, Rebecca V., for the gift of the B.I.C. Box. What a game changer!

Thank you, Marty B., Linnea S., Sheryl B., Joy D., Theresa M., and Judy K. You came, you read, and you shared.

Thank you, Richard B., for your priceless input early on.

Thank you, Jim M., for setting me straight on functions within the church.

Thank you, Ron N., for patiently answering all my "detective" questions.

Thank you, Dale B., for a long conversation about death that brought new life to the story.

Thank you, Sue and Steve R., Robin Z., Bob S., Rich F., and Patsy A., for your ready answers to my fact-checking queries.

Thank you, Dorothea L., for following the Spirit's leading.

Thank you, BookLogix folks. Doing it "your way" has been such a blessing.

About the Author

Janifer C. DeVos is a longtime teacher and storyteller. She's worked in schools and churches in Florida, Texas, Mississippi, and Michigan. Jan currently resides in Western Michigan, where she never tires of watching snow fall in winter. She is profoundly grateful for all the ways God is, and has always been, on the move in her life.